The Bronze Bottle

Book 2

Linda Shields Allison

Published by BookLocker.com, Inc., St. Petersburg, Florida.

Printed on acid-free paper.

The characters and events in this book are fictitious. Any similarity to real persons, living or dead, is coincidental and not intended by the author.

BookLocker.com, Inc.
2020

First Edition

Library of Congress Cataloging in Publication Data
Allison, Linda Shields
The Bronze Bottle by Linda Shields Allison
Library of Congress Control Number: 2020909168

For my father ~

A great storyteller and a man

Who touched the lives of so many

A special thanks to ~

Michael and Tina Canon for their creative technical support.

Terry Nettles Meaney and Claudia Weston for editing the manuscript.

Rudy and Norma Romero for their amazing skill in marketing the books.

A very special thanks to ~

Russell Mars for editing my manuscript and encouraging me to complete the trilogy.

Books in the Journey of the Bottle Trilogy by:
Linda Shields Allison

The Emerald Bottle

The Bronze Bottle

The Amethyst Bottle

The Characters ~

Esther King: The young half-caste slave girl does not fit in on the King Plantation. Taunted by other black slaves in the quarters because she looks different, ignored by her father, and despised by his wife and overseer, Esther comes to distrust both white and black people. She eventually escapes to the North to work as a conductor on the Underground Railroad. A mysterious Bronze Bottle helps her return to her plantation to rescue two adults and five children. In the process, she learns the valuable lessons of love and forgiveness.

Old Jed: The recently arrived slave, considered too old to toil in the fields, works as a trapper to supply extra meat for other slaves. Over a period of three years, he secretly teaches Esther and Bucky to read at *Night School*. The mentor also shows his young students how to survive in the forest so that they may one day follow the North Star to freedom.

Mammy Naira: The kindly mammy offers to raise baby Esther as her own child when her birth mother is sold south. She builds Esther's self esteem with love and praise, but also reminds her artistic daughter that she may be punished if caught creating forbidden drawings with charcoal.

Bucky: Esther makes a special friend while working to cut trees for the King Plantation in the forest one summer. Old Jed teaches the two companions to read the signs of the roads and the signs of the forest in the event they may one day try and escape to freedom.

Steidley King: The master of the King Plantation ignores his half-caste daughter because she reminds him of her beautiful mother. He spends his days painting, hunting, and spoiling his five children, and leaves the workings of the plantation to his mean-spirited wife and cruel overseer.

Wendalyn King: Heartless to the feelings of her slaves, the mistress of the King Plantation thinks little of selling a slave south if they do something to annoy her. When Esther begins to turn into a lovely young woman, she plots to send her away.

Shelby Moss: The cruel overseer is disgusted to look at Esther when she is brought before him for drawing. He despises that she is of a mixed race and viciously punishes her before all the slaves in the quarters with the sting of his whip.

Claudia Grigg: As a station master on the Underground Railroad, the young Quaker woman forms a lasting relationship with Esther and Bucky. Over the years, she helps Esther send and receive special notes about Mammy Naira and Old Jed through the help of her brother, Mark Singer. Claudia leaves her family in Pennsylvania to travel south with Esther to help rescue Esther's family from imminent danger.

Joanne Cody: After receiving her freedom papers and one hundred dollars from her master, Mrs. Cody learns to read and starts an orphanage for abandoned children in Seneca Village.

The Bronze Bottle

Linda Shields Allison

Preface

The system known as the Underground Railroad began in earnest in the 1800s and continued until the end of the Civil War in 1865. Runaway slaves fleeing the southern part of the United States escaped by traveling though a series of secret routes that were neither *underground* nor a *railroad*. Those who assisted the slaves in making their way to the northern part of the United States and into Canada were: freed slaves, escaped slaves, and sympathetic white activists called abolitionists. Among the many non-blacks who gave immense assistance to the fleeing slaves were the dedicated Quakers, a religious group also known as the *Society of Friends*.

In 1853, tension between the northern and southern states made civil war appear inevitable. Two small women named Harriet played unique roles in bringing sympathetic public attention to the plight of Negro slaves and helped accelerate the course of war. Historians speculate that Harriet Ross Tubman, an escaped slave, brought over 300 slaves to freedom on the Underground Railroad. Her indisputable bravery and the fact that Harriet never lost a single passenger made her a legend in her own time. Around the same time, Harriet Beecher Stowe's popular novel, *Uncle Tom's Cabin ~ or Life Among the Lowly*, changed many people's attitudes about black slaves by humanizing them as persons with feelings and emotions. At the height of the Civil War in 1863, Abraham Lincoln met Mrs. Stowe at the White House and referred to her as "the little woman who wrote the book that made this great war."

Prologue ~ August 1853 – New York City

Seventeen-year-old Esther King stood at the bow of the steamship and looked at the skyline of New York City. The population of the island of Manhattan had grown to nearly 700,000 people since a disastrous fire in 1835 had all but wiped out the business district located near Wall Street. The opening of the Erie Canal in 1825 had elevated the importance of New York's harbor. The canal linked the Hudson River to the Great Lakes and made New York the center of trade along the east coast and across the Atlantic to Europe. In the distance, Esther could see the top of the Crystal Palace. The gleaming structure made of glass and iron had recently been erected as a showpiece to honor the nation's first World Fair, which had opened earlier that summer. Scores of visitors from near and far flocked to Manhattan to marvel at the many exhibits that demonstrated the modern advances of a young nation. The New York Knickerbockers baseball team was beginning its eighth season as an organized club. Newspapers like the *New York Post, New York Times* and *The Liberator* punctuated the energy of the city with headlines that told of excitement and apprehension.

Despite its problems with growing pains, Esther loved New York City. She hoped that Bucky would be waiting at the docks to drive her home to Mrs. Cody's orphanage and school in Seneca Village. The village was located to the north of lower Manhattan on a site that would later become part of Central Park. Seneca Village was Manhattan's first significant community of African American property owners.

Esther had telegraphed Bucky from Boston confirming when her steamship was due to arrive in New York. The voyage from Prince Edward Island had been a pleasant one, and had given Esther time to reflect on the journey that lay before her. Instinctively, she reached her right hand to grasp a Bronze Bottle, encased in its leather pouch and strapped across her left shoulder and under her right arm. For the hundredth time, she gently removed the bottle from its case and cradled it in her hands. Esther smiled as she recalled the first time she had seen the bottle.

The former slave girl had successfully delivered a group of slaves to a young Irish woman who had answered her advertisement in the newspaper. Tara Maguire and her family had offered to provide employment for the liberated slaves on their farm in Prince Edward Island, Canada. While visiting with Tara and her mother Elsie in their parlor, Esther's eyes had been drawn to a beautiful Emerald Bottle resting in a china cabinet. With the eye of an artist, she asked Tara about its history. The young Irish girl had smiled knowingly and rose to take it out of the cabinet. When placed into her hands, the bottle had given Esther a deep sense of peace and an unusual feeling of inner strength. For the first time in many months Esther did not feel as burdened by the difficult task of working as a guide on the Underground Railroad. Tara had persuaded Esther to keep the bottle in her guestroom to enjoy during her two-week stay on the island. To Esther's amazement, the Emerald Bottle began to gradually change in color. The beautiful shades of greens and gold became overlaid with patches of bronze, ebony, copper, and gold. The colors of the bottle were brilliant and complex, and sparkled unlike anything she had ever seen. Over the next fourteen days, Esther shared many conversations with Tara to find out all that the Irish girl knew about the mysterious bottle.

Esther learned that Tara had received the bottle from an Irish Tinker woman named Diviña, and that the bottle had been a rich shade of sapphire blue mixed with swirls of silver the first time her eyes had caught sight of it in Diviña's caravan. Tara had explained that the mysterious bottle was very old, and she believed that the bottle had changed colors many times as it had passed through countless hands. The changing overlay of colors signaled to the current owner that the time had come to pass the bottle into the hands of another person in need of its help. Esther had listened in amazement as Tara explained that the bottle appeared to assist each new owner along different journeys. Near the bottom edge of the bottle was an inscription in Latin written in beautiful calligraphy. Translated into English, the words formed a two-line couplet that read:

Into thy hand I come.
Unto thy spirit as one.

Esther ran her fingers over the raised letters and sighed. Tara had told her that she believed that the bottle embraced the spirit or energy of its owner. Esther studied the bronze pigment that seemed to form the base-coat of the bottle. Esther knew from an old blacksmith, named Riley who worked on the King Plantation, that bronze was an ancient mixture of alloys made strong by heating copper and tin to the boiling point and forging the molten liquid into lasting shapes. Esther thought about her racial background. Like bronze, she was a mixture - half white and half black African. Esther knew she was the daughter of Master Steidley King, the owner of the plantation where she had been raised. Her birth mother had been sold to another plantation shortly after she had been born. Esther thought about the fate life had cast her. As a half-caste slave girl working on the King Plantation in Dorchester County, Maryland, Esther did not exactly fit in. She learned early on, that to survive she had to become like bronze – strong in body and in spirit. Esther looked down at the Bronze Bottle again. Tiny flecks of gold and other colors of the rainbow shimmered in the sunlight against the backdrop of ebony and bronze. The brilliant specks of light reminded Esther of the stars that sparkled so brightly at night in the moonless sky. Esther's mind slipped back in time to recall the stars, which had been so important in helping a young slave girl find her passageway to freedom so many years ago.

Chapter 1 ~ May 1846 – Maryland

Ten-year-old Esther King had been sent to the woods to collect kindling for Mammy Naira's fireplace. The ancient fireplace was where the old mammy cooked meals for Esther. Its bricks were blackened from years of constant use. Many other slaves shared the hot embers of the old hearth located inside a small cabin amid rows of identical cabins in the slave quarters on the King Plantation. The young slave girl quickly gathered a large bundle of twigs and branches. Esther knew that her mammy would not expect her back to the quarters just yet, so she rewarded herself with a few stolen moments of peaceful solitude. Life for a slave on a large plantation allowed little time to be alone. Esther slept with her mammy in a cabin that was also home to a dozen other men, women and children. Each night she fell asleep near her mammy's pallet on the ground listening to the sounds of other slaves whispering, laughing, grunting, and sometimes crying in the dark. Privacy was not part of any slave's life. A quiet moment alone was a rare gift.

Esther sat along the edge of the Big Buckwater River near the collected pile of wood drawing a fluffy cloud in the moist earth with a twig. The young half-caste slave-girl captured the sunshine of the low country on her face as the sun dipped in the western sky. Esther studied the wind casting delicate ripples across the surface of the water. The movement distorted the image of the clouds reflecting off its surface. She heard the soft rustling of leaves in the trees, and felt the coarse sticky grains of sand between the toes of her bare feet. The young slave girl sighed with happiness at the intimate beauty of the moment.

You see, Esther observed the details of life. Her unusual green and gold eyes viewed the world, with its varying shapes and dazzling prism of color and light, through an artist's imagination. When others saw a cloud as a white puff in the sky, Esther considered the fragile motion of the vapor – dense gray patches churning against creamy shades of pale pink and ashen white. To Esther, a newly fallen pine branch held the detailed texture of rough bark pocked with complex wormholes, and the sharp piney fragrance of sticky sap. An eagle soaring high above the trees, as its motionless wings imprisoned the wind, intrigued the young artist. Esther noticed the fragile veins in the petals of the pale white water lilies that floated in the marshes and coves of the tidewater country on the Eastern Shore of Maryland. Nothing escaped her vision of the intricate landscape around her.

Esther looked down at her foot. A large black ant struggled to carry a torn bit of leaf across the sand. The ant reminded Esther of the master's slaves who worked on the plantation. Like ants, her people knew nothing but work as they marched in silent lines to the fields just as the morning sun rose in the eastern sky – day after day – sunrise to sunset – uninspiring, endless work.

Suddenly, Esther was pulled from her thoughts. She startled at the sound of laughter and footsteps coming up the worn path that ran alongside the river. Quickly, she crouched into a squatting position and scratched her stick into the moist earth to rub out the detailed sketch of the cloud in the sand.

"Hey, *alligator eyes*," smirked a dark skinned slave-girl named Mandy. "Ya know ya ain't supposed to be makin' dem marks in d'ground with dat stick. Boss Shelby would love to tear at your hide with his whip if'n he was to catch ya." Mandy and three other slave girls circled Esther. They stood with their legs apart and their arms akimbo. "Look at her, gals. She be creepin' in d'mud just like an old gator!" taunted Mandy as she cruelly shoved Esther onto her backside with the push of her foot.

Esther quickly scrambled to her feet. She tried to dart away, but a large pocked-faced girl named Bertha grabbed Esther's hair and pulled her back into the circle of hecklers. Esther's heart pounded in her chest, and her mouth felt as dry as the ashes in Mammy Naira's fireplace. She willed herself not to look frightened, but she couldn't stop her body from shaking. Esther had reason to be scared. These girls had tormented her before.

"Look at dis gal's hair," teased Bertha. She grabbed a fistful of Esther's light brown hair streaked with golden strands from the sun. "It look all pale and limp like de corn-silk on d'cob of corn I shucked for my daddy's dinner last night." All four girls laughed, and another slave, named Rowena, reached in and cuffed Esther on the side of her head.

"What did y'all make for yo' daddy's dinner last night, *leather face?*" taunted Mandy. "Oh, dat's right. I plum forgot dat y'all ain't got no daddy. Least no daddy dat claims ya as his-own blood. All you got is an ol' barren mammy who ain't even yo' real birth mammy," Mandy added in a mean-spirited tone. The girls laughed again as Bertha pushed Esther closer to the river's edge.

Esther looked around helplessly at her tormentors and saw no way of escape. She knew that Mandy washed clothes for the King family up at the Big House. She was several years older than Esther and wielded power over the three other girls who worked in the fields.

"I believe dem yeller-green alligator eyes makes y'all look like a slimy ol' reptile," smirked Mandy. "Best y'all go for a swim *gator eyes*." Mandy nodded at Bertha, and the heavy-set girl grabbed the back of Esther's neck and shoved her down the muddy slope of the riverbank. Esther tumbled forward and landed face down in the churned up water and dirt. Laughter erupted from the four older slave girls as they saw Esther struggle to crawl up the slippery bank of the Big Buckwater.

"You gals best be gettin' on 'bout your business," barked a deep voice coming from the direction of some underbrush. An elderly slave by the name of Old Jed stepped onto the path and stood looking at the muddy Esther. Four rabbits and two squirrels all tied together lay draped over his shoulder.

Old Jed was considered too frail to work in the fields, so he spent his days trapping small animals in the woods to provide extra food for the slaves in the quarters. The overseer of the King Plantation was clever enough to understand that the extra meat kept the Master's slaves strong and healthy to work the fields. The quiet elderly man caused the overseer no trouble, so he pretty much left the ancient trapper to his own business.

Mandy opened her mouth to say something to Old Jed, but instead, she snorted in disgust and jerking her head motioned to the others. Mandy strutted up the path with the three friends trailing behind and laughed defiantly. But in truth, Mandy did not want her friends to know that she was somewhat afraid of the curious old slave who had only recently come to Master King's plantation. The peculiar trapper, who stayed mostly to himself, was unlike the other slaves in the quarters. Mandy thought he talked and acted different, like maybe he thought he was better than her. His interference in their fun mocking Esther annoyed her. Mandy mumbled something amusing to her friends and laughed a bit too loud as she strolled up the path. She felt if the other girls sensed that she was frightened by the old man, she knew it might lessen her position as leader of their group.

Esther stayed crouched on the muddy bank until the muffled laughter faded in the distance. Old Jed peered down pensively at

Esther and held the green-eyed slave-girl in his gaze. In turn, Esther stared up at Jed's dark ebony skin, which glowed like the color of Mammy's ancient cast iron pan. She saw almost black eyes, a straight broad nose, and snow-white crinkly hair. Esther studied the deep creases in the man's face, and thought the lines gave wisdom to the lean old trapper who had clearly lived a long time. He was medium in build, but as he stretched out his hand to pull her up the bank, Esther thought he moved gracefully with nimble muscles despite his advanced age.

"You best come with me, child," he said kindly. "I'll take you home to your mammy."

Wiping the soggy strands of hair from her eyes, Esther nodded and grabbed her bundle of firewood. She took off after Old Jed whose long strides had already carried him several yards up the path that led to the slave quarters.

Old Jed delivered Esther to the door of her mammy's cabin, a kindly woman known as Naira to the slaves in the quarters and Nancy to the white folks up at the Big House. Naira looked at Esther and frowned. Mud was splattered on Esther's arms, across her face, and in her damp matted hair. The mammy then crossed her large arms over an ample chest, which blended into a sizeable stomach and clucked her tongue as though she were calling chickens to feed. Naira shook her head and stared at her daughter through kindly dark eyes.

"Esther, what happened to ya, child?"

Esther looked at Old Jed and then at her mammy. "I slipped and fell into the muddy shore of the Big Buckwater. Old Jed came along and…well, he helped me out."

Naira looked down at Esther and shook her head again. "Y'all must be more careful, Esther. Ya don't know how to swim, child. D'spring runoff from de rains can cause dem swift waters of Big Buckwater to suck you downstream like dishwater down a drain. Now ya best git inside and clean yo'self up for dinner."

Esther looked at the old trapper and mumbled, "Thanks for what ya done for me."

Old Jed looked as though he wanted to say something to Esther, but he only nodded and watched the young girl scurry inside the cabin. "Naira, I had particular good luck in the forest today. Take this here rabbit and add it to your pot," said Old Jed as he untied the fattest hare from his catch.

"Why Jed, dat be mighty kind of ya. Dere ain't nothin' like a plump ol' rabbit to flavor-up a pot of stew. Why don't ya stop back later and join us for a bite to eat?" Naira asked hopefully. The mammy, a widow for seven years come Christmas, was secretly fond of the old trapper who had arrived at the King Plantation last summer, and she had been looking for an excuse to ask him around to dinner.

"I'd like that, Naira," said Old Jed warmly. He tipped his ragged felt hat and strolled away from the cabin.

Later that night, after a relaxing dinner of rabbit stew with rice and collard greens in the company of Old Jed, Esther cuddled with her mammy under Naira's colorful handmade quilt. Together, they whispered softly on their pallets in the dark, while watching tiny red embers flicker in the fireplace and listening to the familiar sounds of the other slaves in the cabin.

"Tell me the news from the Big House Mammy. Did ya have a good day?

Mammy Naira sighed. "Cookin' for dat family sure do wear me out, child. But that weren't nothin' compared to what went on for Ivy in the Big House."

"Tell me, Mammy!"

"Mistress King was in a powerful bad temper today. I heard it whispered from de servers dat Ivy dropped Miz Wendy's favorite crystal punch bowl while she was cleaning it, and dat bowl shattered on de floor lookin' like de tiny chips of ice dat float in de Master's Bourbon. Dey said dat de Master's wife thrashed dat young girl with de handle of a broom until Miz Wendy got so tired dat de rage finally left her body. But, child, de slaves dat witnessed de beatin', said de rage never left dat woman's face."

"What will happen to Ivy, Mammy?" asked Esther with a shudder.

"Miz Wendy done told dat poor gal dat she would be sold South, cuz every time she be lookin' at Ivy, she'd be thinkin' of her favorite crystal bowl smashed to pieces on her floor. Den, she sent Ivy to Boss Shelby to work in de fields."

"But, Mammy, Ivy is married to Benjamin and they have four small children," whispered Esther in a worried tone of voice.

"Dat never stopped Miz Wendy before, child. When she be gettin' somethin' in her mind, she be like a vulture waitin' for a meal, and dere ain't nothin' gonna sway her."

Esther shuddered. She knew that the Master's wife, a pale pinched-faced woman, had sold Esther's birth mother to the Deep South two months after Esther had been born. Esther was scared to shivers when she thought of Wendalyn King. She recalled the many times Mistress King had given her a hard stare with eyes that bore into her like the crazed muskrat she had once found with its paw clamped in a metal trap near the Big Buckwater.

But as terrified as Esther was of the Master's wife, she loved to cuddle with Mammy Naira on their pallet at night and listen to the story of how Naira came to be her mammy. Each time, Naira softly retold Esther's story with the emotion of a narrator from an ancient Greek tragedy.

"I know your tired, Mammy, but would ya tell me the story of how you came to be my Mammy?"

Mammy Naira sighed with pleasure and began the tale. "Master King had been sorely dejected to learn dat his favorite slave, Janet, had been secretly sold south by de jealous wife, Miz Wendalyn King. Many of de slaves took notice dat de Master seemed to wander 'bout his plantation as sad as a dreary winter day for many months after she departed. De graceful fair-skinned Janet, had begged de Master's wife to let her take her baby Esther with her south," Naira's voice always softened to a whisper at this point in the story. "But de mean-spirited wife turned a deaf ear to her slave's courageous plea for mercy. And de baby Esther was given to de barren slave, known as Nancy to de white folk up at de Big House, to raise as her own precious child on dat very day dat de beautiful Janet was dragged away from de plantation in chains."

Naira slowed her pattern of speech at this point in the tale for an added touch of drama. "Now, de barren kitchen slave, known as Naira in de quarters, and Nancy at de Big House had pleaded with Miz Wendy dat she might mother d'child because she had never been blessed by de Lord with children of her own. Miz Wendy snarled dat it mattered naught to her who raised de brat, as long as de task did not interfere with Nancy's chores in de kitchen. So de barren slave, Naira, found a wet nurse for baby Esther and proudly raised de cherished child as her own."

Esther loved Naira's story of her mother, and never tired of hearing it told.

"Would ya tell me what my birth mammy look like again, Mammy Naira?" whispered Esther.

"She was small-boned with warm brown skin de color of pecans, and her face looked a lot like yours, child. She was very beautiful, 'cept dat her eyes were light brown and her hair was darker and curlier."

Naira yawned, "We best git some sleep, Esther, cuz dat rooster be crowin' afore long, and we don't want to give Miz Wendy any excuse to use her switch on us tomorrow."

"Goodnight Mammy. I love you," whispered Esther as she snuggled closer to the only mother she had ever known.

As loved as Esther was by Naira, life was not easy for the half-caste slave girl. She looked different from most of the other children in the slave quarters. They had dark hair that crinkled into tight curls, whereas Esther's hair was golden brown, and her curls fell in soft waves around her face. Some of the children in the quarters teased her, and called her *alligator eyes*, because Esther's eyes were green with tiny flecks of gold that sparkled like dew drops on dried hay. Her skin was the soft tan color of the Master's saddle and some children sniggered and nicknamed her *leather face*. Esther was not tall, but she stood erect and was gracefully proportioned. She endured the taunts of her tormentors with a silent look that held no judgment in the alligator green eyes. Esther might have held herself in low esteem had it not been for Naira, but the mammy so often assured Esther that she was special, that the praise took root in her heart like the ivy vines that plastered themselves to the tall white columns that surrounded the Big House.

Earlier that spring, Naira had presented Esther with her first bandanna and took her to work with her in the kitchen quarters. The bright red and yellow headscarf and the new work-dress made Esther feel very grown up and far removed from the younger children who ran around the quarters barefoot in one-piece tow–linen shifts. The shapeless white garments were made from the cheapest cotton fabric.

As Esther and Naira walked up the dirt path to the kitchen near the Big House, the excited young slave girl chattered, "Mammy, I think red and yellow are my favorite colors. Thank ya for my bandanna. I'll work hard and make Master King and y'all proud of me."

Naira's breath had caught in her throat. She stopped to look down at the young girl standing by her side. Esther grabbed Naira's waist and buried her head in her mammy's ample belly. Naira lifted Esther's face between her hands and looked down at her daughter. "Yes child, I do believe dat dis scarf be makin' yo' eyes look mighty pretty."

Slowly, Esther dropped her chin on her chest and mumbled, "I don't like my eyes, Mammy. They're…colored odd and not like the others…"

Naira raised Esther's face upward. "Esther, now look here and listen to your ol' mammy. I hear what dose other children be sayin'. I know dey be callin' you *alligator eyes* and other such names, but child, yo' green eyes are special. Esther, your birth mammy was beautiful, and so are you. Be proud of who you are and where you came from. Don't be tryin' to look and act like everybody else on dis ol' plantation. De Lord made ya just de way *He* wanted ya to look," pronounced Naira as she bent over closer to her daughter, "and de Lord don't make garbage."

Esther looked up at her mammy and smiled. Naira always knew just what to say to make Esther feel cherished. Esther let out a deep sigh. "I love you, Mammy."

"I know dat you do. Now, we best get to work, child. Don't want us to be late on yo' first day. And we don't want to be givin' Miz Wendy any reason to lash out at ya, Esther. Remember what I done said last night? Keep yo'self busy at all times, and keep yo' eyes cast to de ground when she be nearby." Esther nodded her head somberly and clutched her mammy's hand as they walked to the cookhouse.

As with most plantation houses in the south, the cookhouse had been built twenty yards away from the Big House. The constant threat of fire and the stifling humidity of the eternally hot summers made the kitchen arrangement more practical. Three times each day, food was brought in large trays to the dining room to feed Steidley and Wendalyn King, their five children, and the many guests who visited their plantation. Like Esther, the servers who carried the trays to the household staff were trained to whistle in a loud nonstop flow as they walked the twenty yards from the kitchen through an arbor of honeysuckle vines to the French doors that led into the dining area. In this way, the white folks could be assured that the slaves would not taint their food by sneaking a bite from a platter that would soon be put before them to eat. Esther was never allowed inside. A house slave stood waiting at the French doors to relieve her of her burden. Sometimes she would steal a peek inside.

Once she saw the slave girl, known as Pixie, standing silently in the far corner of the room. Beads of sweat trickled from beneath Pixie's headscarf as she gently tugged on a long cord. The action motivated ostrich feathers to gently sway across the table to fan the heavy humid air and scatter fervent flies. Pixie stared past Esther toward the arbor with a vacant look in her eyes, and for the first time in her young life, Esther had been glad that she was never permitted to enter the Big House.

Esther was certain that Master King knew that she was his daughter. Although he never spoke to her personally, and at times seemed to go out of his way to avoid her, she sometimes noticed him staring at her from a distance when she went about her chores – pulling onions in the garden located behind the cookhouse or fetching buckets of water from the well. Esther thought that she detected a sad look in his eyes, like he was perhaps remembering the past. Once, she smiled at him. He had started to smile back, but the muscles in his face suddenly twitched causing his mouth to set into a stiff frozen stain. Steidley King had held Esther in this granite stare for several seconds before he jerked his head away, turned on his heel, and quickly walked away.

Chapter 2 ~ Summer 1847 – King Plantation

During Esther's eleventh summer on the King Plantation, she boarded wagons with many other men, women, and children and was sent to work miles away in the woods. Only the most trusted slaves were allowed to cut lumber in the forest. The slaves who were chosen to chop trees for the Master considered it an honor to work unchained under the cool canopy of tall trees, and not have to labor in the hot fields with their bare backs glistening with sweat under the burning summer sun.

All that summer, Esther cut branches off large oak and pine trees that had been felled with axes by broad-shouldered slaves who cut the timber so that it could be shipped to the Master's lumberyard in Baltimore. Esther enjoyed the work and became friendly with a tall fourteen-year old boy with soft brown eyes, large white teeth, and a faded scar on his left cheek. His name was Bucky.

Bucky's father, a tall intelligent slave with a reputation for *catchin' on quick*, had been sent to work at the Master's lumberyard when the boy was four-years-old. Young Bucky spent much of his youth with an ache in his heart looking down the oak-lined road that led to the entrance of the King Plantation hoping to see his father walk up the path. Sadly, Bucky never saw his father again. The young boy clung to his mother each night when she returned to the quarters from scrubbing clothes for the King family up at the Big House.

He became heartbroken when she died from cholera a few years later, but he had no time to mourn. At seven-years-old, the young slave was in charge of his own destiny. The mammies in the quarters looked out after him, but Bucky was just one of many slave-children who had been orphaned by a parent. A displaced family was a common occurrence in the slavery system of the South. The boy quickly learned to wrangle for a spot at the large trough of cornmeal mush set out each evening for the stray children so he wouldn't starve. Bucky worked alongside other young slave children on the plantation. He pulled weeds and killed the aphids in the rose garden near the Big House. He knew that only the slaves who worked were entitled to receive a portion of the monthly food delivered to the slave quarters on *issue day*.

The quiet young boy was exceptionally bright. Bucky had a lot of time to think, as he toiled at meaningless jobs, and he pondered the mysteries of life. He wondered why the moon changed its shape each month. He studied the efficient flight of a hawk as it bore down on a young duck floating on the Master's pond to grab the fowl in its claws with one swooping movement. The graceful action reminded Bucky of the slaves who sang and danced with elegant dipping motions around the large mountain of corn husks that were shucked by the slaves each year in the fall. Corn shucking time was a joyous event for Bucky and the other slaves on the King Plantation. Next to Christmas, when the master's slaves were given new clothes and shoes for the year on *issue day*, it was his favorite event.

The curious young boy was fascinated by the idea of printed words, and the way the master's children would hide their noses in books for hours – reading on the porch or in the hammock, which was attached to a giant oak tree that grew on the lawn in front of the Big House.

Once, as Bucky squatted over the grass uprooting dandelions in front of the Big House, he noticed an abandoned book lying on the lawn near the hammock. Cautiously, he lifted his head and looked around, but he could see no one nearby. The twelve-year-old boy slowly inched closer to the object, weeding as he crawled, until the book was close enough to touch. Bucky stared in awe at the forbidden object – too scared to pick it up. A picture of a white man in tattered clothing was etched on the front of the brown leather cover. The setting seemed to be a tropical island, like the ones slaves described from their voyages over on slave ships. The image showed a beach with tall mop-shaped trees in the background. The man, in torn clothes, was signaling to a black man who wore a bone in his nose and a necklace made out of shells. There were other strange markings on the cover, which the boy knew to be letters. Bucky had often seen similar symbols on the sides of wooden crates or on signs planted alongside the roads, and he recognized that he was looking at words. Lost in the dream-world of words, Bucky's heart raced with yearning as he sat crouched on his haunches staring at the illicit item in wonder.

All of a sudden, the snap of a riding crop struck him full force across his left cheek, and Bucky fell flat onto the grass. At first, the stunned boy felt nothing, but then a sharp stinging pain, almost like the crack of thunder which crashes a few seconds after a flash of lightning, smacked him full force. Acting on impulse, Bucky smothered the stinging wound with his hands as he stared up into the face of Wendalyn King standing over him. The hand, which held the menacing riding-crop trembled against her hip. The other hand gripped the reins of a small gray mare. Despite his pain, Bucky noticed that she wore a dark brown-velvet riding outfit and a matching brown hat with a pheasant feather sewn into the side.

Mrs. King looked down at Bucky and sneered at him through thin clinched lips, "I swear, boy, I do believe that you were about to lay your filthy black hands on my son's book. Were you thinking of fouling that book with those black dirty hands, boy?" the angry woman questioned with scorn. Bucky saw her thin lower lip quiver with rage.

Bucky slowly rose to a kneeling position with his heels resting against his bottom. He lowered his head to the grass. "No Ma'am. I was just looking at the picture."

"Look at me, you stupid monkey!"

Bucky fearfully looked up at Mrs. King and observed that her small squinty eyes perfectly matched the dark brown color of her dress. Tears welled in the rim of his eyes as the frightened boy stared up at the mistress of the plantation with both terror and shame.

The Master's wife stood over Bucky for a few moments and not a hint of compassion embraced her soul. Her eyes fixed upon him with a brooding stare. When she spoke again, she measured her words slowly as though she were speaking to someone mentally impaired. "Boy, it is a crime in Maryland for slaves to learn to read. Do you want to go to prison?"

"No, Ma'am."

"It's the law! Books are forbidden to slaves, so you had better get back to work, and stay away from things that will only get you into trouble. Consider this lesson as my favor to you, boy. It will remind you to keep your rightful place amongst the more cultured people in the South. Now with that said, you may attend to the task of pulling dandelions from my lawn."

Bucky felt that he was expected to say something to Mrs. King. So, he lowered his head and watched in fascination as two large beads of blood fell onto a blade of grass. "Yes'um," he mumbled.

Bucky stayed bent in that position picking weeks until he heard Mrs. King stoop to pick up the book, mount her horse, and ride away. "I want my mammy," he cried.

From that day forward, a small straight scar about two inches long cut a diagonal line across Bucky's left cheek. The incident with Mrs. King taught Bucky to be more cautious, but it did not squelch his spirit.

To nourish his desire to learn, Bucky liked to squat unnoticed behind the woodpile and listen to broad-backed slaves swap stories around the campfire about the personal or legendary tales of slaves on other plantations.

Once he recognized the rich baritone voice of a slave called Tucker talking to the circle of men. "I heard tell 'bout a young slave over near Bucktown who had a powerful yearnin' to run away from his master. First time dat boy got caught, d'overseer cut off his two smallest toes. When he got a notion to run off again, De master's dogs tracked him to d'swamp and tore into him until most of his clothes and skin were in tatters. Slave-catcher's dragged dat poor bleedin' boy back to d'quarters and chopped *all* de toes on his left foot. Now, dat slave don't be goin' nowhere after dat. He be spendin' his days on his knees pullin' weeds in the master's cornfield."

"Why didn't de master just sell dat boy south?" asked someone sitting around the circle of men.

"D'master be wantin' to make an example of dat boy so no other slave be gittin' an idea to be makin' tracks north."

From the stories told in the quarters, Bucky came to know the name of the free Negro known as Denmark Versey who bought his freedom from his master when he was thirty-three, then set out to preach the virtues of freedom for all slaves.

Bucky listened to the men discuss the story of Nat Turner in guarded whispers inside the cabins. A blacksmith named Riley, who used to live on a plantation in Virginia, loved to tell the tale of Nat Turner whenever anyone would listen.

"Now, old Nat Turner was a slave out Virginia-way who claimed to be called-on by the Lord to become a preacher-man. Some folks even called him a prophet. He said dat his mammy told him as a youngin' dat he would lead slaves, just like Moses done led de Israelites out of Egypt. Each night, his mammy recited chapters from d'Bible, and he memorized her words, 'specially dose passages from d'Old Testament. Old Nat grew up believin' that he was born to do somethin' special."

Bucky held his breath as he listened in the dark.

"One day, Old Nat decided he weren't gonna be a slave no more. So Nat Turner ran off to live in some caves where he claimed to have visions from d'Lord. He gathered a cluster of other runaway slaves around him to listen while he preached. He got it in his head to do something, and Nat Turner and six of his followers set out on a mission to kill white folks. He said God told him to deliver his people from bondage by slaying all white people. Soon, other slaves joined Nat and his band of six, until their numbers swelled to nearly seventy. Before Nat and his followers were finally caught and hanged, I heard tell he had killed sixty white men, women and children within a circle of twenty miles."

Bucky shuddered. He wanted his freedom as much as any slave, but fretted about what Nat Turner did in Virginia. He wondered – *Should unsuspecting people die so that others might be free?* Bucky reasoned that there must be a better way.

Being chosen to work in the forest all summer pleased the fourteen-year-old boy, and he enjoyed getting to know Naira's daughter, Esther, as they trimmed branches off the big logs felled by large-muscled men. One night Bucky woke Esther while she slept under the stars near a makeshift camp and silently motioned her to follow him into the woods. They walked without speaking for twenty minutes until they came to a clearing where Esther saw Old Jed sitting by a small campfire warming his hands. The trapper had been sent to the forest that summer to catch small game like muskrat, squirrel, and rabbit during the day so that the women could turn the rabbit and squirrel into a red bean and rice stew to feed the hungry slaves chopping logs for the master.

"Sit and warm yourself by the fire, Esther," instructed Jed in a serious but gentle tone of voice. With a quiet reverence, Esther sat on a log. "Listen to my words, child, but do not speak. When you have heard all that I have to say, you may stay, or you may walk back to the camp and never utter a word of what has been spoken around this fire to anyone. Do you understand?"

The flecks of gold in Esther's green eyes sparkled as they reflected off the flames in the fire, and slowly she nodded her head.

"I have watched you work. You tend to your job with a steady pace, and stay mostly to yourself. I can see that your character is strong. Naira has done well in raisin' you as her own child. Bucky tells me that you have a gift for drawin' critters in the dirt. That is a wonderful and useful gift from the Lord." Old Jed paused and looked closely into Esther's eyes. "I have begun to teach Bucky his letters so that he may one day learn to read, and I am willin' to teach *you* as well. What we do here at Night School in secret is dangerous and forbidden to all slaves. If you would care to stay and learn with Bucky, sit where you are. If you are scared, you may leave now and return to your pallet and allow this night to fade into your memory like a distant dream. There is no shame in the choice you make. Old Jed waited and looked at the green eyes of the girl thoughtfully wrinkling her brows. After a measure of time he said, "Good, Esther. We will begin with the letter **A**."

Throughout the summer, Bucky and Esther met in secret with Old Jed at night to learn to read, but he taught them other things besides their letters. The old man convinced the field boss that Esther and Bucky would be useful in helping him hunt for food to keep the workers strong, so part of their day was spent alone with Old Jed setting and retrieving traps in the forest.

There gradually came to Esther a wild and free spirit because of Old Jed. The old trapper showed Bucky and Esther where to look for that one special star, known as the North Star, which stayed fixed in the sky when all the other stars appeared to rise in the east and set in the west. Old Jed pointed out how a person could tell which way was north when clouds obscured the stars in the sky. "Feel the moss on the bark with your hands," he instructed. "Moss always grows thicker on the north side of the tree trunk. This knowledge could be useful to you on a rainy night." He showed his students how the thickness in the coat of a muskrat or squirrel signaled the coming of winter. He taught them how to set traps along the edge of the river to catch the brown muskrat that lived in burrows near its shore. The fur of the river rodent could fetch a little money or could be traded for useful supplies for a slave. Old Jed showed them which berries and roots were good for eating and those that would make them sick. He pointed out the leaves, roots, and bark that could heal a scratch or calm a stomach disorder. Old Jed taught his pupils how to trek through the underbrush like a cat without rustling a leaf or breaking a twig. He trained Esther and Bucky to listen to the sounds of the forest. "A flock of birds startled into flight might signal the approach of a wildcat, or a bear…or a pack of men." He showed them how to calm a dog with a bit of dried meat. The trapper told them many wondrous things about the world beyond their reach. "The waters from the rivers and creeks of the Eastern Shore run southwest all the way to a large bay called the Chesapeake with water so salty you can taste it by dipping your finger into its shore."

"Why are you teachin' us these things?" asked Bucky one day.

Old Jed looked at Bucky and Esther through his almost black eyes, which shaded the depth of wisdom buried beneath them. "You may one day find that you no longer want to be owned by another man. Readin' the signs of the roads and readin' the signs of the forest might come to be useful in makin' your way north where slaves are free."

"Why don't you go north, Old Jed?" asked Esther.

"Been north."

"Why did ya come back?" she asked with surprise.

"When I lived in the north, I learned to read and had many other wonderful experiences. I was mighty content. Then, one night I had a dream. An egret with large white wings spread about its head told me that it was my destiny to fly south to give others the gifts I learned up north – so they might know how it feels to be free. So, I traveled back to the low country of tides and marshes and got myself caught by some bad-tempered slave-catchers who sold me to this plantation for not much cash because I was so old." Old Jed chuckled softly as if remembering some private joke.

Bucky and Esther looked at each other. Clearly, there was a lot to consider, but Esther couldn't imagine a life away from her mammy.

All summer long the cicadas hummed while eager dragonflies flickered far above the ground amid the trees, and lazy clouds rolled gently across the sky. The days and weeks pressed forward until the last logs were finally loaded on creaking wagons and bound with heavy rope. All the way back to the slave quarters, the workers sang as they wearily marched behind the weighted wagons, which cut deep wheel ruts in the road.

Esther hugged her mammy with joy. "You've changed over de summer, Esther. Let me look at ya. I swear, child, I do believe you have grown like a weed in a cabbage patch. I sorely hate to admit it, but my little girl be growin' up."

Chapter 3 ~ April 1848 – The King Plantation

Esther could not remember exactly when, but it seemed from a very early age, that she discovered she had a talent for drawing. Because slaves were forbidden to learn to read and write, any tools for such purposes were banned to slaves. Esther had to feed her intense desire to draw in creative ways. Usually, that meant scratching in the dirt with a stick that had been rubbed hard against a rock until a sharp point formed the needed tool for the task. She found that her best drawing surface appeared after a gentle rain had saturated the earth. Then, the texture of the ground was perfect for creating a butterfly in flight or bringing the image of a water lily to life in the moist soil. Sometimes she would sneak a half charred twig from Mammy Naira's fireplace to sketch the form of a bird on the soft underside of a chunk of bark, or a firefly on one of the smooth flat stones that rested near the river.

On many occasions, while squatting on her haunches scratching a stick in the dirt, Esther had experienced the sting of a slap to her head, or the blow of a kick leveled into her backside by one of the adult slaves or a field foremen.

Naira would wag her finger and warn, "Child, what ya's doing will only lead to misery and heartache."

"I know, Mammy. I've learned my lesson." Esther would cease for a few days, until the powerful desire to draw overtook her pledge to stop. Common sense would yield to her yearning to sketch, and she would resume the act again with furtive caution.

When Esther turned twelve, a scrawny field foreman with buckteeth and crossed eyes, named Jasper, caught her behind one of the tool sheds. She had been drawing a spider with a fly in its web on an old plank of wood using a thin shard of charcoal she had pulled from the edge of a cold pit-fire that morning. Jasper dragged Esther by the roots of her hair to the overseer, a pitiless person known to the slaves as Boss Shelby, who was sucking on a blade of straw as he watched a dozen slaves stack bails of barley onto flatbed wagons.

Shelby Moss was a large-bellied man with yellowish-brown teeth stained from the mushy wad of tobacco that seemed to always rest inside his left cheek. The ill-tempered taskmaster had worked on the King Plantation as overseer for two years, and he insisted that all the slaves address him as Boss Shelby. Esther, however, had secretly imagined that it would be a lot more interesting to use his last name as part of the demanded title. Then he could be known in the slave quarters as Boss Moss.

The bored overseer swatted a large green horsefly, which was biting into the soft fleshy underside of his chin and looked at the scared half-caste slave who had been dragged before him. He stared at the mulatto girl with disdain. Shelby did not like the fact that some white man had obviously *jumped over the fence* with a black slave-woman to produce the abomination that stood before him. Shelby Moss considered such relationships evil and a sin against maintaining the purity of the white race.

Boss Shelby hawked a jellied glob of brown spit onto Esther's right foot. "What be yer name, gal?"

Esther looked up at the overseer and stared wide-eyed as a slow stream of brown spit oozed down the side of his mouth; painting his lip into a crooked frown. Her throat suddenly felt as though she had swallowed a lump of dried clay. Gulping, she barely choked out, "Esther."

"Jasper, why have you brought this lazy picaninny before me whilst I be busy directing this vital operation?" Shelby asked while picking his nose.

Esther saw one of the slaves, known as Sam, tilt his head toward the overseer and softly grunt, then quickly lower his eyes to pick up a bail of barley from the dirt.

"I caught this gal here using writin' tools in secret, behind the shed," announced Jasper. Then, he proudly produced the charcoal drawing of the spider web from behind his back, and beamed as though he was presenting an apple to his teacher.

Esther looked at the realistic illustration she had created on the wooden board with some pride, until it abruptly occurred to her that she was about to become a fly in the trap of the human spider, Boss Shelby Moss. She had witnessed the overseer's wrath on many occasions, and shuddered with the crushing thought that she was about to become his next prey.

Shelby bent over until he was four inches from Esther's face. An acrid stench from sour whiskey and wet tobacco hammered Esther, but she willed herself not to pull away in disgust. "Looks like this worthless excuse of a maggot needs a lesson as to where her rightful place might be in this here world!"

Esther, like every other slave on the plantation, knew that the "lesson" was a whipping – carried out by Boss Shelby in front of all the slaves in the quarters as a reminder of what might happen to any one of them if they did not conform to the overseer's rules for all slaves on the King Plantation. The truth was, Shelby Moss enjoyed using his whip. It excited him and provided a sick form of amusing entertainment from the monotony of his job. "Jasper, remove this abomination from my sight! barked the overseer.

"Yes, boss."

One hour after the work bell signaled that it was time to quit for the day, every slave on the plantation was called to watch as Boss Shelby made an example of Esther. Naira could hardly contain her anguish. Large tears trickled down her cheeks like rain on a windowpane, and she had to be supported by Old Jed and another woman who stood next to her.

A somber slave bound Esther's hands together with rough hemp. The rope was then pulled through a large metal hook located high on a sturdy whipping pole. Esther wore a coarse tow-linen garment that hung loosely around her body. The slave mumbled something under his breath as he tore the garment from her neck to expose her tender young back. Out of the corner of her eye, Esther was mortified to see Bucky standing off to the side by himself. The skin on his face seemed to have faded to the color of the gray slate that covered the roof on the Big House.

Boss Shelby cracked his large black whip over his head releasing a snapping sound that vibrated menacingly through the air. Smirking broadly, he faced the slaves in the quarter like a preacher addressing his congregation. "We have before us an uppity half-breed who has broke a rule. This good-for-nothing piece of slime seems to have forgot her place in life. She thinks that it be her station in life to be an artist or some other such nonsense."

The overseer placed the whip under his armpit and spit out a glob of tobacco near Esther's feet. He slowly grabbed a small pouch from his shirt-pocket, pulled out a pinch of tobacco, and stuffed the brown shreds into the left side of his mouth. Clearly, Shelby Moss was enjoying the moment before his captive audience. He wanted to build a measure of drama to the occasion, and took pleasure in making the slaves squirm. "It be the responsibility of yer overseer, Boss Shelby, to teach this sneaky baboon a lesson, so that she might never again believe that she be better than the rest of you slaves."

Shelby Moss continued to preach. Low murmurs of, "Yes, Mas'r," "No, sah," and "Amen, Boss" issued from the slaves as they were forced to hear Shelby sermonize his interpretation of the Bible's prophecy for the children of Hamm. At its conclusion he pronounced. "This ungrateful gal will receive ten lashes of the whip, which be the punishment for female children under the age of womanhood."

Esther wanted to be brave and not scream, but the pain was too great. After the whip had cut into her back five times, she remembered being surprised to hear a crack of thunder just before she fainted.

Naira took pork grease from the shelf in the cabin to mix with ashes from the fireplace. She gently spread the mixture on the wounds laid open across Esther's back like a platter of fresh fish that had been gutted for supper. Esther might have scarred horribly had it not been for Old Jed. He appeared at Naira's cabin late that night carrying a large burlap sack filled with large wet leaves he had gathered from the marsh. He instructed Naira to abandon the grease and soot, and lay the fresh leaves over the cuts and bind the back with strips of clean cloth. "These leaves will draw out any infection that might've formed and will help the scarring."

Naira looked at Old Jed with even more affection for this gentle friend. "Will she be alright Jed?" Naira whispered as she walked him outside the cabin.

Jed shook his head and sighed. "I don't know. The scars on her body should heal well enough." He peeked through the door before turning from Naira to leave and said, "It'll be up to us to help her mend her spirit."

Esther could not stand up for three days. It took another week to restore her health so she could resume her job working with Naira in the kitchen. All the slaves in their cabin took turns caring for her. Jed continued to bring the wet leaves to Naira each night, and Bucky stopped by when he could to check on her progress. He tried to cheer his friend by telling her amusing stories that had happened on the plantation during the day. Esther listened to Bucky, but she did not say much.

While the wounds across her back healed, the half-caste slave girl had plenty of time to think. When awake, she recalled the many lessons taught to her by Old Jed. At night, bright shiny stars consumed her dreams.

Chapter 4 ~ 1849 – Summer of Enlightenment

After receiving the whipping from Boss Shelby, Esther grew cautious and distrustful as she tended to her chores. Thanks to Old Jed, the lashes on her back eventually faded to thin raised scars. But the scars inside her body refused to heal.

A tiny kernel of hatred came to live inside Esther's heart. It lay buried within her like the tender nut of the pecan encased inside its hard protective shell. She went about her chores with an energy that earned her the praise and respect of being a good slave worker. Whenever possible, she avoided all white people on the plantation. She especially shied away form Boss Shelby and Wendalyn King as though they were an infection that could cause her to break out with the pox. Gradually, Esther came to despise the fact that, without wanting it to be so, white blood pumped through her heart. It appalled her to know that she possessed the same blood as the mean-spirited white oppressors who forced her mammy and all the other slaves on the plantation to work hard until they became old and dried up like the wild grape leaves that withered in the forest after an autumn frost.

Esther gave these matters serious thought as she went about her daily work, but she was not completely prejudiced by her feelings. She had to admit, that she had never seen Master King hit or abuse any of the slaves he owned on his plantation. It seemed to Esther that *his* great sin was one of indifference to the workers on his plantation. Without knowing it, Esther had come very close to the truth.

Steidley King existed in a private realm of his own making. Esther's father had grown up as the only child of parents who had immigrated to Maryland from Norway. He had been raised in an environment of luxury and privilege. The handsome fair-skinned child with straight pale-blond hair and soft-blue eyes lived in a fantasy world. As a boy, he had read all the works of William Shakespeare and found poetic creations of himself in most of the tragic figures featured in Shakespeare's later plays. His favorite was the brooding prince of Denmark featured in *Hamlet*. When the boy turned eighteen, Steidley inherited the King Plantation after his parents died from a typhoid epidemic. The incident shattered his world, and the young man felt lost and alone.

At twenty, Steidley King exchanged wedding vows with the daughter of Mason Waverley, the owner of a nearby plantation. His parents had prearranged the marriage when Steidley was fourteen. It had been their belief that the union would strengthen the family's position in southern society. Steidley King married Wendalyn Waverley to honor his dead parents' wishes. It was a loveless marriage almost from the start. Wendy's unpredictable fits of rage and hateful nature drove a wedge in their marriage almost form the start. Over time, he became drawn to the kind nature of a shy house slave named Janet. Her gentle spirit and thoughtful ways filled a longing within him that he had never before known.

Naira's bedtime story was, in fact, close to the truth. Master King *had* been brokenhearted when Wendalyn sold Esther's mother to the Deep South. But, he was also a coward and more than a little afraid of his wife and her family's social position.

So he avoided his half-caste daughter, not only because he feared further retribution from Wendalyn, but also because it saddened him deeply to gaze at her. The child looked so much like her mother. In truth, Esther was a mixture of both her parents.

So, while Esther grew up in the slave quarters under the loving guidance of Mammy Naira, Master Steidley King hunted in the woods with other men from nearby plantations who were equal to his social class. He sat hidden in his duck blind to shoot the wild ducks that landed on his lake with the same shotgun his father had given him for his sixteenth birthday. Master King filled his time playing cards one night each week with his father-in-law's poker group. He gave and attended lavish parties. He doted on the five children from his marriage with Wendy, and spoiled them just enough to make them unattractively self-indulged. Steidley King reread his favorite fictional plays written by William Shakespeare, and the many other books that lined the shelves of his library. He painted beautiful portraits of his children, or still-life oil paintings of fruit or other contrived arrangements. He had no interest in farming, and left the intricate workings of the plantation to his wife and the overseer named Shelby Moss, whom she had interviewed and hired.

On the day Esther was being whipped by Shelby Moss, Steidley King had been losing in a chess game at the home of his father-in-law, Mason Waverley. He never knew about the incident because his wife thought it best to keep him ignorant about what went on in the quarters. Besides, she was unsure of how her husband might react to the beating of his own daughter. Wendy, on the other hand, had been rather pleased that Janet's daughter had received a whipping. In truth, she would have sold Esther long ago had it not been for Naira. Wendalyn King was somewhat fond of the old mammy, and she knew how much the barren kitchen slave loved the little girl. But that would all change soon. The little girl was no longer a child, and plans were being made to sell the girl, who was growing into a lovely woman, to the Deep South when she turned fourteen.

The summer following the whipping, Esther was again invited to work in the woods with the slaves who chopped wood for the master. She and Bucky continued to learn from Old Jed, but now Esther had grown more reserved. The wild spirit of the previous *summer of enlightenment* left Esther. A new passion of spirit embraced her senses. She memorized the lessons of Old Jed with the fury of a student who wanted to absorb every ounce of knowledge stored inside the teacher's brain. If Jed noticed a change in Esther, he kept his thoughts to himself.

Once when they were setting traps for Jed, an irritated Bucky asked, "Why are you so serious all the time, Esther? I never see you smile anymore."

"I don't have time to smile, Bucky. There's too much work to be done, and too much learnin' to be learned. When I'm free, then I'll have time to smile."

Feeling somewhat ashamed, Bucky looked at his companion and nodded. He was deeply concerned about his friend, but understood the solemn gravity of Esther's words that said so much.

As much as she missed drawing in the dirt, Esther vowed that she would *never* again use her extraordinary gift until she was a slave no more. Then, she would draw, and sketch, and paint using the special oil paints that Old Jed had told her about. Then, she would create a thousand landscapes like the beautiful painting of a lake in a lush green valley she had once seen along the wall of the master's dining room.

The four seasons of Esther's thirteenth year came and went like the ebb and flow of the tides in the rivers and marshes of the low country. Esther spoke of her feelings of hatred to no one. Not even to her mammy when they lay in the dark on their pallets to discuss the gossip of the day. At night as she slept, the murky pain of hatred stained her heart like the smoky haze from the fireplace, which saturated the walls of the cabin. The idea of freedom consumed her every waking thought and engulfed her dreams at night.

Chapter 5 ~ Summer 1850 – The Forest

The summer of 1850 was to be Esther's last *summer of enlightenment* helping Old Jed trap food for the slaves who cut timber for the Master. Bucky and Esther could read as well as Old Jed from the books he mysteriously produced from hidden places in the forest. Once the students asked him where he got such precious items, but he only smiled and shook his head. "Best you not know 'bout things that could only get y'all in trouble."

There was a buzz among the slaves that summer that Steidley and Wendy King would be selling some of their slaves for a cash-profit to a master over in Hurlock because they had lost money from their lumberyard business in Baltimore the previous winter. Rumor had it that both Esther and Bucky were slated to be sold sometime before Christmas. Everyone in the quarters was on edge.

Rumors often spread in the quarter as fast as the wild Virginia creeper vines that covered the forests each summer, so Esther could not be certain that what was being said was true. Sometimes the overseer and field bosses would start a rumor to scare the slaves into submission, or to coax more work out of them by telling them the master would never sell his *hardworking* slaves.

Jed's students had become so good at trapping small game that he often let them venture into the woods alone. One day while setting traps deep in the forest, Bucky and Esther spotted a handbill tacked up high to the trunk of a tree. It was an advertisement from a slave trader that read:

Will Pay Top Dollar for
Strong Hard-working Slaves
Must Be
Sound of Body and Mind

Contact Norman Willy at:
P.O. Box 19 Easton, Maryland

Esther stared at Bucky and said, "This is a sign, Bucky."

Bucky looked confused. "I know it's a sign, Esther."

"No, Bucky, this is a *sign*, a symbol...a signal that the time has come for us to go north. I can feel it in my bones. The rumors about us being sold have been weighing on my mind and now that I see this, I am certain that something horrible will happen if we don't go." Esther spoke calmly, but her heart was beating as fast as the wings of a small blue hummingbird drinking nectar from a nearby honeysuckle flower.

Bucky looked at Esther for a long moment before nodding his head. He reached up and tore down the paper and ground it into the dirt with his foot.

That night, seated around a small fire on a starless night, Bucky told Old Jed about the rumors and the handbill and what they had decided to do.

"You sure this is what you want?" asked Old Jed.

"Yes," whispered Bucky, "and we want you to come with us."

"Too old, Bucky," said Jed, "and my bones are too weary. I would only slow you down. You can find your way north by following the light of the North Star, and putting into practice all the other things that I have taught you. Remember?"

Bucky smiled and said, "We remember, Old Jed. Read the signs of the road and the signs of the forest."

Esther remained unusually quiet, and left the talking to Bucky. Finally, Old Jed turned to Esther and asked, "What about you, Esther? Are you sure you want to leave this plantation and your mammy and travel north?"

Esther looked into the ruby embers of the fire and let out a deep sigh. "I have been gripped with the desire to be free every waking moment and within every nighttime dream since Shelby Moss whipped me in the quarters." Old Jed noticed that the muscles in Esther's face tensed as she spoke about Shelby Moss and her eyes narrowed as if remembering that horrible nightmare. "Yes, Old Jed, I truly do want to go to the North. I so much want to be free! But...I'm afraid."

"What are you afraid of, Esther?" asked Jed in a gentle voice.

Esther held Old Jed with her eyes. "Once, you told us that there are a lot more white folk up North, and...well...I *hate* white people, Old Jed. I want to live up North in a place where there are *no* white people."

"If you go north, child," chuckled Old Jed, "you're sure to have some dealings with white folk, because there are a powerful lot of them up there. So you best listen carefully to what I'm gonna tell you now, Esther."

The old man took a deep breath and let out a sigh. "Now Esther, I have met some white people in my day that were meaner than a muskrat with its paw caught in a trap. And I have met some white folk that were dumber than the babies in the quarters who would walk into a pit of fire if one of the mammies weren't there to grab them up. I have also met white folk that were hateful and ornery just for the sheer pleasure of it. But, child, it would be foolish for me to say that *all* white folks are bad."

Esther took in every word that Old Jed was saying. She held her breath and it was almost as though the forest had stopped breathing with her. When Jed thought that she had time to absorb this first information, he continued.

"I've also met some crooked Negroes who would sell their own mammies to a slave catcher if they thought it would advance their own selfish interests. I've met others who are lazy and shiftless, and some who possessed other undesirable vices. I don't particularly like that large-bottomed slave, named Mandy, who scrubs clothes up at the Big House 'cause I think she is mean-spirited by nature." Esther nodded, remembering how Jed had pulled her from the Big Buckwater when Mandy had tormented her with her friends. "Therefore, it would be downright foolish for me to believe that all black folk are good."

Jed took in another deep breath of air and continued. "Esther, I've met some white folk up north who went out of their way to show kindness to a frightened Negro slave who didn't even know how to read or write his own name. And I met others who handed me a meal from their kitchen door when I was half-starved. When you go north, child, some folks'll be good to you, and others will try and trick you so they can take your last penny. But I expect that you and Bucky will be smart enough to know who's for ya and who's not."

Esther stared down at a glowing log and her green eyes sparkled in the flickering light of the fire.

"Look at me, Esther," requested Old Jed in a gentle voice. "I know the weight of pain you've carried in your heart like a heavy stone these past months, but it would be unfair for you to judge all white folk using Shelby Moss and Wendy King as a measuring stick."

Large hot tears began to well in Esther's eyes. They fell down her cheeks and onto her chin. The silent tears fell in a stream wetting the front of her dress. It was the first time Esther had cried since that day at the whipping post when she screamed out in pain.

Old Jed looked kindly into Esther's eyes and said, "I think the hardest test that the Lord asks of his children is the lesson of forgiveness. But, child, if you can find it in your heart to release the burden of pain from those who have harmed you, your spirit will be set free."

"It's hard for me Old Jed!" Esther cried out in anguish. "No one understands what it was like to be whipped by that cruel man...or to look different from everyone else in the quarters...or to have my birth mammy taken from me when I was a baby so I could never know her love." Pain distorted Esther's face as she sobbed.

Without uttering a word, Old Jed stood up and slowly took his shirt off. By the glow of the fire, Esther and Bucky could see his chest. They gasped to catch sight of a succession of horrible scars that mutilated his upper body. The skin on his chest seemed to have been branded in many places with some instrument of torture. Bucky and Esther felt suddenly sick inside. It appeared as though a heated metal poker had been held against Old Jed's body and had scorched his skin into the hideous wounds that he exposed to them now. Bucky and Esther stared in horror at the grotesque scars. Each could only imagine the pain he must have endured at the hands of another human being. The two sat in stunned silence.

The old man looked kindly at his students and began to tell his tale. "When I was in the middle years of my life, I worked for a man who owned a tobacco plantation over near Williamsburg. That sack of manure beat his slaves purely for the pleasure of watching them scream for mercy. One day, I came upon this dung beetle of a master as he stood over a pretty young slave girl named Joan. He was beating the girl raw with a cane because, despite hours of labor, Joan had been unable to get a wine stain out of the large rug she had spread over a clothesline. He screamed that she was a useless wad of crap and hurled other horrible insults as he twisted her arm as he beat her with a stick. I winced with horror as the poor girl begged for mercy. To this day, I don't know what lead me to do it. But I walked over and grabbed the cane out of his hand, and broke it over my knee. The brute was so stunned that he stood planted in that spot like a dead tree stump and watched me walk to the slave quarters."

Bucky and Esther looked at each other and trembled at the thought of Old Jed's bravery.

"That night he came to my cabin. I knew that he would. He brought three large black field hands with him. The three slaves held me down as their master heated an iron poker over the coals in my fireplace until it glowed red. It took, what seemed like an eternity for him to torture me until I passed out," said Old Jed as he shuddered. "To this day, I can still hear the sound of his wicked laughter and smell the stench of burning skin as he pressed the hot metal rod into my flesh."

Esther was openly sobbing now, and Bucky came over and sat next to her. He wrapped her in his arms, like he was her mammy, and stroked her hair. At length, she composed herself and spoke. "I'm sorry, Old Jed. I never knew."

"Don't fret over this child," said Old Jed as he slowly buttoned his shirt and sat back down on his log. "It happened a long time ago. I was traded to another master shortly after that, which was probably wise, because I could think of nothing but how I was going to deliver revenge on my master...regardless of the consequence to me. In truth, I think he lived in fear of the same thought." Jed chuckled. "I went around my new plantation fairly consumed with anger. I'd get in fights to temper the burning ember of hatred in my soul."

Old Jed shrugged and poked a log on the fire with a stick. "Then one Sunday while delivering some muskrat to a trader, I came upon an old woman with no legs. She sat on a soiled blanket selling roasted peanuts by the side of the road. Stopping, I looked down at her as she heated the peanuts in their shells in a small cast iron pan over a simple fire.

For the first time in months, I stopped thinking about my own sorry-self. I felt so sad for her. I wondered how she had lost her legs, but I didn't ask. The most beautiful smile graced her face as she looked up at me from her place near that small fire on the ground. Without a word passing from my mouth, I pulled some pennies from my pocket. She gently took one penny from my hand and placed a handful of her roasted goobers into a newspaper cone. As she looked up to thank me, I felt certain that the warmth from the nuts in my hands fully matched the warmth of her smile. I caught my breath and wondered how a woman with such miserable circumstances could be so filled with happiness.

"I took her offering and walked up to the top of a hill where there was a pretty view of the valley and a majestic range of snowcapped mountains in the distance. It was the kind of day that takes your breath away. An early morning rain had wet the leaves of the trees, and they sparkled like tiny crystal beads in the sun. The nutty taste of the warm peanuts satisfied my hunger, and I began to think about the wondrous creations of the Lord. I thought about the woman with no legs, and how she'd found a productive way to make her way in the world. And, like a bolt of lightening it occurred to me, Esther, that no matter what trouble I might have in my life, there are so many others with worse troubles of their own. Slowly, I reached up and touched my face, and I was surprised to find that it was wet. I hadn't even known that I'd been crying. I cried, not for myself. I cried for the woman who had no legs, but could still smile. I cried for the beautiful day, and the peanuts that tasted better than any food I had ever put in my mouth. I cried, because at that moment I knew that to heal myself, I had to forgive that man for the pain he caused me."

Old Jed adjusted a log in the campfire and the action caused the flames to leap a foot into the air and send sparks flying skyward like dancing fireflies. He looked at his students and smiled.

"Esther, a weight lifted from me at that moment, and I felt as light as the clouds that floated before me in the blue sky. I then noticed a beautiful rainbow arched behind the snowcapped mountains. I felt that it had been put there just for me. I wiped the tears from my eyes, and with that simple gesture, I became whole again. It was shortly after that experience that I made plans to escape to the North."

No one spoke for several seconds. Esther looked at the fire and listened to the crackle of the wood. The tiny yellow sparks that flew into the night air reminded Esther of the stars in the sky. Finally, she looked at her dear friend and teacher with a face that was calm but determined. "Thank you for sharing your story with me, Old Jed. I know it must've been hard for you," said Esther emotionally.

"Child, I don't know if you're ready to forgive Shelby Moss just yet, but I do know that you'll never be able to get on with your own life until you do. Esther, I believe that every person put on this earth is on a journey to learn and grow. Shelby Moss and Wendy King are on their own journey, and I believe that one day they'll have to answer for what they've done in this life. But you, Esther, are on your own journey. Forget about Shelby Moss, and get along with your own life. Try to take *that* unspeakable experience and turn it into something good." Old Jed coughed the winded rasp of the elderly. "Now, I know I'm just an old man talking too much, but you think about what I've said. Promise me that you will, Esther."

Esther got up from the log where she had been sitting with Bucky, and crossed over to where Old Jed was sitting on his log near the campfire. She knelt in the dirt before him, threw her arms around his neck and mumbled into his chest. "I promise. How can I ever thank you for what you've done for us? Whatever happens in my life, Old Jed, I will never forget the lessons you taught Bucky and me. You'll always be a part of my journey."

Chapter 6 ~ September 1850 – The Slave Quarters

When Esther returned from the forest that summer she was surprised to see that her mammy had lost a considerable amount of weight, and that she had been having a lot of trouble with her legs. Her ankles were so swollen and sore that large veins bulged under her skin. Sometimes her legs sweat with a sticky puss that oozed from open sores, and her limbs had to be wrapped with cotton rags. Mammy Naira had trouble standing for long periods of time and had been dismissed from her work in the kitchen.

As often happened in the plantation slave system, when slaves could no longer perform an assigned task, they were given a new job. The old mammy, who had worked so long and so hard for the Kings at the Big House, was placed in charge of the young babies who ran about in the quarters, so their own mammies could work in the fields or up at the Big House. Naira loved the little children, and she was happy to spend her days in the quarters. Sometimes she could sit during the day, and this relieved the swelling in her legs.

Esther had only been home for a few days when she told Naira what she and Bucky were planning to do. They were alone in the cabin while the other slaves were gathered outside for *issue day*.

Each month, a wagon rolled into the slave quarters and Shelby Moss and some of the other field foremen unloaded an allotment of food for the slaves. Salt, pickled pork, salted fish, corn meal, dried beans, rice, and other food items were handed out to the slaves. The food kept the slaves alive, but the portions were not plentiful. The extra rabbits and squirrels caught by Old

Jed and some of the other old slaves added variety to an otherwise boring diet. Once a year, usually at Christmastime, clothes, blankets, and shoes were distributed along with the food.

Naira sat on an old stool and soaked her feet in a warm bucket of water. Esther knelt at her mammy's feet chopping the root of a water lily she had gathered from the marshes to place in the water. Jed had taught her that the root contained healing medicine that would ease the swelling. Esther then sat on the hard earthen floor and gently rubbed her mammy's swollen legs. "Dat sure do ease d'misery in my legs, child," said Naira as she looked lovingly at her daughter and wondered where the time had gone. Her little girl was suddenly fourteen and growing prettier by the day. "Ya seem distracted as of late, Esther. Is dere something on yo' mind?"

Esther did not know how much time she would have alone with Naira, so she decided to speak to the point. "I don't know how to tell you this any other way, Mammy, but Bucky and I are going away. I will not say other than that. If you're questioned up at the Big House, you can say, with honesty, that you don't know where I've gone. I know that you've always put great stalk in telling the truth, and if you don't know any details, you can look Master King and Miz Wendy in the eye and not have to lie for me. I won't tell you when, and I won't be able to say goodbye, so you need to listen to me now. We may never have another chance to be alone."

Large tears trickled from Naira's eyes, as she rocked back and forth on her stool. Naira started to say something, but Esther reached up and put her hands to her mammy's lips. "Please, Mammy, let me get through this while I still have the courage. For fourteen years, I have loved you as much as any daughter could love her mammy. And I'm grateful for all that you've given me. You taught me that I was special. You told me it so often that you convinced me to believe in myself. There's no greater gift a parent can give a child. I love you, Mammy, and I'll never forget you. If I could stay here with you, I would, but there's a burning inside me to be free." Esther's voice started to choke. She stopped talking and buried her head in her mammy's lap.

After a time, Naira spoke, and Esther was surprised that her mammy's voice sounded so calm. "Daughter, I knew dat dis day would be comin', and I'm happy with de choice you be makin'. 'Cause if'n you don't be makin' dis choice, down de line, somebody else will be makin' a different choice for ya. I know dat Miz Wendy has been unhappy dat you's been here dis long. I be hearin' de rumors on dis plantation my own self. So, don't you go frettin' about your old mammy. I will be missin' my little girl, but I will be just fine knowin' dat you be free and in a better place."

"Mammy," cried Esther, "I promise that I'll find a way to get word to you that I've made it north, and I'm safe. I don't know how, but I *will* see you again someday."

"If dis be somethin' dat can be happenin', it would make your old mammy mighty glad. But if it don't come to pass, I will see you again, child, in d'house of de Lord."

Esther looked lovingly into the face of her mammy and whispered softly, "Amen to that, Mammy."

Chapter 7 ~ September 1850 – Escape to the North

Old Jed had advised Bucky and Esther to leave late on a Saturday night because Sunday was the Lord's Day and the only day of rest for the slaves on the King Plantation. "With luck, you might not be missed 'til Monday morning when you don't show up for work. By then, you will have left two whole nights of travel behind you, and the men who will surely ride out after you."

Bucky and Esther decided to leave after work on the second Saturday in September because the moon would be a thin crescent in the sky and would give off little light. Esther began hoarding a few scraps of food that week, but she didn't want to stockpile too much. She was scared that the gesture might tip off a snitch in the slave quarters; someone who might pass the word along to Boss Shelby or to somebody up at the Big House. The overseer encouraged slaves to spy on other slaves for a reward or special favors.

Esther knew that she would be able to take very little with her, the clothes and old shoes she would be wearing, and the shawl that Naira had knitted her last Christmas. On the day of her departure, she added a piece of salt-herring, a chunk of baked pumpkin, and a dry slice of cornbread (known as ashcake to the slaves because it was often baked in the ashes of the fireplace) to an old bandanna she had hidden in the crotch of a tree located behind the outhouse. Esther knew that she and Bucky would not starve. Thanks to the lessons of Old Jed, they could survive on the edible roots and berries from the forest. There would be no point in trapping animals to eat because a fire would be far too dangerous for the runaways.

If Mammy Naira suspected that Esther was leaving that night, she never let on to Esther. She had promised Esther that if she went missing some morning, she would just tell everyone that her daughter must have gone trapping with Old Jed and Bucky. It was a reasonable explanation, as the three often went out together.

The women chatted about their day before turning in to bed that night. Esther was so nervous that she only pretended to sleep. She waited until the fire in the hearth had turned to tiny yellow embers while listening to the familiar sounds of her mammy and the others in her cabin sleeping. In the distance, a barn owl hooted softly. It was the signal that Bucky was ready to leave. Esther reached for her knitted shawl and slowly stood up. She looked one last time at Naira asleep on her pallet. The cabin was so dark that she could barely make out the face of the woman who had given her so much. *I love you, Mammy. Please do not grieve too much for me.* Esther slowly walked to the door and gently slipped out of the cabin that had been her only home.

Esther walked over to the outhouse like she meant to do some business inside and bumped smack into Mandy stepping out the door. The slave girl looked at Esther through drowsy eyes and scowled. Mandy spit onto the dirt before swaggering back to her cabin. Esther's heart leapt in her chest, and she worried if Mandy might come back to check on her. She entered the small wooden structure and waited for five minutes. She removed her nightdress to reveal the skirt and blouse she wore underneath. Later she would tie the garment to a rock and throw it into the river so its scent would not attract the dogs that were sure to follow after them. Esther cautiously emerged from the outhouse. She saw no one. A quiet stillness floated over the quarters, broken by the sporadic sounds of slaves snoring in their cabins. Esther quietly walked away from the quarters and grabbed the bandanna from its hiding place in the tree. The sky was filled with stars sparkling overhead, and Esther breathed a sigh of relief. From the shelter of the tree, the young girl lingered briefly for one last look at the quarters wondering how she could walk away from her mammy and the security of the only life she had ever known. Once again, she heard the hooting of an owl coming from the direction of the woods. Esther turned away and walked into the shadowy darkness toward the forest.

Esther followed the trail until she found Bucky and Old Jed. Her heart beat rapidly in her chest, and her mouth was as dry as the dirt at her feet. She could barely swallow. Old Jed was dressed like he was going trapping. He told the pair that he did not want to be near the slave quarters on Sunday so that folks might assume that the three had gone trapping together.

"Walk all night, but stay off the main roads," cautioned Old Jed. "There are always slave-catchers out looking for a runaway. You must trek alongside the Choptank River northeast until it splits into a fork. Then y'all will want to follow the river called the Tuckahoe, which is on the northern end of the split, so find a shallow place to cross on the Choptank when you can. The Tuckahoe veers in a northeasterly path and it'll take you in the general direction of where you want to go. When the river peters out you'll be more than half way to Pennsylvania. Follow the North Star and in time you'll cross the Mason Dixon line to freedom. It's vital that y'all find a safe place to hide during the day, and you must move with a fast pace each night. With luck, no one'll miss you until working-time on Monday morning. By then, you should be far enough away from the plantation that the overseer and his men will soon tire of chasing after you.

Now, travelin' at a steadfast pace should get you to Pennsylvania in about five days. I know that there are folks on the Underground Railroad who could help you, but I'm not sure how you might find 'em. When y'all get to Philadelphia, you'll be out of the south, and there are many good folks, especially the Quakers, who'll help get y'all settled." Both Esther and Bucky had been told how to spot a Quaker by the noticeable way they dressed with plain clothes and similar hats and bonnets.

Finally, when there was no more to discuss, Old Jed held out his hands to Esther. She thought he intended to bid her goodbye so she happily reached for his grasp. She was surprised when he placed a thin bundle of cloth into her palm. Esther could feel the weight of round metal coins beneath the cloth. "It isn't much," the old slave muttered, "but it will see you to a meal or two until you can find work."

Esther knew that Jed traded the muskrats he trapped to a man from a local store for a few pennies. The coins felt heavy and cold in Esther's hand. The simple slave girl had never possessed any money in her young life. She held the bag clumsily as if it contained precious jewels and parted her lips to speak.

Old Jed placed a calloused hand over her lips. "Don't say a word, child. Y'all will be havin' a need for this money, and I've not much use for it these days. Anyway, as long as there are muskrats in the river, I can get more coins where these came from. Now, I don't want any argument about this from you youngsters."

"Thanks, Old Jed," whispered Esther with sincerity. Tears welled in her eyes as she carefully placed the coins inside her bandanna next to the food.

Bucky cleared his throat and added, "You've been so kind to us, Old Jed. Sort of like the daddy I never got the chance to know. I'll always be grateful to you." Bucky hugged his friend, and for the first time realized that over the many *summers of enlightenment,* the student had grown taller than his teacher.

Old Jed smiled and looked at the scared young children. "I had a dream last night that you two were eating biscuits with a white woman who lived on a farm. She was a slender woman with a kind face who wore a white bonnet on her head and a long white nightdress. Don't know what it might mean, but you seemed content enough in her company, so maybe the dream is a good sign."

Esther nodded her head slowly, looked at Jed through wet green eyes, and spoke to him earnestly. "I've given much thought to what ya shared with me that night by the fire, Old Jed. I promise that I'll try to look for the good in the people up North and not to blame all white folk for the ugly deeds of those like Shelby Moss."

"I know that you will, child," Jed said lovingly. "Now, I hope that you two might see fit to pass the things that you've learned from me on to someone else. I believe that it'll be in your nature to want to do something nice for others who may need a lift up."

"We'll do our best to make you proud of us," declared Bucky.

A lump suddenly crowded Esther's throat as she realized that she might never see her old friend again. She quickly shook the thought from her head. "We'll try and get word to you, if possible, to let you know that we're safe," whispered Esther.

Old Jed nodded and smiled warmly at the two children who had given him so much joy. Tears were beginning to well at the bottom of his eyes. He cleared his throat and urged, "Y'all best get going now. Every moment is important."

The teacher and students hugged one last time before quietly parting company, each slipping away into the woods in different directions.

Chapter 8 ~ September 1850 – The Pursuit

Esther and Bucky threaded softly through the low underbrush of the woods well off the main road. The night sky, though studded with stars, was dark, but the darkness did not hamper their movements. The pair had spent many nights in the woods with Old Jed, and they moved with soundless ease as they made their way northeast toward the Choptank River. Neither spoke. They used animal calls and silent gestures to communicate with each other. When the runaways had been walking for several hours, they heard the pounding sound of horses' hooves galloping on the road in the distance.

In an instant, they lay flat on the damp ground of the wooded area. Anxiety gripped Esther's thoughts. The frightened girl's head began to swirl, and her hands shook so hard that she grabbed moist fistfuls of soil from the ground. In her imagination, she could see Shelby Moss sitting astride his big white horse, cracking a whip in the night air. Esther willed her mind to connect with her surrounding before the nightmarish vision took complete hold of her. She forced herself to breathe deeply and smell the leaves, moss, and dead twigs rotting on the moist floor of the marshy woods. The musky scent was so soothingly familiar to her that it covered her like the warmth of mammy's quilt, and she was gradually comforted and calmed. When the horses had long passed, Esther continued to breathe deeply from her position on the ground until her heart rate slowed. She sighed as Bucky placed a reassuring hand on her back. On impulse, she took the wad of soil still grasped tightly in her hand and placed it in the pocket of her skirt. As she braced herself to stand, Esther prayed that the forests in the north would give her as much comfort as the lowlands of her youth.

"We must get up and move as quickly as we can, Esther," whispered Bucky nervously. It was clear that he too had been shaken by the incident. "If we can make it to the fork in the river that Old Jed told us about, I think we'll have a good chance."

After midnight, clouds covered the stars and patches of rain showers came and went throughout the night. The fugitive slaves could not see the North Star, but it was not important because they could follow the course of the river and know that it was taking them in the right direction. At length, they came to a shallow place near a bend in the running waters of the Choptank.

Bucky directed, "Take my hand. I think we should cross here, Esther. Up ahead, when the river breaks into a fork, we will be on the proper side to make our way up the Tuckahoe River." The chilly water crept past Esther's knees, and she gripped Bucky's hand fearing that she might be swept away into deeper water. Neither could swim, so the terror of deep water weighed heavily on their minds. Although the water moved swiftly, it never washed past their waists, and the pair made it safely to the shore. Esther's thin dress was soaked through to her skin. She noticed that the clump of dirt in her pocket had vanished, leaving nothing behind but a muddy stain on her dress. She wondered if it was a sign. *I can't think about that now,* Esther said to herself. The determined girl was cold and sore as she trudged into the unfamiliar night. Her spirits perked a bit when she saw in the distance that the river split in two directions just as Old Jed said it would, and they were indeed on the right side.

The exhausted friends walked throughout the night until a gentle indigo glow began to light the eastern sky. Bucky whispered in a soft voice. It broke the silence of the night much like the light of the sun yielding on the horizon. "We'd best find a place to hide."

Esther nodded her head, but was still too anxious to speak. She followed Bucky to a small marshy cove. Years of erosion from the ebb and flow of the river had created a shallow cave in the bank of the river to form a sheltered hiding place. The cave would hide them from people walking along the upper bank of the Tuckahoe River. Esther could see from her vantage point in the cave, a tiny marshy island in the middle of the river about twenty yards away. The water raced swiftly, and Esther thought it looked deep. Wild reeds grew thickly along both sides of the river. Bucky and Esther agreed that the riverweeds would keep them dry and off the damp ground near the river. They quickly searched the area and gathered enough reeds to make a nest in which to lie down. The rest they pulled over them like fire kindling to hide their bodies from people walking on the trail above them near the bank of the river.

Esther pulled her shawl around her shoulders and burrowed her face into the folds of the wrap to get comfortable. The yarn, knitted so lovingly by her mammy, contained the smoky residue from the poorly ventilated fireplace that had warmed her cabin and cooked her meals each day of her life. Esther breathed into the shawl and sighed with longing. She wondered if Mammy Naira was up stirring the embers in the fire to make ashcakes for breakfast. Esther had not eaten since yesterday's dinner, but she and Bucky were too tired and scared to think about food. In the distance, a rooster crowed and the soft yelp from a dog answered its call just as Esther drifted into a fitful sleep.

Esther did not know how long she had been sleeping before it began to rain. The drops pelted against the river reeds and began to soak through the cracks in the reeds. The shallow overhang protected their upper bodies, but the cold downpour soaked them from the waist down.

Bucky whispered, "Don't worry, Esther, the rain is a blessing and will keep most folks indoors today and away from the river." The day passed with a miserable slowness and neither friend was able to sleep much, but Bucky had been right. On that particular dreary Sunday, no visitors came within earshot of their hiding place.

Bucky and Esther calculated from the position of the moon poking through a cloud that it was close to ten o'clock on Sunday night when they emerged from the soggy reeds. They freshened up from the waters of the Tuckahoe and shared the roasted chunk of pumpkin and stale ashcake before heading away from the river into the safety of the woods. Rain showers continued to come in spurts. The rain was irksome but just as Bucky had predicted, it seemed to keep people inside their homes and huddled around the comfort of their fireplaces. After several hours of walking, the fugitives felt a little easier about whispering an occasional comment.

"Bucky, I've been praying that we'd get the gift of this night before Shelby Moss realizes we're gone." With sadness in her voice, Esther murmured softly. "I keep wondering what Mammy did in the quarters all day Sunday to keep her spirits up, yet knowing in her heart that I was probably lost to her forever."

Bucky nodded his head and added. "I pray that Naira and Old Jed can convince Boss Shelby that they're not involved in our escape from the plantation." Bucky started to add that the overseer would love to look for an excuse to use his whip on the fugitive slaves, but thought better of it. There was no point in worrying Esther more than necessary.

The rain continued on and off throughout the night. Esther's wet clothes soaked through to her skin, and she was cold, tired, and sore. While stepping over a log, Esther snagged her shoe on a jagged branch and split the sole of her right shoe. Mud and dirt rubbed against her skin causing blisters to form on the bottom of her foot. She made a mental note that she would repair the split by lining the inside of her shoe with fresh leaves the next time they stopped to rest.

The fugitives kept up a forced march throughout the long hours of darkness. Lack of sleep and food impeded their progress, but the runaways stumbled onward with a purpose fueled by fear. In her mind, Esther started to sing the Negro spirituals and work songs the slaves had invented over time to ease the monotony of their long days in the fields. The cheerful rhythms helped to keep her tempo up and her pace from slowing.

Gonna jump down, turn around, pick a bail of cotton.
Gonna jump down, turn around, pick a bail of hay.
Oh, Lordy, pick a bail of cotton.
Oh, Lordy, pick a bail of hay.

By early morning, Esther and Bucky were exhausted, and they wearily searched for a hiding place to sleep during the light of day. Away from the river, they found a large stack of hay in a field that had been partially harvested. In the distance, a hazy smear of smoke escaped from the chimney of a small farmhouse built next to a large red barn. The pair agreed that the haystack would be a warm place to spend the day sleeping.

"If it rains again today, we will stay warm and dry inside this haycock," whispered Esther.

Bucky smiled and nodded. "Esther, you climb up to the top, and I'll follow."

Being careful not to disturb too much of the hay, the fatigued fugitives climbed to the top of the fragrant heap and carefully carved out a hollow space in the center of the hay. They crawled inside, and Bucky pulled the straw over them to recreate the original shape of the mound. The hideout was deep enough to keep them warm, and a small air hole provided sufficient circulation for breathing.

"I pray that no one notices that this mound has been tampered with," said Bucky earnestly. "We're worn out, Esther, and need to get some sleep."

Esther felt like a muskrat in its burrow. The hungry girl wished that she could eat the hay that sheltered her so amiably like the muskrat that eats the grasses and roots that grow inside its marshy cave. The famished runaways decided to share the last bit of salted herring from their food supplies. That left only the hunk of jerked pork that Bucky was saving to calm a nervous dog if the need should arise. Exhaustion soon took hold, and the pair fell into a deep slumber.

Loud voices pulled Esther and Bucky from a deep sleep. Esther's heart began to beat rapidly as the blast of Shelby Moss's distinct drawl bellowed at someone nearby. Bucky reached over and placed a gentle hand on Esther's arm. The gesture calmed her, and reminded her that she was not alone. Bucky and Esther concentrated on the muffled-conversation taking place outside their hideout in the haycock.

"We been looking for two slaves that run away from the King Plantation over near the Big Buckwater. They came up missin' Sunday night when one of our slaves thought it were suspicious that they were nowhere to be found. The missing slave gal was last seen late Saturday night using the outhouse. My men and me have rode our horses hard all night hopin' to run 'em down. Any chance you boys have seen a tall black buck with a scar on his cheek, or a half-caste female abomination with greeny-eyes and light brown hair? There'd be a reward in it for ya if you were fixin' to help us out. What'd you say yer name was again, friend?"

The farmer cleared his throat and offered, "My name is Frank Milford, and these are my sons, Adam and Clayton. Sorry, but I can't help you. I don't think your slaves are in these parts. My boys and me have been working in this field all day, 'cept for a break at around two-o'clock for dinner with the wife and daughter. We haven't seen anyone but the circuit judge ride by in his buggy on his way to Templeville. If you're slave hunting, where are your hounds?"

"My bitch just gave birth to a litter of puppies, and this mornin', my male hound stepped in a metal trap and broke his foreleg as we searched the swamp a few miles north of our plantation." Shelby Moss spit a wad of tobacco in the dirt and shook his head in disgust. "I had one of my men carry the dog on his horse back to the barn to get him tended to."

Bucky listened as the men chattered on for a few minutes. Esther's spirit collapsed when she heard Shelby Moss request a favor from the farmer. "We sure would be obliged if we could help ourselves to a little feed for our horses off your haystack. The beasts be plum tuckered out, and they are surely weak with hunger. I can pay ya for the hay."

"I'll get my son to pitch a little hay onto the ground for your horses from our haycock." The farmer stretched his head back and searched the sky. "Looks like rain clouds are forming again in the west. We gotta get this hay harvested before it's ruined by the next storm. If this rain don't let up, the hay'll never dry properly. You're welcome to take shelter in the barn for the night if you want."

"We appreciate yer offer, but I think we best be backtracking south after we feed and rest the horses a bit. We have posted handbills with a description of them runaways all over the area, and a reward for information leading to their capture. The mistress of my plantation is particularly anxious to have these two back. Wants to make an example of them before she sells them further south, so we best keep movin'. We appreciate yer time and yer hay," grunted a weary Shelby Moss.

The muscles in Esther's stomach twitched with a sickening fear as she heard the tines of the pitchfork penetrate the outer edges of the haycock. The pair willed their bodies to remain still as the sides of the haycock were pulled away from the mound. Luckily, the farmer's sons took hay from the base of the mound and did not come near their hideout. The fugitives were high enough in the stack to avoid detection.

Chapter 9 ~ September 1850 – The North Star

"I don't know, Esther," groaned Bucky. We may be heading north, but the foggy night has me mightily confused. We could be going in circles for all I know." Bucky squinted with his eyes in an effort to see into the distance. "Are there any berries left?"

"We ate the last of them when we rested earlier," answered Esther in a worn out tone. "If we can get to some woods again, we may be able to find something to eat. I could use a rest. My blisters hurt, and the leaves in my shoes need to be changed again."

"The last sign I saw said Wilmington – 15 miles," declared Bucky, "but I don't know if that's where we want to go." Bucky and Esther plodded through the fog for another hour until Bucky spoke. "Look, over there. I think I see a stand of trees. Let's take shelter there for a while to get our strength back."

Esther nodded.

The runaways had been traveling hard for four nights. Since their encounter with Shelby Moss in the farmer's hay field, they had not met with any other trouble. They had found the opportunity to sleep some during the day in the cove and the haystack. Another day had passed in an abandoned chicken coop and their last day was spent hidden in the woods. Although they were exhausted, their slumber was never relaxed. Any sound threw them into a state of panic. Both youngsters were weary and in need of nourishment. Water had not been difficult to find as small rivers and streams ran freely with the continual rain showers. But they were very hungry, and had once even looked for a few scraps of food in a pigpen. The lack of nourishment made it difficult to walk at a steady pace, and they had to rest often. The wounds from Esther's tender blisters oozed with pus. A throbbing pain in her foot made walking very hard. Earlier, Bucky had found a patch of water lilies at the edge of a cove and tugged up the root from the floating white flower and stashed it inside his shirt, knowing that it would help Esther's foot.

"How're your blisters, Esther?"

"They hurt," Esther said with a purpose, "but the pain won't keep me from walking to where I want to go. We have come too far, Bucky."

"Try and hold on for a few more hours. Morning will be upon us soon, and we'll find a place to rest during the day. I'll smash the water lily root with a rock and make a mash. We can pack it onto the tender area of your foot and leave it there while you sleep. The root will draw out the infection from the blisters and make it easier for you to walk tomorrow."

"Thanks, Bucky," said Esther gratefully. Mentally she thanked Old Jed for teaching them about the healing powers of the pretty plant.

The tired friends approached a small stand of trees near a swift-running creek. They drank some water and dropped to the base of a large pine tree. Esther and Bucky curled into two balls on a bed of pine needles to keep warm. The tired runaways only intended to rest, but sheer exhaustion took hold of them, and they both collapsed into a fitful sleep.

Esther felt the nudge of a foot against her back. "I'm sorry, Bucky. I didn't mean to fall asleep. Give me a minute…"

"It wasn't me that bumped you, Esther. Ya better get up."

Esther's heart leapt in panic, and she winced with a bolt of pain as she jumped up from the ground and put weight onto the forgotten blistered foot. The girl was shocked to be staring eye-level with a short Negro woman peculiarly dressed in a man's suit and carrying a tattered felt hat in her hands. The woman smiled at her warmly. She began to speak, and Esther marveled at the deep throaty resonance of her voice.

"Are you two runaways?" asked the woman.

Bucky swallowed hard, but was too scared to speak. Both Bucky and Esther knew that a dishonest slave would sometimes betray one of their own people and turn in a runaway to a slave-catcher for a cash reward.

"You can talk freely with me, friends, 'cause last year I be makin' this very journey my own self. Just now, I'm on my way back to my old plantation to convince my husband to join me in traveling the road north to freedom." She looked down and grabbed the corner of her jacket. "I wear these men's clothes 'cause they're more practical for travelin' through the underbrush," shared the mysterious woman as she clutched the soft felt hat to her chest.

Esther looked down at her own tattered skirt. Large rips at the bottom made her feel like she was wearing a filthy old rag. She peered at the woman again, but still she could not find the courage to speak. The woman before her bore a deep scar in the middle of her forehead. She was about Esther's height with chestnut-colored skin. The wiry woman had dark eyes, a straight broad nose, and full lips. There was a quiet strength about her. She was not handsome yet she possessed a gentle tenderness in her smile, which made her eyes shimmer with kindness. Esther suddenly felt calmed in her presence.

"We've been traveling for four nights now, but I think we may be lost," said Esther with a tired voice.

"Y'all headin' up north to Pennsylvania?"

"Yes," Bucky declared, "I saw a sign that said Wilmington back a piece, but I don't know if that is where we want to go."

"Y'all know how to read?" the stranger asked in amazement.

"Yes," said Bucky, "we both know how to read."

"Well if that don't beat all. I'd give my pennies if I could read. How'd you learn?" she asked hesitantly. "Readin' is forbidden to slaves," the woman added.

"We were taught in secret by an old Negro man who once lived in freedom up North, but came back to the South so that he might share his gifts with others. He's the one who taught us to read and write and learn all the other things we needed to know so that we might one day escape north to be free," said Esther lovingly.

"Your friend's a good man," said the stranger. "Listen, there's a decent Quaker gentleman over in Wilmington, Delaware who'll help y'all out. His name is Thomas Garrett, and he is a station master on the Underground Railroad."

"There really is such a thing?" asked Bucky with excitement. "We heard about it from our teacher-friend, and…well… there are always rumors around the quarters."

"Why, of course there be such a thing. I was a passenger on the railroad when I escaped from my old plantation, almost from the start. I'm plum amazed that y'all made it this far on your own accord. You should be right proud of what you've done."

"I know we couldn't have done it without the help from our friend," Esther modestly admitted.

"Well, you listen to what I'm gonna to tell you, and y'all will be passengers on the Railroad startin' now," the mystery woman said with a smile. "Follow the signs from that road over yonder," informed the woman as she pointed in the general direction of the road, "Keep to the side of the road and out of sight. Wilmington is about two hours up the road." Using detailed landmarks, the extraordinary woman gave the runaways directions to Thomas Garrett's house. "If you can get to Quaker Garrett, he'll give ya each a new pair of shoes, a good meal, and a ticket on the Underground Railroad to the next station house."

Esther looked down at her worn and tattered shoes and then into the remarkable face of the stranger. "An angel sent you to us, Ma'am," said Esther tenderly. "Could ya at least tell us your name so that when we speak kindly of you in the future we can tell others about the helpful lady who came to our aid?"

The stranger looked uncomfortable and the sudden change of her tone of voice suggested her anxiety. She lifted her hand to the deep old scar on her forehead and touched the wound gently with her fingers. Esther wondered what horrible accident could have caused the gash. "It's best we just leave it alone, friends. If slave-catchers should happen to capture either of us, they might try to get more information out of us than we want to give. If I don't know yer name, and you don't know mine...there isn't plum much of anything we can tell them...right?"

"I guess what you say makes a lot of sense," said Bucky.

The strangers chatted for a few more minutes. Then, the three shook hands, said their goodbyes, and walked away in opposite directions. Esther turned back to look with admiration at the woman dressed in men's clothing, but she had already slipped quietly into the night. The young fugitive wondered if *they* would ever have the courage to travel alone into unwelcome territory.

As Bucky and Esther wandered in the general direction of the road, Bucky remarked, "She reminds me of Old Jed, Esther. Think of the generosity of what she is doing! A woman who made her way safely to freedom is traveling all the way back to her old plantation to come to the aid of her husband. I hope he appreciates the danger she has placed herself in for his benefit."

Esther nodded, and then stopped suddenly.

Bucky turned and looked at his friend. "What's the matter Esther? Does your foot hurt?"

"Look, Bucky. I see it!" Esther whispered breathlessly as she stared in awe at the night sky. "The misty fog must've lifted while we were resting. The sky is finally clear of clouds, and I can see it at last, Bucky!" exclaimed Esther.

"What is it, Esther? What do you see?" asked Bucky smiling.

"There," said Esther pointing with excitement, "the North Star!"

Chapter 10 ~ August 1853 – New York City

Esther twitched when a young sailor tapped her on the shoulder. "Sorry, Miss King, I didn't mean to startle you. I just wanted to let you know that the ship will be docking shortly."

"Thank you," answered Esther gratefully. She stared at the tiny specks of gold sparkling on the surface of the bottle in her hands and smiled. "I guess I was daydreaming." The friendly sailor tipped his hat and continued walking along the deck.

Esther gently placed the Bronze Bottle back in its leather case. She scanned the busy dock and found Bucky waving at her from the crowd. Adjusting the bottle at her side, Esther stood up on her tiptoes and flashed Bucky a huge smile as she waved back at him.

Upon disembarking from the steamship, Esther threw herself into the arms of her old friend, who welcomed her warmly and escorted her to a wagon parked several hundred feet from the dock. The boy, who had learned so much from Old Jed during the *summers of enlightenment*, was now a mature man of twenty. The tall lanky boy with large white teeth had grown into a handsome young man. Warm chocolate eyes set off a chestnut brown face, which still bore the faded scar on his left cheek suffered at the hands of Wendalyn King. Since he and Esther had finally managed to escape from the King Plantation in 1850, much of Bucky's time had been spent furthering his education. Bucky was extremely intelligent – a brilliant self-taught scholar. When not teaching at the orphanage or working as a guide on the Underground Railroad, Bucky generally had his nose buried in a book. Twice each week he met with a group of both black and white men at the office of the Seneca Vigilance Committee. Over the years, many Vigilance Committee offices had been set up throughout the North to assist freed and runaway slaves find work and get settled. Some of the members of Bucky's committee also used the office to discuss all varieties of subjects like astronomy, history, mathematics, engineering, literature, Greek and Roman philosophers, and theology. Bucky considered freedom and knowledge to be man's greatest gifts.

"It's mighty fine to see you again, Esther," said Bucky as he helped Esther up the step of the rickety old wagon. You look different," Bucky added as he squinted his eyes and cocked his head to one side. "I can't quite decide what it is...I guess you look rested."

"I do feel rested, Bucky," said Esther as she settled into the seat of the buckboard wagon.

How was your trip north to Prince Edward Island? Did Big Jim and the others settle in with the Maguire family?"

"Yes, Bucky. The Maguires are good people. It was a special trip in many ways, Bucky, but I'll tell you more about that later," said Esther as she adjusted the bottle at her side. "First, tell me the news of the school."

"Much has happened since you've been away, Esther. Final preparations are being made to move the orphanage and school out of Seneca Village. Mrs. Cody has leased a compound in a town north of Niagara Falls just across the Canadian border called St. Catharines. I think we'll be safe there," said Bucky solemnly. "I never thought that it would come to this, Esther, but recent circumstances have made it unsafe for many of our people in New York," Bucky added sadly. "Last week twenty-three more men and women were kidnapped off the streets at night. Those unfortunate folks were bound in chains, forced onto wagons, and sent to the South before anyone could protest. There are many who are upset, Esther, but the Fugitive Slave

Law of 1850 has made it nearly impossible for us. We now must deal with an assortment of unscrupulous scoundrels. Those men who were once indifferent to Negroes living in New York are suddenly tempted to sell fugitive and even *freed slaves* back into bondage for money. Last week, several freed slaves who possessed the proper papers tried to get a judge to listen to their story, but if just one white man is willing to testify under oath that a person is a fugitive, the judge will not make a ruling in favor of the freed slave."

"Oh, Bucky, this is a mighty sad time for our people and our situation seems to be growing worse by the day."

"Yes, Esther, but there's still hope. Many articles have been printed in the newspapers expressing anger over the unfairness of this law, and many good people have promised that they'll not lift a finger to help southern slave owners catch their runaways. In fact, Mr. Garrison recently wrote in his newspaper, *The Liberator*, that if conditions on the plantations are as good as the masters say they are, then why are so many slaves hightailing it to the North?" Bucky reported.

"Then maybe there's still hope for us. What's the news of our headmistress, Mrs. Cody? She must be worried about the safety of the children."

"Oh, you know that nothing much ruffles Joanne. She guards her brood with the resolve of a mother hen watching over her chicks. We've enrolled seven more orphaned children to the school these past weeks. When you rescue the five children in Maryland, our enrollment will be forty-seven."

Bucky glanced again at the girl sitting next to him and scratched his head with the thought that Esther looked so different to him. "Esther, I wish I could make this trip south with you, but Mrs. Cody has asked me to take ten of the older children to the new school in St. Catharines to help ready the compound for the *big move*. I'm worried about you. You've never made a trip back to your own plantation, and that brings an added measure of danger. Someone might recognize you. Esther, you must promise me that you'll be extra careful."

"I promise, Bucky, but don't you go worrying about me. I've made these journeys before, and you know how cautious I am. Anyway, I must free Mammy Naira, Old Jed, and the children from the plantation. Their safety is in jeopardy." Esther paused and looked at her friend. "This may be my last trip as a conductor, Bucky," said Esther with emotion. "When these five children have been collected and safely installed at the *Thomas Garrett School and Orphanage* in St. Catharines, I'll become a fulltime teacher at the new school. I'm happy to start a new chapter in my life, but I'll miss being a conductor on the Underground Railroad and helping others follow the light of the North Star to freedom."

Bucky patted Esther's hand. "You'll make a wonderful teacher, Esther. Your students will blossom under your guidance," said Bucky with sincerity. "It was decent of Mrs. Cody to make a place at the new school for Naira and Old Jed"

"I know. She's been an angel. And I'm so happy that Mrs. Cody chose to honor Thomas Garrett by naming our new school after him. He not only helped us, but he's done so much to help hundreds of runaway slaves, Bucky."

"We were talking about him at the Vigilance Committee meeting the other night, Esther. Lewis Cook shared the best story. He told us that when Quaker Garrett was found guilty of breaking the law as a stationmaster for the Underground Railroad in 1845, the fines imposed on him took his every dollar and all of his property, but through it all, he never lost his resolve. When the last of his household possessions was finally sold at public auction, the sheriff who conducted the sale remarked, 'Thomas, I hope that you'll never be caught at this again.' But the feisty sixty-year-old just looked squarely at that sheriff and replied, 'Friend, I haven't a dollar in the world, but if thee knows a fugitive anywhere on the face of this earth who needs a breakfast, send him to me.' Bucky slapped his knee and laughed at the retelling of Lewis Cook's story. "He's a remarkable man," praised Bucky. "It's estimated that despite the setback of losing all his worldly goods in '45, thousands of slaves are still being offered food, shelter and a free pair of shoes at Mr. Garrett's *station* in Wilmington, Delaware."

"I know, Bucky. Remember when we were lost and scared coming north to freedom? Our mystery woman pointed us in the direction of his station, and it was Quaker Garrett who gave us shoes, money, and the courage to go on."

Bucky nodded his head and remembered the trouble they might have encountered had it not been for that strange angel dressed in men's clothes who came out of the night to show them the way to get a ticket on the Underground Railroad. "It strengthens my faith to know that even though there are some who would falsely sell another human for *thirty pieces of silver*, there are just as many who'd give all their worldly possessions, like Mr. Garrett, to do what's right in their hearts."

"That reminds me, Bucky, have you had word from our Quaker friends in Philadelphia?" Esther instinctively lowered her voice, even though the sound of the horse's hooves and the creaking wagon muffled any conversation that might be heard by people going about on the busy streets of the city. "Next week, I'm supposed to meet with the Griggs at their farm. Donald and Claudia have been mighty kind to offer me assistance," said Esther.

Bucky smiled and produced a letter from his inside coat pocket. He handed the envelope to Esther as he coaxed the horses up Fifth Avenue.

Esther carefully unsealed the envelope and read its contents.

Dear Esther, August 10, 1853

I trust, and I have prayed that thy trip to Canada was successful. My husband, Donald, and our two children, Hannah and Seth, look forward to seeing thee again on the tenth day of September, as was prearranged in our earlier correspondence. We will meet thee at the train station and take thee to our farm. I have had recent news from my brother Mark in Maryland, but I will wait to share this information with thee until I see thy face.

Our prayers are with thee for a safe journey.

Thy faithful friend,

Claudia Grigg

Esther and Bucky had first met Claudia Grigg when they were offered food and lodging at her Philadelphia farm home. The scared youngsters had finally crossed the Mason Dixon line into Pennsylvania and to freedom. Guided to his home by their mystery woman, the same Thomas Garrett, who lost everything in 1845, had given the runaways directions to the next station, which turned out to be the Grigg farm. As the horses headed north out of the city, Esther called to mind the woman who was to become her special friend – the kind woman who had opened her heart and her home to strangers traveling to freedom as passengers on the Underground Railroad

Chapter 11 ~ September 1850 to
July 1853 – The Quakers

A hungry and cold Bucky and Esther nervously knocked on the door to the farmhouse late that chilly Thursday night of September in 1850. A woman's voice asked, "Who are thee?"

Bucky anxiously answered, "A friend with friends," which was exactly what Quaker Garrett had told them was the password for runaway slaves traveling to various stations along the Underground Railroad.

The door opened and an attractive young woman dressed in a long white nightgown with matching robe and a white night cap stood smiling before them. Esther and Bucky looked at each other and smiled remembering Old Jed's dream about meeting a woman dressed in white who would help them on their journey north. The woman introduced herself as Claudia Grigg, and quickly motioned the pair inside. Mrs. Grigg scanned the area around the farm for movement. When all looked quiet, she slowly closed the door to the house. A small fire burned in a large fireplace. Its glow cast the only light in a plainly furnished sitting room that extended into a small dining room and neatly organized kitchen.

"My husband, Donald, is away buying stock for the farm, and the twins, Hannah and Seth, are asleep. Come warm thyself by the fire while I heat thee some biscuits. Thee must be very tired." The uneasy runaways could only nod as they looked into her kind face.

Claudia served tender biscuits with butter and a large pitcher of milk to the famished travelers. "Friends, I am heating thee some lentil soup on the stove, but this will take the sting out of thy hunger." A hungry Esther and Bucky tucked into the platter of warm biscuits. While they ate, Claudia put the pair at ease by sharing a few bits of information about her and Donald and their life on the farm. When she sensed that the couple had finally satisfied the hunger in their bellies she asked, "Where did thee live before making thy way to freedom?"

"We worked on Master King's plantation in Dorchester County Maryland, near the Big Buckwater River," said Bucky. "Have you heard of it?"

A radiant smile spread across Claudia's face. "Why, this is a small world indeed. My brother, Mark Singer, runs a dairy farm with his wife and two boys on fifteen acres. I believe it's just a few miles north of the King Plantation." Did thee not use his home as a station coming North?"

"No," explained Bucky, "we left late on a Saturday night and walked through the swamps and back roads for two nights. We hid in a haystack all day Monday, and walked on for two more nights. Each time we heard the sound of horses' hooves in the distance, we would crouch in the underbrush until they passed by. We would have starved if it had not been for Old Jed," said Bucky.

"Is Old Jed thy friend?"

"Yes," said Esther, "he is an old Negro slave who used to live free in the North. He taught us what roots and berries to eat to stay alive while we followed the North Star. But even with all of his teachings, we may not have made it to freedom but for a chance meeting with a small wiry Negro woman dressed in a man's suit and wearing a shabby felt hat. This strange angel appeared silently from nowhere and told us where we might find a man named Mr. Garrett who would give us shelter and a good meal. From that moment on, we were passengers on the Underground Railroad, and that led us to you, Miz Grigg," added Esther with affection.

"Please my friends, thee must call me Claudia. I must say, thee were fortunate to meet thy mysterious woman."

Claudia Grigg was pleased to have company that evening. The Quaker farm wife had recently been through a personal tragedy, and she surprised herself by sharing certain intimate details of the experience. Until that night, she had kept her sorrow buried inside her heart like the tiny casket that lay buried on a small hill near the back of the farmhouse. Later, she wondered what had prompted her to open up to the unknown fugitives.

Perhaps, she had reflected, it was because the strangers were visitors who would pass out of her life like the many other runaways she and Donald had helped find their way north. Maybe, it was because she was lonely with Donald away from the farm, and she felt forsaken. Whatever the reasons, she was never sorry. The story she shared and the compassion Esther and Bucky extended to her, helped heal Claudia's wounded spirit.

The slim twenty-six-year old farm wife with hazel eyes and light brown hair began her sad tale by telling Esther and Bucky that she had recently given birth to a baby girl who had died when the infant was only three days old.

"The twins, Hannah and Seth, are now seven years old, and I was surprised and saddened when there had been no other babies after them. Donald and I love children and always assumed that we would have many. Our hearts were gladdened when the Lord finally blessed us with the joyous signs of a new baby. Donald spent many nights sanding and painting the old baby cradle, while I happily sat by this very fireplace stitching and knitting new clothes for the child growing in my womb. Late one night, the pains of labor came, and Donald took our wagon to fetch the local midwife from her bed."

Claudia stared past Esther and Bucky and continued her story with a pained expression on her face. "The birthing went poorly, and the little girl that I delivered was so small. I tried everything, but my sweet cherub would not take my milk, and she struggled for life with every breath. Our beautiful little Emma passed to the angels on the third day of her short life. I was devastated to lose the little daughter I had named Emma to honor my loving grandmother," she sighed. "It was a further shock to be told by the local midwife that there would be no more children for Donald and me."

Esther and Bucky listened to the young mother's tragic tale with genuine concern. It suddenly occurred to Esther that she and Mrs. Grigg had much in common. Esther identified with the sorrow of a mother never knowing the love of her daughter, much in the same way Esther had never known the love of her own birth mother.

Claudia Grigg *had* been broken-hearted to lose little Emma, and the distraught mother took to her bed for a week. Donald fretted over his wife, bringing her calming medicines from the local doctor, which she promptly set aside and ignored. While grieving the loss of her daughter, Claudia's naturally positive outlook on life and her strong faith led her to believe that the Lord must have another plan for her. On her seventh day of mourning, she tossed aside the quilts and asked Donald if he would take Seth and Hannah to the barn to help with the milking so that she might bathe and wash her hair.

The Grigg family was happy to have the young wife and mother back. Claudia tucked her sorrow away like a treasured hymn that is too sad to sing. She never spoke of losing Emma to her husband or anyone else until the night Bucky and Esther knocked on her door. But each Sunday, after attending First Day Meeting with other Quakers in the district, Claudia would walk alone up to the top of a small hill where the child lay buried near a stand of dogwood trees and place flowers on Emma's grave. It was the only time she allowed herself to dream of what might have been.

That evening in 1850 marked the beginning of a deep friendship between Claudia and Esther. For the next three years, Esther happily corresponded with Mistress Grigg, who shared precious information about life on the King Plantation. They wrote each other often, and in that time Claudia became a lifeline to Mammy Naira, Old Jed, and the many others slaves Esther knew in the quarters. News from Naira would secretly thread its way to Claudia's brother, Mark Singer, the dairy farmer who produced cheese in Dorchester County.

Like so many other Quaker friends, Mark and Rebecca Singer had given a great deal of assistance to the many scared runaways who knocked on their door in the dead of night seeking food and shelter. When Claudia told him of Esther's desire to know about her family, Mark agreed to offer his assistance. Through coded correspondence, Claudia gave Mark a detailed description of the trapper known as Old Jed, and the places where he liked to set his traps. Mark roamed the river for about a week before he stumbled upon the old trapper as the hunter checked his traps near a favorite cove where the muskrat liked to burrow.

Over the years, news of Naira came by means of Old Jed, who shared the news with Quaker Singer. Gradually Old Jed began to set more of his traps along the river where the dairy farmer watered his cattle. Usually only brief and guarded words were exchanged between the two.

Every now and then, a tattered worn letter written in Jed's familiar script would secretly pass along the stations of the Underground Railroad, and find its way to New York and into Esther's grateful hands. At other times, Mark would send news from Naira, which he disguised in his letters that were sent through the mail to Claudia. In turn, she would pass the information on to Esther. It was dangerous work. Both Claudia and Mark knew that mail traveling from the South to the North was sometimes opened and read by the postmaster. All correspondence had gone without mishap until the summer of 1853.

Claudia had been baking bread on that beautiful July morning when Donald handed her a letter from her brother. The news was jarring. Mark had written a shocking message about a group of orphaned children from the King Plantation whom Naira and Old Jed had cared for and nurtured since the mammy had grown too old to carry out her duties in the kitchen. He informed Claudia that the five children were in grave danger. An informant who worked inside the Big House, named Mandy, was blabbing to the overseer that she overheard some children talking in the quarters about learning their letters. He said the overseer was investigating the claim that an unknown slave from the plantation might be schooling some children in secret. He also relayed that Shelby Moss had held a general meeting in the slave quarters warning that if the rumor proved to be fact, he would whip the culprit responsible until he or she bled to death. Then, he threatened to drown the children in the waters of the Big Buckwater. Mark ended the letter by saying that the state of affairs on the King Plantation was so turbulent that a rescue might be the only solution.

A stunned Claudia had read Mark's letter again and thought of the children from the slave quarters. She thought of little Emma, who would have celebrated her third birthday on that very day. The coincidence sent a jolt through her body like a flash of lightening in a storm. She suddenly felt *enlightened* like so many of the elders she often witnessed at Meeting when they broke the silence of private prayer and meditation to share a spiritual thought with the rest of the congregation. "Since the day thy left me, Emma, there has been a tiny hole in my heart," Claudia whispered out loud, "but I never lost faith that there was some other purpose for me that would help heal my pain and make me whole again." *I always knew the Lord might have another plan for me*, she sighed in thought.

Chapter 12 ~ August 1853 – New York City

Pulled from the memories of her friendship with Claudia Grigg after meeting her as a runaway, Esther looked fondly at her tall friend as he skillfully drove the wagon further north away from the busy city toward the more rural section of Seneca Village. "Oh Bucky, I can't wait to see Mammy Naira again, but I'm terrified for her and Old Jed," Esther remarked while clutching the letter written in Claudia's neat hand to her stomach. "Claudia's been such a dear friend to me these past years. She and Mark have risked much, so that I might have this lifeline to my mammy. I still can't believe her kind offer to make the journey to Maryland with me to rescue the children. It's a mighty courageous gesture."

"It gives me great comfort to know that you'll not be alone, Esther," whispered Bucky caringly.

Esther shyly glanced at the tall young man with whom she had been through so much and smiled. She wondered if he still thought of her as a child or a little sister.

"Oh, I almost forgot, Esther, I have some exciting news to share with you," said Bucky.

"What news?" asked Esther as she carefully placed Claudia Grigg's letter into the leather case containing the Bronze Bottle.

"Mrs. Cody's friend, Harriet Tubman, is here in New York, and we have been invited to meet her tomorrow night at the Seneca Village Methodist Church. Joanne says she's making her annual autumn trip south to rescue another group of slaves. Esther, we'll finally get the chance to see if she *was* the woman traveling south who came to our aid...the miraculous woman who pointed us north and told us where we could find a good meal at a safe house when we were so hopelessly lost."

"She certainly fits Mrs. Cody's description of her friend, Harriet," said Esther. "Remember how the woman wouldn't tell us her name, but told us she was traveling south to bring her husband north to freedom?"

"Yes."

"Bucky, remember how Mrs. Cody said that Harriet Tubman had gone to get her husband, John Tubman, in that same autumn of 1850?"

Bucky inwardly smiled at Esther's excitement. "Yes, and I remember Mrs. Cody saying how broken hearted Harriet had been when John wouldn't come north with her because he had met and married another woman named Caroline even though he was still wed to Harriet. It *has* to be her, Esther," Bucky said catching Esther's enthusiasm.

"Bucky, that chance encounter was the turning point in making our way to freedom. I can't believe that we might finally have the honor to meet the woman known to our people as Moses," murmured Esther.

"I have other wonderful news," beamed Bucky.

"Bucky, you are a mighty torrent of information, but I can't imagine that there'd be anything that could surpass the news that you shared with me but a moment ago."

Bucky chuckled. "What's your favorite book, Esther?"

"Why, Bucky, you know for a fact that my most prized possession is the book that you gave me last Christmas, *Uncle Tom's Cabin*, by Harriet Beecher Stowe. I've read it so many times that I mostly know each word by heart. You also know, first hand, that I have shed a river of tears at the deaths of Uncle Tom and Little Eva, and that I've trembled with fear over the brutality of the cruel Simon Legree because of his likeness to Shelby Moss. Why do you ask me what you already know?"

Bucky's eyes sparkled mischievously as he chortled out loud. "You'll not believe the treat that Mrs. Cody has in store for us. To celebrate your return, Joanne got tickets for us to see the stage drama of *Uncle Tom's Cabin* which has been playing at the *National Theatre of New York* all summer."

Esther gripped Bucky's forearm with her hands and shrieked. "This *is* the most amazing news! I've been reading in the newspaper that the play is a huge success, with scores of folks going night after night."

Esther released Bucky's arm and sat in thoughtful silence for a few seconds before she spoke. "The thought of meeting Harriet Tubman, and seeing the drama of my favorite author Harriet Beecher Stowe all in one week is a dream come true. Bucky, I believe I'll call this…the week of the Harriets!" Esther flashed a huge smile at her friend, and Bucky noticed that the gold flecks in the alligator green eyes sparkled in the sun.

Chapter 13 ~ August 1853 – The King Plantation

Clumsily holding a glass of icy lemonade to his forehead with thick clammy hands, Shelby Moss slouched in a wicker chair on the shaded veranda of the Big House. Wearily, he listened to Wendalyn King as she interrogated the slave, Mandy. In the distance, Shelby could see Master King painting a portrait of his youngest daughter sitting on a swing, which hung from a great oak tree shading the large manicured lawn. The day was hot, with not a whisper of wind to offset the dank humid air, and he found it difficult to focus as Mrs. King questioned the house slave, again, about the rumor of slave children learning to read. He itched to place a wad of tobacco inside his mouth to ease the edgy feeling he got whenever he went too long without the shredded brown leaves resting between his cheek and gums, but Mrs. King did not allow the overseer to chew tobacco in her presence.

"Mandy you are trying my patience! It has been two months now and still we have no proof of any slaves learning to read. I do swear gal, sometimes I think you just cleverly make things up so that you can get in my good graces and profit from a quick reward."

"Oh no, Miz King! No sir, Boss Shelby! Y'all hafta know dat I be tellin' de truth." Mandy looked at her mistress and overseer with dark wide eyes that conveyed a look of terror. Words continued to sputter from her lips like the crackle of bacon grease on a hot skillet. "It's like I done told y'all before. I wuz doin' my...ahem...business in de outhouse, when I heard a small child's voice tellin' another child dat dey be learnin' all d'letters of de...afabet...or somethin' dat sounded close to dat strange word. But it were unfortunate at dat partic'lar moment dat I...well...happen to generate some unexpected and loud noises from my...uh...lower insides, and...well...it were unlucky for me dat d'children must of heard a loud discharge comin' from d'area of my bowels."

Shelby Moss attempted to stifle his laughter by placing the edge of his lemonade glass against his lips when Mrs. King shot him a menacing glare.

"For goodness sake, girl, spare me the graphic details of this horror and get to the point," groused Wendy King.

The nervous Mandy raced ahead with her story in an effort to convince her mistress that she was not making up rumors for cash profit – a trick that she had, in truth, used in the past. "Miz King, I tried to hurry my...ahem...course of action but dose children just ran off afore I could finds out just who dey was. Den shortly after, I reported what I heard to y'all. And shortly dere after, Boss Shelby spoke to all de slaves at de quarter, tellin' dem what would be in store for dose learnin' to read, and dat dere would be a sizable reward for information 'bout *any* slave on d'King Plantation teachin' readin' and writin' to other slaves in d'quarters." Mandy fidgeted with her apron and chewed on her lower lip at the end of her account.

A loud burp erupted from Shelby Moss's mouth. Wendalyn King rolled her eyes skyward before turning in the direction of the disgusting overseer. "Mr. Moss, might you have the courtesy to control your bodily functions in the presence of a genteel southern lady!"

The uncouth man, who had little regard for women (southern or otherwise) who interfered in men's work, slowly placed his lemonade on the table. "I apologize, Mrs. King. It appears that *bodily functions* seem to be a problem for a number of your workers at this moment."

He sat up a little straighter, and cleared his throat. "Yes," drawled Shelby Moss, "in hindsight, I think that it may have been a mistake on my part to talk about the offense to the slaves. Unfortunately, I may have tipped my hand. I did not expect that a secret of that magnitude could be kept hidden from me. And now that it be out in the open, I have eliminated the element of surprise. It is my judgment that very few slaves in the quarters must actually be aware of the culprit responsible for this loathsome crime. Otherwise, why else would they not come forward with the information? We all know that there are always slaves, like our clever Mandy here, who are willing to turn in a fellow slave for a cash reward."

"Why thank ya, Boss Shelby. I do try and..."

Wendy King cut Mandy off with a flap of her hand as if swatting an annoying gnat from her face and turned to her overseer. "Those who may be teaching my slaves to read, *will* be caught and severely beaten," she snapped. "An example will be made once and for all, and I have the weight of the law to support me!" The mistress of the King Plantation flared her nostrils as if some distasteful smell had just floated under her nose.

Shelby slouched back in his chair and stared at his female boss in silence. He had witnessed these outbursts of Mrs. King, regarding her slaves, numerous times before. But today he considered it wise not to ruffle her further. It was just too hot.

Ice clinked against the sides of Mistress King's glass, as she raised her lemonade to her thin lips. The cold liquid seeping down her throat seemed to mirror the icy blood that flowed through her heart. "No slave on this plantation is crafty enough to deceive me." Nodding her head at each of the workers before her, Mrs. King ordered, "Keep your eyes and ears open, Mandy, Mr. Moss. I will reward you handsomely for your trouble.

Something is certain to show itself – and when it does, we will be ready."

"What we need to do is start easin' things up a bit in the quarters," stated Shelby Moss in cunning tones. "When the culprits be feelin' safe again, they will most likely drop their guards. Let the mice come to the cat. We'll be ready to pounce on them."

There was a quiet bustle in the quarters that same day, as the evening drew to a close. The once robust Mammy sat on her stool in the cabin talking with Jed. Although Naira had lost considerable weight in recent years, the swelling in her legs continued to give her fits during the warm humid months of the summer, and she sat whenever she could to ease the pain. Five young children, between the ages of twelve and four shared a large wooden bowl of cornmeal mush flavored with salted pork and cabbage.

"Look how d'children be growing, Jed. My, but dey just seem to sprout as fast as de marsh reeds dat shoot up along de bank of d'Big Buckwater each summer."

"They're smart too," commented Old Jed. "They know that *all* our futures depend on everyone having their wits about them," he added in a soft whisper.

Naira nodded slowly but said nothing.

The old mammy was currently responsible for fifteen young slave children during the day, but most of them were collected to their cabins by tired mammies after finishing a long day's work. The remaining five were orphans. Naira and Old Jed gradually took on the responsibility of caring for the neglected children. In the years since Bucky and Esther had run away from the King Plantation, Jed and Naira had grown very close. Over time, their friendship deepened from a shared sense of loneliness and discovering a fervent love for young children – especially the downtrodden.

The oldest of their five charges was a twelve-year-old boy named Sampson. Although a federal statute signed into law by Thomas Jefferson in 1807 prohibited importing slaves into the United States, the increasing demand for cotton in Britain made black market slave trading a highly profitable industry. Seven-year-old Sampson had been smuggled into New Orleans on a bootleg slave ship and eventually ended up on the King Plantation with a group of other slaves when he was nine-years old.

Greedy slave traders had kidnapped the boy and his mother as they fetched water from the Volta River near their village in Ghana on the coast of West Africa. Sampson was loaded on board a filthy ship with his mother and other frightened men, women, and children by cruel white men cracking whips and yelling harsh-sounding words that made no sense to the scared youth. During the long cruel voyage to the West Indies, the boy's mother had finally collapsed on the deck of the slave ship, while being forced to dance to music with other slaves as a form of exercise, and amusement for the crew. The seven-year-old boy had been too stunned and scared to cry, as he witnessed a sailor unlock the shackles that bound his mother's ankles and carelessly toss her wasted body over the side of the ship. The sound of his mother's body slapping the surface of the choppy sea still haunted the child in his dreams.

The young slave boy was renamed Sampson because his first master did not like the name *Osombo*. Sampson had been cruelly cast about different plantations before finally being sold to the King Plantation. When Sampson was nine-years-old, the slave boy was purchased on an auction block by Shelby Moss, as an after thought, for two hundred dollars, along with fifteen more profitable adult slaves. Since the death of his mother, Sampson had never known a day of compassion until being taken under the loving wings of Mammy Naira and Old Jed. It was then that his natural spirit of kindness, together with a desire to learn, slowly began to emerge.

Twelve-year old Sampson's face was as dark and smooth as the hard black ebony wood, hidden inside the ordinary looking trees from his African homeland. His keen insightful charcoal-colored eyes quietly absorbed the information taught to him by Old Jed – much like the moss that grows on the master's pine trees after a summer downpour. The long-legged boy with tight curly hair the color of night had been working long hours with other adult slaves in the fields for over a year. Sampson kept mostly to himself. He worked hard and didn't cause trouble. The field hands, who foolishly considered the quiet young slave to be somewhat dim-witted, left the boy alone.

Two young girls sat next to Sampson. The twins, Florence and Frances, were nine-years-old. Flossy and Franny, as they were affectionately called in the quarters, had lost both parents when their mother and father had been sold to a plantation in North Carolina when the girls were seven. The new master refused to take any children in the sale, so the girls were left behind on the King Plantation. Mammy Naira promised the devastated parents that she would look after the girls until the day in which they might be reunited again. It was a hollow pledge, but the gesture made the parting a little easier.

The identical twins possessed dark brown skin the color of the waxed walnut wood dining table in the Big House. Short upturned noses and large dimples gave the petite girls an impish doll-like appearance. Together, they could charm almost anyone in the quarters, and often did. It would have been difficult to tell them apart, except for one astounding difference. Flossy talked all the time. Nonstop babble poured from her mouth as steady as the chirp of a cricket on a hot summer night. And as if to balance things out, Franny hardly said a word and seemed content to leave most of the verbal chatter to her twin sister. Flossy and Franny worked with other children their age tending to the mistress's rose garden on the south side of the Big House. Each morning, the children were given a small burlap rag filled with tobacco leaves tied at the top with twine. They were instructed to chew the leaves and spit the tobacco juice on the rose plants to kill aphids and other bothersome insects so that Mistress King's roses would bear beautiful blooms. Each evening Naira would listen as Flossy complained in rapid bursts.

"We hate the taste of the tobacco leaves, Mammy Naira," declared Flossy with an agitated tone. "Sometimes 'dat ol'nasty brown juice slips down our throat and makes us dizzy with sweat. It gets mighty bad when we're hungry. But there's nothing we can do 'cause Miz Wendy has that older girl, named Daisy, watch over us. If Daisy sees us slackin' on the job, she whacks us on the neck with a switch. Mammy Naira, I ain't never seen anyone love to use a switch as much as Daisy – unless of course it's Boss Shelby, 'cept that he uses his whip." Flossy's nine-year-old body shuddered for an instant remembering the many times she had been made to watch the overseer lash out his fury on some hapless victim. ""Dat Daisy gal's switch really stings, Mammy!"

Franny, who had been quietly listening to her sister Flossy talk, tugged on Mammy Naira's dress and pointed to a long red mark on the side of her neck.

The tenderhearted mammy clucked her tongue in silent disgust as she shook her head. "I know, girls, but dere is nothin' dat Mammy Naira can do for y'all. Spittin' tobacco on Miz

Wendy's roses is what young children do on dis plantation. When you gals grows old enough to get yo' first bandana, I'll try to get y'all work in da Master's kitchen."

Two other little boys completed the circle of children eating from the wooden bowl in the cabin. The older child's name was Noah. He was five years old. The other boy, a lively lad of four years, was called Moses.

During the spring rains of 1852, Noah's mammy had drowned when she waded too far into the waters of the Big Buckwater and slipped into a hole. The panicked slave did not know how to swim, and she was dragged screaming downstream with the swift flowing current. Slave-workers searched the banks of the river for two days. They finally found her body wedged in the branches of a tree that had become jammed onto a sandbar.

Moses was orphaned at three when his mother suddenly dropped dead from a blood clot to the brain while picking tobacco. Mercifully, she never knew what hit her and was dead before she hit the ground.

Neither child remembered their mammies. The cheerful boys with chubby cheeks and dimpled legs loved Old Jed and Mammy Naira as ardently as any child loves his parents. The boys spent their days toddling around the quarters in the same one-piece tow-linen shirts worn by all young children on the plantation. The aging Mammy Naira carefully watched over Noah and Moses and all the babies in the quarters as they squatted in the dirt and played with rocks and sticks or fiddled with bugs and worms. The boys played, and wrestled, and laughed together like frisky puppies. At night, they lay bundled together on their mat with arms and legs entangled like a knot of wild grape vines.

Old Jed turned his attention away from the five children sharing a meal and leaned closer to Naira. He lowered his voice to a whisper, "I ran into Quaker Singer today as I cleared my traps near Pickle Cove. He expects a visit from his sister sometime near the end of next week." The old trapper looked around the cabin, but none of the other slaves were paying much attention to the two old folks quietly talking in the corner. "We've made plans to meet up in a few days to go over the final arrangements. Can you be ready?"

"Dere's not much to get ready, so I guess we be ready."

"The little ones don't know our plans, and that's best. It'd be too hard for them to keep the secret. Everything must seem as normal, Naira. That's the key to not arousing suspicion."

Naira nodded her head and said, "We must be mighty careful. Boss Shelby has been terrorizing all d'slaves in the quarter. He be as determined as a duck on a June bug to find out what he wants to know." Mammy Naira lowered her head and rubbed the back of her calf as she spoke in soft whispers. "I see dat serpent Mandy lurking in d'shadows as de men swap stories 'round de campfire, and nosin' 'round as d'women chatter while dey wash clothes in d'river. I know she be hoping to hear some useful gossip so she can run over to de Big House and blabber to Miz Wendy."

Jed patted Naira on the knee and smiled. "Just a few more days, my dear," he whispered, "and we'll take flight like the geese that go north each spring."

Mammy Naira sighed. *Oh Lordy, please let dis ol' mammy have de joy of seein' her daughter, Esther, at least one more time 'fore I make it to de Promised Land. Amen and hallelujah.*

Chapter 14 ~ September 1853 – Meeting Moses

A large crowd of people gathered at the Seneca Village Methodist Church to meet the woman known to her people as Moses. Mrs. Cody had arranged a potluck supper and a baked goods sale to raise a little money to aid her friend, Harriet Tubman, in her efforts to bring enslaved people North on the Underground Railroad. But even the usually composed Joanne was surprised by the huge turnout.

Twice each year, in the spring and in the fall, Harriet would travel south to rescue slaves from different plantations. Her daring reputation had grown in the years since she had made her own escape in 1849. Without knowing it, the small fearless conductor was becoming a legend in the slave quarters and mansion houses of the many plantations in the southern part of the United States.

Slaves and masters along the Eastern Shore of Maryland, including Wendalyn and Steidley King, talked in whispers about the mysterious bandit known on the plantations as *Moses*. The stories they shared were fantastic and astonishing. It was rumored around campfires in the quarters that the shadowy pirate called Moses could see as well as an owl in the night. Overseers overheard the gossiping whispers of field hands declaring that Moses, like the legendary Paul Bunyan, was strong enough to carry a grown man across his back for twelve straight hours. House slaves swore in hushed tones as they polished wooden floors on their knees that the slave stealer could trek though the underbrush with the silent grace of a lion. Young children, gathering twigs in the woods, brazenly boasted that their hero Moses could smell a slave-tracker's scent floating in the wind from miles away, just like a deer.

All over Maryland, large rewards were offered to capture the mystifying man called Moses. Too many prime slaves were disappearing into the night. To help the slave-catchers hunt the fugitives, resentful plantation owners purchased extra dogs at an unwanted added out-of-pocket expense. Woods and marshes were searched – roadblocks set up. But season after season, the legendary conductor slipped away into the night with scores of slaves worth thousands of dollars – as elusive as mist evaporating with the warmth of the morning sun.

Bucky and Esther scanned the crowd as they moved through the church hall to find Mrs. Cody. The busy headmistress had worked at the church all afternoon to prepare for the fundraiser. Joanne had promised Bucky and Esther that she would introduce them to her special friend.

"Can you see Mrs. Cody, Bucky?" asked Esther fretfully. "I wish I were taller."

"Not yet. Lordy, there sure are a lot of folks here. This crowd must outshine the number of people that Mrs. Cody expected to participate in the bake sale." The tall young man cut a path through the throngs of people in the hall. "Let me take your cake, Esther, before it gets smashed in this crowd."

Gratefully, Esther handed the chocolate cake to Bucky. He hoisted it up high, and the pair made their way to the baked-goods table where it was added to the other offerings. Bucky turned and scanned the crowded room. "There in the corner! I think I see Mrs. Cody's back in that group," pointed Bucky.

Esther caught her breath in excitement. "I wonder if she's talking to our mystery woman, and if so, will she remember us?"

Bucky grabbed Esther by the hand and said, "I guess there's only one way to find out, Esther. Let's amble on over."

Joanne Cody turned briefly and caught sight of her two young friends as they maneuvered toward her. She waved the long fingers of her hand to help guide them to her corner. Everything about the middle-aged headmistress seemed elongated. She was tall and thin with lengthy facial features and strong white teeth.

The former slave had received her freedom ten years earlier after her husband, George, died of diphtheria. The dedicated couple had worked as house slaves for a decent master in Delaware for twenty years. He appreciated the couple's loyalty, and had planned to give them both their freedom upon his death. After George's funeral, the kindly master took the grieving woman into his study and said, "Joanne, over the years, I have watched you bring five children into the world and bury them all before their first birthday. And, although you grieved, you never complained. I watched you care for your good husband with the grace and compassion of an angel before he died. You are well aware that it is written in my will that you and George would have obtained your freedom upon my death, but I will not make you wait another moment. You have suffered enough in this life." The master then reached into the drawer of his desk and handed his house slave an envelope. It contained her freedom papers and one hundred dollars.

Joanne had known immediately that she would use the money to begin a school for orphaned children. She worked long hours at a hotel in Philadelphia and saved almost every penny she earned to add to her nest egg. Each Sunday she attended church. After the service, she stayed on with other members of the congregation and learned to read and write from the minister. After six years of backbreaking work during the day and practicing to read and write at night, she moved to New York to search for a suitable site to open her school for abandoned children.

It might have been easy for Mrs. Cody to fail. Finding the right house to begin her school was a daunting task. Then her luck prevailed once more. A kind society woman heard of Mrs. Cody's intention to start an orphanage for homeless children and commissioned the renovation of an old rundown boarding house in Seneca Village. The three-story brownstone house was a perfect place to shelter and teach the many unwanted children who lived like rats in a rundown area known as Five Points and other similar slums on the Lower East Side.

"Bucky, Esther," exclaimed the headmistress, "can you believe it! All these folks came to meet my dear friend." The usually unflappable Mrs. Cody raised her voice to be heard over the crowd. "Come. Come. Let me introduce you to Harriet Ross

Tubman." Mrs. Cody gently tapped Harriet on the shoulder, and the petite woman turned to face Bucky and Esther. The woman before them looked completely different from the woman they had seen dressed in a man's suit of clothing. Harriett wore a dark blue dress with a cream-colored lace collar. Esther thought she looked about the same size as their mystery woman, but couldn't decide if she was the same extraordinary woman who had come to their aid. The night had been so dark, and the brief encounter had taken place almost three years ago.

"Harriet, I would like to introduce you to the two friends I was telling you about earlier," said Mrs. Cody. "This is Bucky and Esther. They work at the orphanage with me." Bucky shook the outstretched hand of Mrs. Tubman. He marveled at the strength in the hand of a woman so small. Mrs. Cody continued, "Harriet and I worked together for a time in a hotel in Philadelphia in 1849, before I moved to Manhattan."

"It's a pleasure to meet you, Ma'am," said Esther as she too grasped Harriet's hand firmly. "You're doing wonderful work on the Underground Railroad."

Harriet smiled cordially at Esther and acknowledged her with a firm handshake, "I understand from Joanne that you and your friend, Bucky, have worked from time to time as conductors on the Railroad. Now that I think about it, I believe my good friend, Quaker Thomas Garrett, has mentioned your name to me as well."

Esther looked at Bucky and broad smiles of recognition spread across their faces. Esther turned back to face Harriet. "I wasn't sure if it was you from the way you are dressed tonight, but I would *never* forget the sound of your lovely deep voice," said Esther warmly. "It *was* you, Mrs. Tubman! I don't know if you remember us, but we remember you. We had a chance encounter with you about three years ago. You were dressed in a man's suit and you wore a floppy felt hat. You found Bucky and me asleep under some trees. We were completely lost just outside Wilmington, Delaware. It was you who kindly gave us directions to Mr. Garrett's station and made us passengers on the Underground Railroad."

Harriet Tubman put her hand to her forehead, pushing aside her hair just enough so that Bucky and Esther could see the same deep scar in the middle of her brow. Harriet narrowed her eyes and scratched the old wound as if she were relieving an itch from a phantom flea. "Y'all weren't those two scared runaways I found whilst making a trip south to convince my husband John to come north with me? Why, you two were nothin' more than youngsters!"

"Yes, I'm afraid that was us," said Bucky grinning. "We were hopelessly lost and very tired and hungry. You wouldn't tell us your name that night, but you said that you were on your way to bring your husband north. Bucky lowered his voice. "I'm sorry that your trip didn't work out as you had hoped."

"No, it didn't," whispered Harriet sadly. "I felt like a darn fool dressed in those dusty men's clothes the night I came a knocking at the door of John Tubman's cabin. I was shocked when he told me he had remarried. Why, the snake was still married to me! His new wife was so pretty standing at his side, and they just stood there at the door and laughed at me."

"It took me a long time to get over it, but I finally reckoned that the Lord just had another path for me to follow," Harriet sighed. "I'm glad you kids made it safely to freedom, and I'm happy that y'all have gone back to help others find their way north."

The three former slaves swapped stories about some of their experiences as conductors on the Underground Railroad. Finally, Esther got the courage to ask Harriet how she got the scar on her forehead.

"When I was still a young girl," recalled Harriet, "but old enough to wear a bandanna, I got in the way of an overseer who was trying to stop a slave running away from our plantation. The overseer found the poor man hiding behind some crates inside a small store. That scared slave jumped up like a jackrabbit and bolted out the front door. The boldness of the slave so startled the overseer, he picked up a two-pound scale-weight off the counter and hurled it at the man. Problem was, he hit *me* square in the forehead as I stood frozen near the front door. I darn near died from that blow," Harriet recalled as she touched the old gash in her forehead. "Funny thing though, ever since that day, I have been prone to violent headaches and sudden fits of sleep, which produce strange visions that come on me as quick as a dog on a bone."

Harriet continued, "Now, I always warn my passengers that I might drop like a sack of cornmeal in the dirt for a nap, but not to worry too much over it." Harriet chuckled. "Once, I was leading a group of eleven slaves away from a plantation, and I could feel a doze comin' on strong. We was in a pretty tight situation because of travelin' by day and close to the road. We could hear the faint sounds of hound dogs barkin' in the distance. I tried singin' to stay awake, but I knew it weren't no use. In the end, I tumbled to the ground and was out like a candle without a wick. I don't know how long I slept, but when I woke, my group was squattin' over me like a flock of crows around a corncob. I jumped to my feet and ordered the group to follow me. I ran like a crazy woman for my beating heart told me that we were in grave danger. I plunged into the woods. Then, I came to a meadow with a winding river at the bottom of a slope. It was there that I froze in my tracks, for it occurred to me that the scene before me was already branded in my brain."

Harriet looked at Bucky and Esther and chuckled. "Why, I'd just seen the same vision while I'd been asleep! I eagerly urged my passengers to cross the river with me. We were mighty scared for none of us could swim. I plunged in, and 'fore I knew it, the icy water had crept to my waist. I looked around and noticed that the others had stopped at the shore. I guess they figured to let me test the waters, so to speak," Harriet winked. "When the water reached my shoulders I shuddered but kept on going, 'cause in my dream I had reached the other side. The chilly water numbed my chin, but I treaded forward putting my faith in the Lord. At that moment, the water suddenly began to retreat to my shoulders, and I impatiently waved the others to follow on. We were cold and numb and dripping wet when we finally reached a clearing. It was there that I saw a cabin, and I knew we were safe because I had seen that very cabin in my dream as I slept alongside the road. I boldly knocked on the door, and a family of free Negroes welcomed us inside. They gave us food and shelter for the night, and showed us a safe way out of the area in the morning. I have learned, over the years, to pay particular attention to my dreams."

Esther told Harriet about her up-coming trip to rescue the five children from her old plantation in Maryland and how it would probably be her last journey south.

Harriet looked at Esther for quite sometime before she spoke. "You must be extra careful, Esther. There's always an added degree of danger going back to a place you where you might get recognized."

"I promise that I'll take care not to get captured," said Esther solemnly.

"I must confess. The thing that struck me most about y'all the night we met-up, was tellin' me that ya both could read. You said that an old man had taught y'all in secret. I thought 'bout that a lot after we parted ways. Teachin' young children to read and write is a mighty noble line of work. Heck, any old John or Mary can do what I'm doin'. But y'all have a special gift. It's best you leave conducting to a simple ol' gal like me, who can't read nor write a lick. You kids can best put your gifts to a better use by teaching children readin', writin', and 'rithmetic, and the future will be better for all our people."

Chapter 15 ~ September 1853 – National Theatre of New York

Esther was excited to see the stage production of Harriet Beecher Stowe's story of *Uncle Tom's Cabin*. The young woman trembled slightly as she walked down the creaking staircase from her small bedroom on the third floor of the orphanage. She grasped tightly the Bronze Bottle at her side for support. Esther had spent the previous evening sewing an elegant new evening bag so that she could bring the bottle to the theatre with her. She could not understand why, but she felt compelled to keep the bottle near her at all times. The beautiful bottle gave her a sense of comfort, and tonight she knew that she would need all the courage she could muster. Esther had never worn a long frock, and she had never been to a theatre to see a play. The moss-colored velvet garment suited Esther. The skirt flowed softly from her waist. A stylishly tailored jacket fitted with tiny pearl-toned buttons ran from her waist up to a graceful Mandarin collar, which flattered Esther's slender neck.

Earlier that evening, Mrs. Cody had insisted on coming to Esther's bedroom so she could style her curly locks into an intricate up-swept hairstyle. Joanne had recently seen the fashionable hairdo in the latest edition of the popular magazine, *Godey's Ladies Book*. When she was done, tiny wisps of curls framed the young girl's face. To finish the look, the pleased headmistress carefully positioned a narrow coral comb extending six inches long into the back of Esther's hair. Mrs. Cody's deceased husband had affectionately given her the comb to mark their tenth wedding anniversary. "There, the comb finishes the look perfectly, if I do say so myself," the headmistress said with pride as she compared her handiwork to the lithograph picture in the magazine.

"Mrs. Cody, you mustn't loan me your precious coral comb. Mr. Cody worked on his days off to earn the money for that gift. It means so much to you," declared Esther earnestly. "I might lose it!"

"Nonsense, Esther, hair-bobs should be worn by the young," said the efficient headmistress with a quick wave of her hand in the air. "I know you'll take good care of it. Anyway, the comb compliments the moss green color in your new velvet dress, which I must say sets off the striking shade of your eyes."

Esther looked at Mrs. Cody with affection. She had long since ceased to feel embarrassed about the unusual color of her eyes. "I'm truly grateful for the gift of this lovely dress, Mrs. Cody. The material is so soft, and unlike any fabric I've ever felt before. In all my life, I've never worn anything as beautiful as this. I can't thank you enough for buying it for me."

Mistress Cody stepped back and looked at her young friend fondly. "Well, you deserve to look nice, Esther. You and Bucky have worked hard to make this orphanage a decent place for our children; it is the least I could do. Anyway, you're going to see the stage production of *Uncle Tom's Cabin* at the *National Theatre of New York*, child. You had nothing appropriate to wear for such a fine occasion. Now, let's hurry. You don't want to be late for the opening scene. I saw the play when you were in Canada. It's very moving. I cried during most of the last act."

Bucky looked up to see Esther coming down the stairs followed by a smiling Mrs. Cody. His mouth slid open slightly, as he stared at the striking young woman and wondered. *Could this be the young girl I have always thought of as a little sister? All of a sudden, the little girl has grown into a beautiful young lady. Why didn't I see it before?* In that instant, the thoughtful young scholar was completely besotted.

During the several seconds it took to process this notion, Bucky thought that he detected a knowing grin on the face of Mrs. Cody. He wondered if his thoughts were that transparent. Bucky coughed and said in a flustered voice, "Esther, you look...very nice...er...really lovely in your new dress. The color is beautiful...and I like what you've done with your hair." Bucky suddenly realized that he was poking the top of his head with his hands, and that he must look like an idiot.

Esther blushed and then smiled. She felt slightly flustered to have Bucky suddenly pay so much attention to her appearance. "Mrs. Cody styled it for me, Bucky. I could never have done it myself. And, she graciously let me borrow her elegant coral comb," said Esther as she turned to show off the back of her hairdo.

"It's lovely," Bucky mumbled.

"Your new suit fits you very well, too," Esther complimented, hoping to move the conversation away from her.

"You *both* look very handsome," interrupted the amused headmistress, "but your carriage is waiting outside. Here are your tickets," she said as she handed them to Bucky. "Now, you mustn't be late for the first act, so you'd better hurry. Have a wonderful time, my dears, and *please* be careful," Mrs. Cody instructed as the efficient headmistress shepherd the young couple outside the front door of the building.

Bucky supported Esther's arm as she climbed up the steps to the interior of the coach hired by Bucky to drive them into the city. Esther was grateful for the assistance because she still felt a bit clumsy in her new leather boots with the delicate little heels, and weighted down by the heavy folds of fabric in the velvet skirt. Bucky climbed into the cab and settled onto the seat next to Esther as the driver urged two black horses up the street.

"You look very pretty tonight, Esther," Bucky said sincerely as he gazed at his old friend. "The moss green color of your dress compliments the beautiful color of your eyes."

Esther was surprised and secretly pleased to know that Bucky liked the greenish color of her eyes.

"You *should* be exhausted from the long voyage back from Prince Edward Island, meeting Harriet Tubman, and shopping for your dress, but you look serene. It's as though you've become a different person since you stepped off the ship." Bucky was still a little tongue-tied. "I'm sorry. I can't seem to express myself very clearly tonight, Esther." Bucky sighed. "I guess what I'm wondering is, where do you find the energy?"

"I do feel exceptionally rested, despite the fact that I *have* been very busy." Esther turned in the seat to face Bucky. "I'm so happy to have a few minutes alone to talk to you, Bucky, because something fantastic happened to me while I was staying on the island with Tara Maguire and her family." Esther looked down at her lap and felt the outline of the bottle inside its case. "I don't quite know where to begin, Bucky."

"Well, start by telling me about your trip, Esther. We haven't had much time alone since I picked you up at the docks, and I'd love to hear about your fantastic adventure."

Esther reached for her evening bag. Slowly, she slid open a drawstring cord and reached into the green and gold brocade bag, which she had so painstakingly stitched. She gently removed the Bronze Bottle and positioned it on her lap. Even in the darkened interior of the confined coach, the bottle sparkled with a soft glow. Esther placed the bottle into Bucky's hands.

An unusual warm feeling briefly rippled through the palms of Bucky's hands. The sensible young scholar shook off the episode as a fluke and turned his head toward Esther.

"Bucky, this bottle was a gift to me from Tara Maguire."

The beauty of the bottle immediately charmed Bucky. He held it near the window hoping to catch the light from a gas street lamp. The specks of gold glittered against the bronze and ebony background. Bucky studied the bottle. "This is a very beautiful bottle, Esther. What's it made of?"

"I think it's glass infused with brightly colored hues of paint."

Bucky shook his head as he studied the bottle. "I don't think that I've ever seen anything quite like it. It was very nice of Miss Maguire to give it to you. It looks pretty old and, I imagine, somewhat valuable. The glass bottle is covered with such beautiful colors, and the gold speckles remind me of something...I can't quite think...yes, that's it...stars! They sparkle like all the brilliant stars in the sky."

"I know," Esther agreed with excitement. "I think so too." Esther's voice faltered slightly. "There's something else, Bucky. You're right, the bottle *is* old, but it's also very mysterious." Esther stopped to compose her thoughts. "Please don't think that I've lost my mind, but what I'm about to tell you is completely true. You must believe me. It's very important to me that you know that I would never exaggerate the truth where this bottle is concerned."

Bucky looked at Esther again and slowly nodded his head. He could see that the young girl was very serious about what she wanted to say to him. He placed the bottle into her hands and said, "We have a fairly long ride to the theatre, Esther, so tell me everything you have discovered about your mystery bottle."

"Well, to begin with, Bucky, a month ago this very bottle was *emerald green!*"

Bucky listened intently as Esther shared the joy of discovering the bottle in the china cabinet of the Maguire's parlor. Esther relayed the unusual history of the bottle, and the incredible distance the bottle had traveled through time. She told him of the many interesting places to which it had journeyed, and the various different people it had helped before the bottle had ultimately found her. She described the fantastic feeling of contentment when Tara had placed the beautiful Emerald Bottle into her hands. Esther tried to accurately convey her utter amazement when the beautiful shades of emerald green gradually became overlaid with the rich shades of bronze, copper, ebony, and gold. And, finally, she explained how the brilliant speckles of light gradually appeared like the twinkling stars at twilight.

"Look, Bucky, there's more!" Esther held the bottle up again to catch the light of the full moon outside. She pointed to the inscription at the bottom of the bottle.

Bucky studied the two-line couplet. "This inscription is written in Latin."

in tuam manum venioad
tuum spiritum tam unus

"I know that *manum* means hand and *spiritum* is spirit in Latin, but I cannot accurately say what the rest is. What does it mean, Esther?"

Esther read the couplet at the bottom of the bottle. "Tara told me that translated into English, the Latin poem simply says:"

Into thy hand I come
Unto thy spirit as one.

"Tara believes that the bottle somehow embraces the spirit of its present owner which is signified by the expression of new colors," added Esther. "That's how she knew that it was time to pass the bottle on to me."

"I must admit, it's certainly a curious story." Bucky gathered the bottle into his hands for a few moments more. He looked down at it, as if it might speak to him in reassuring tones, but the bottle lay silent. At length he looked into Esther's eyes. "I'm not sure what to make of it all, Esther, but I'm very happy that this bottle has found you. You know that it's weighed heavily on my mind that I'll not be able to make this trip south with you. Somehow, I feel better about your journey now that you have the bottle to protect and guide you."

Bucky escorted Esther by the arm as they strolled down the steps of the National Theatre amidst the other members of the audience. Bucky had arranged for the same carriage driver to pick them up after the play. The driver had asked them to meet him around the corner where it would be less crowded. As the two walked along, they noticed from the dampened street that it had rained while they had been inside the theatre. But now, bright stars twinkled in the sky, and Esther inhaled the balmy night air. The friends spoke with excitement as they ambled away from the crowded theatre.

"I have never seen a story told so magnificently in all my life, Bucky. The saga of Eliza and Uncle Tom came to life for me on that stage. When Little Eva fell sick and died, I knew it was going to happen, and yet I cried anyway! The man who played Simon Legree was so evil. The audience booed every time he came on stage."

"I'm glad you enjoyed it so much, Esther. I must admit to you that I choked up a bit myself when Uncle Tom died at the hands of Simon Legree at the end of the play."

The friends chatted amiably as they rounded the corner. The crowd had thinned out as the couple moved away from the theatre, and the two were not aware that two men lurked in the shadows of a side alley. The taller man had red hair, which was covered by a navy blue knitted hat. His shorter partner had a crop of black hair sticking out the sides of a short-brimmed tweed gray cap. The smaller of the two stepped into the road and walked casually toward the approaching couple.

"Say friends," he asked with a grin on his face, "could you tell me where I might buy a newspaper?" He turned around and fell into step with Bucky and Esther.

Bucky said, "We saw a newsstand across from the theatre. It's back around the corner."

"Why, that's terribly nice of you, friends. Did you just come from the play? I heard that it's a real pipper. People been coming here every night all summer long."

As Esther and Bucky passed the darkened alley, the stranger engaging them with animated chitchat was distracting them. Silently, the taller partner slipped in behind the three and with the swift movements of an experienced pickpocket, pulled the coral comb from Esther's hair and tore her silk brocade purse from her hand in one fluid motion. In an instant, the two thieves raced back into the alley and disappeared before Bucky and Esther had time to react.

"Bucky, the bottle and Mrs. Cody's comb – we must try and get them back!"

Without thinking of the consequences to their safety, Bucky and Esther turned and chased the pair up a narrow alley lined with tall brick buildings on both sides. They could see the thieves dodging puddles while running toward the lights and carriages on a busy street at the other end of the alley. Esther's heart sank. She knew that once the scoundrels reached the crowded street, they could easily disappear among the people on the busy avenue. It seemed that all was lost to Esther, and she grieved that she might lose the bottle and comb that had been so faithfully entrusted into her care.

All of a sudden, the taller of the two thieves screamed out in pain and dropped to the floor of the alley. The bottle, still in its case, and the coral comb were abandoned on the cobble stone. The pickpocket continued to grimace in pain as he plunged his hands in a nearby puddle of rainwater. His shocked partner stopped and looked down at the groaning man as if he had gone mad.

"What's the matter, Mick? Have you got a cramp in your leg? Get up and run, you idiot, or the coppers will be on us!" The shorter thief could see Esther and Bucky closing in on them. Deciding that it was every man for himself, he bent down and snatched up the stolen property.

"Don't touch it, Willy!" screamed Mick.

"I'm not gonna stay here..." But, before Willy could take two steps, he too, screamed and dropped the pilfered bootie in the alley.

By the time Bucky and Esther reached the thieves, they were surprised to see them writhing on the ground in obvious pain.

"Are you crazy?" asked Willy as he stared up at a confused Esther. "What've you got in that bag, hot coals?"

Esther's heart throbbed in her chest as she bent to pick up the comb and bottle in its brocade bag. *Please don't be broken*, she prayed.

With puzzled stares, Esther and Bucky looked at each other and then at the thieves. "We'd better get out of here, Esther, before these two stop thrashing in the puddles." Bucky grabbed Esther's hand and quickly led her back in the direction from which they came. They were panting by the time they found the driver of the carriage.

"You kids are all out of breath. Did you think I was going to take another fare and leave the theatre without you?" he joked as he helped his passengers into the coach and shut the door.

"That was a very close call, Esther. What do you think happened back there with those two on the ground?"

Esther loosened the cord of her evening bag and pulled the bottle from its case. She felt its surface with her hands to make sure that the bottle was not cracked or broken.

The bottle seemed unharmed. "Bucky, place your hands on the bottle and tell me what you feel?" asked Esther.

Bucky did as he was asked. He looked at Esther with a confused stare. "Warmth, Esther, the bottle feels amazingly warm. What could possibly have caused that to happen?" Bucky asked with amazement.

"I'm not sure, Bucky, but I think the thieves dropped the bottle because it became too hot for them to hold onto. I can't be certain, but I think the bottle may have been burning their hands. Perhaps that's why they had plunged their fingers in the puddles of water." Suddenly Esther looked at her friend and flashed him a mischievous smile. "I don't think the bottle wanted to go with them, Bucky."

Bucky looked at Esther and smiled as he slowly shook his head. "This bottle seems to possess certain mysteries that are beyond my comprehension, Esther. It's made of glass, and yet it appears to be very strong. I'm afraid it's going to take me a few days to absorb everything that's happened to me tonight, and I'm not just talking about the bottle, Esther." Bucky looked into the green eyes of the young girl sitting next to him. "Since you've come back from your trip, you seem like a whole new person to me," he whispered shyly. "I would like to explore this feeling more when you get back from Maryland, if that's acceptable to you."

Esther looked at her old friend and slowly nodded her head. A feeling of warmth passed through her body as Bucky gently placed the bottle into her hands.

Bucky cleared his throat. "Here, let me help you attach the coral comb to your hair. I think, we'd best not tell Mrs. Cody about what happened tonight in the alley. It would only spoil the gift of this special evening, and after all, no real harm was done."

Esther turned her head to let Bucky reattach the coral comb into her hair. "I agree with you, Bucky." When the comb was back in place, Esther slowly turned around and took the hands of her old friend into her own. "Bucky, the day after tomorrow I'll take the train to Philadelphia to meet up with the Griggs. I don't know if we'll get a chance to spend time together alone again. If something happens and I don't see you for a while, I want to thank you for...well, so much, but especially for escorting me to see the play," she said with emotion. "I'll never forget this night."

"Nor will I Esther." Bucky looked down into the green eyes of his friend and surprised Esther by gently lifting her hands to his lips. There, he placed a kiss so soft, it felt like the whisper of a butterfly wing brushing against her skin.

Chapter 16 ~ September 1853 – Philadelphia

The train slowly chugged into the Philadelphia station on time. The trip to Pennsylvania had been uneventful, and Esther had spent the time reading the newspaper. The New York Times reported that Uncle Tom's Cabin was so enormously popular, that it was being held over at the theatre for another two months. The Liberator wrote that twenty-nine unsuspecting Negroes had been stolen by bounty hunters off the streets of Manhattan near a dangerous area known as Five Points. The article speculated that after facing a municipal judge, the doomed captives would surely be sent to the South to face a life of hard labor under the absolute control of indifferent masters. Esther sensed that the tension building between the sympathetic abolitionists and the southern slave owners was bound to collide at some future point.

Esther stepped off the train holding her small bag. The Bronze Bottle had been placed back into its sturdy leather pouch and hung safely across her shoulder. Esther always felt especially happy to carry the beautiful Bronze Bottle at her side. She looked at the faces of people welcoming passengers off the train. At the far end of the platform, Esther noticed the Grigg family scanning the coaches to catch a glimpse of the many travelers streaming out the doors. Deep dimples formed on Esther's cheeks as she smiled at Seth and Hannah Grigg. The twins had broken away from their parents and were racing toward her.

"Esther!" shouted Seth as he threw his arms around her waist. "It is so good to see thy face again."

"Seth, you've grown taller than the cattail reeds that grow along the banks of the Big Buckwater!" said Esther.

"I thank thee for thy words of compliment," answered Seth proudly.

"Hello, Esther," added Hannah shyly.

"Look at you, Hannah. You grow to look more like your beautiful mother with each passing day. How old are you now?"

My brother Seth and I are ten-years-old," said Hannah warming to the special attention from Esther.

"You both must be a big help to your parents on the farm," praised Esther.

"I am learning to plow the fields using our mare, Dolly. Father let me plow two rows of earth all on my own yesterday," revealed Seth with obvious pride.

Claudia and Donald Grigg approached the group and greeted Esther with warm hugs.

"Seth," instructed Donald, "where are thy manners, son? Relieve Esther of her burden." Donald nodded his head toward Esther's bag.

Esther smiled as Seth who took her small satchel into his hands.

"It is so good to see thy face, Esther," welcomed Claudia. "Thee have grown into a lovely young woman during this past year. How is Bucky?"

"Bucky is very well, Claudia, and he sends his best wishes to y'all. He's gone to ready the new compound for our move to St. Catharines."

"Esther, thee must be tired from the long train ride from New York. Let us ride out to the farm. We can get caught up with all the news from my brother Mark on our trip home."

Donald scanned the platform and noted that no one at the busy train station seemed to take any unusual notice of the half-caste girl with light brown hair and green eyes talking to a family of Quakers.

Esther had not been to the Grigg farm since bringing a group of slaves through their station a year ago. There was something strangely pleasant about driving up to the property in the bold light of day, and it occurred to Esther that she had never enjoyed the view of the farm in this manner. Small white clouds floated in the pale blue sky. The neat white farmhouse and matching white barn, flanked by shady elm trees, were pleasing to the eye of the artist. Esther noted that there was nothing fancy or pretentious about the property. The orderly rows of green crops and several small-enclosed pastures filled with various farm livestock represented the vigilant work of an industrious family.

The family and their guest entered the house. "Esther, sit by the light of the window. Seth and Hannah will visit with thee while Donald and I bring the plates of fried chicken, biscuits and buttermilk to the table. Lunch will be ready in a moment. I know thee must be hungry from the long train ride."

"Please, allow me to help, Claudia."

"Not just now, my friend. It gives Donald and me pleasure to serve thee as our guest. Later, I will let thee help." Claudia

Grigg smiled at her friend, and Esther knew that it would be pointless to insist, so she let her friend spoil her for the moment.

As Esther listened to the twins recite a poem they had learned at school, her eyes examined the very room, which she and Bucky had sat in the night they had first met Mistress Grigg. The room was exactly the same with the exception of the walls. A dozen pencil sketches, positioned in identical pine frames, hung in various spots on the walls of the sitting room. Esther smiled as she looked at the sketches illuminated from sunlight streaming through the large window. She reflected on the night when she and Bucky knocked on Claudia Grigg's door.

After their extended late night visit and dinner, Mistress Grigg had given Bucky and Esther shelter for the night. The following morning, Esther and Bucky sat eating breakfast around the dining room table when Esther noticed a stack of white paper and some drawing tools on a small desk in the corner. Esther inquired about the materials. Mistress Grigg explained that Donald had tried his hand at sketching, but found that he did not have a talent for drawing. Esther asked if she might repay Claudia's kindness by trying her hand at sketching a portrait of the children and her.

"Did thee learn to draw as a slave on your plantation?" Mistress Grigg had asked in amazement.

"No ma'am," answered Esther shyly, "I've never had lessons, but sometimes when I was a young girl, I'd sneak away to a quiet spot and draw clouds with a stick in the dirt or sketch insects with a shard of charcoal from the fire on a smooth bit of river-wood." Esther looked over at Bucky and their eyes locked for a moment as if sharing the same private thought. Slowly Esther turned toward Claudia and spoke. "I've not had the…uh desire to draw for some years now, but at this moment there is a powerful yearning in me to take up your drawing tools and attempt to create the images of you and your children." Claudia was only too pleased to oblige the young girl's request.

Nervously, Esther picked up one of the pencils and looked at it with wonder. Until that moment, the young slave girl had never held a pencil in her hand. Tentative in the beginning, Esther began to sketch a portrait of the twins. Soon, a rhythm took hold of her efforts, and she continued to draw with the spirit of one who is in a dream-like trance. Faster and faster flew the nib of the pencil. Using the edge of a sharp knife, Claudia kept a supply of fresh pencils at hand for Esther to grasp as the lead of each one wore down.

No one spoke. All who were present recognized that they were witness to an extraordinary event. By the time Esther was done, a dozen sketches lay scattered upon the table. The drawings of the twins and Claudia Grigg accurately portrayed the details of their facial features and captured each person's spirit with realistic clarity.

"Oh, I'm sorry Mrs. Grigg," apologized an embarrassed Esther, "I thoughtlessly used all of your drawing paper. I can't for the life of me imagine why I would do such a careless thing. I don't remember…I mean…I did not intend…" A clearly stunned Esther looked at the Quaker women and helplessly shrugged her shoulders.

"Do not apologize, Esther. It is clear that thy God-given talent as an artist is immense. I believe it has lain dormant inside thy soul for some time now, and today it just needed to be exposed and nourished. These lovely drawings will hold a place of honor on the walls of our sitting room. I thank thee for sharing thy incredible gift with us."

"I can't reckon the way I feel," declared Esther to the people sitting around the dining room table looking at her artwork, "but I'm happier than I've been in a very long time.

The sound of Claudia's voice calling Esther and the children to the dining room table pulled Esther away from her memories.

Later that afternoon, Claudia and Esther walked up the small hill that held little Emma's grave, and Esther laid some wildflowers at the base of the simple cross.

"We leave tomorrow afternoon on the train to Maryland. Mark will pick us up at the station and bring us to his farm," explained Claudia. "It will be dark, so the three of us should not cause too much attention riding in his wagon. Most folks will be indoors for the night. We will rest there Friday night and most of Saturday. Naira and Old Jed will be on the lookout for thee late Saturday night. Are thee nervous, Esther?"

"Yes, I'm very nervous, but I am also excited to see my family. Mammy Naira is so old, and she has trouble with her legs. That'll make what we need to do that much harder, but I will not leave her and Old Jed behind. I think it'd kill them to have to say goodbye to those five children. They're like a family. No, they are a family. And, God willing Claudia, we'll find a way."

"Well, I am committed to helping thee, Esther. Donald does not fully understand why I am doing this, but he is a good man and supports what my heart is guiding me to do." Esther nodded and patted the hand of her dear friend. The two friends stood watching the sunset, each lost in private thoughts, until finally Esther broke the silence.

"You know, Claudia, I've never traveled to Maryland on a train," chuckled Esther. "Although, it's true that a Negro woman traveling with a white woman south would not signal the same alarm as one traveling by train alone to the north."

"Thee speak the truth," laughed Claudia. "However, if anyone should inquire as to our purpose, I can always say that thee...I mean *you* are my servant," added Claudia. "I will not wear the clothes of a Quaker woman, and I pray that I will remember to adjust my manner of speaking so that I will not set off a warning signal. It is common knowledge that no Quaker would ever own a slave. My brother Mark will have had contact with Old Jed by now to make the final arrangements, and I am certain that Naira and Jed will be ready for us."

"Claudia, I must remember to control my emotions for I know that all of our lives depend upon keeping my wits about me, but I'll be overjoyed to see Mammy and Old Jed once more. I've dreamed of this moment for so long."

"It will be an emotional journey for all of us," whispered Claudia Grigg as she looked down at the small mound of earth at her feet.

Chapter 17 ~ September 1853 – Maryland

One half-caste black woman traveling south on a train to Maryland with a white woman caused not the slightest stir of attention. On the surface, the pair looked like any other slave girl traveling with her mistress. Claudia had decided to wear black. She rationalized that a woman wearing a mourning veil would be less likely to attract an unwanted visit from another friendly passenger wishing to pass the time with idle chatter. The ploy worked, and the women were left to themselves.

It was long after dark when Esther and Claudia finally pulled into the train station in Dorchester County. A clear night sky was sprinkled with stars, and the air still held the gentle warmth from the day. The station was almost empty but to keep up the pretense, Esther followed behind her friend carrying both of their bags as they stepped out of the coach and onto the platform. Before the women had taken ten steps, Mark Singer stood before his sister. He hoisted Claudia off the ground in a giant bear hug. Esther noticed that Mark possessed the same striking good looks as his younger sister, and it was clear to see that they were very close. Mark's long hair was a slightly darker shade of brown, but the hazel eyes and other facial features were much the same. The dairy farmer was tall and slim. Long hours of hard labor hauling heavy bails of hay to his cows had endowed him with muscular shoulders and arms. And yet, Esther detected a quiet gentleness in his bearing.

Esther looked fondly at the brother and sister embracing and wondered what it might be like to have a brother or sister of her own. For all she knew, her birth mother may have had other children – all living completely different lives in some other part of the South. Esther sighed and then suddenly thought. I *do* have brothers and sisters, and I will meet them tomorrow – all five of them.

"Esther, please come and meet my dearest brother Mark," beckoned Claudia enthusiastically. Mark grabbed Claudia's arm and shot her a warning glance. He looked around to see if anyone had been listening to a woman treating her servant more as a friend than a slave.

Esther looked at Claudia with a shielded expression then slowly turned to Mark and said, "It be mighty fine to finally meet ya Massa Singer." Esther bent low and cast her eyes to the ground. "Miz Grigg, why she be goin' on all de time, speakin' so highly of her favorite brother. Now, if'n y'all will be kind enough to point me in de direction of your wagon, I'll be loadin' up our baggage for d'trip home."

Claudia's face reddened at the foolishness of her blunder. *If I don't have my wits about me, I will be more of a burden than a help to Esther,* she thought shamefully.

"It's just over there," Mark said solemnly. "I'll show the way." Mark took Claudia's arm and led her to his wagon as Esther followed a few paces behind.

No one spoke until the wagon pulled well away from the station and onto the main road leading out to Mark's farm. Finally Claudia broke the silence and turned to Esther who had climbed into the back of the wagon with the luggage. "I'm sorry, Esther. If I am not more careful, I will thwart this mission before we even get started. I promise thee that I will do better in the future."

"Don't be so hard on yourself, my friend," instructed Esther. "It's not in your nature to treat people with anything but kindness. This experience is new for you, but I know that you're going to be a mighty big help to me. There were not many people around and no harm was done."

Mark turned around and spoke. "Esther, I met with thy friend two days past. Old Jed said that they would be ready for us tomorrow night. The children know nothing of the planned escape. We both agreed that it would be best if they were kept in the dark until the last minute. It would be too risky a secret to keep, and surprise is the key to our success. Old Jed will tell the oldest boy, Sampson. The boy must know the plan so that he might play his part in the distraction to get Naira and the children out of the cabin and away from the quarters."

"I can't thank you enough, Mr. Singer, for all you've done for my family. Without you and Claudia, I'd have lost all contact with my mammy. Over the past three years, you two have been a lifeline to the people I love the most."

"Esther, it would please me if thee would call me Mark. It is contrary to everything the Society of Friends believes in for any man to own another or take up arms against another. My dear sister and I have merely done, for thee, what we believe is right by decree of a higher power. We will continue to help all those oppressed until they are forever free."

"The Quakers have been wonderful friends to my people for many years now, and I'm certain that one day you'll be rewarded for your efforts. Mark, did Old Jed speak well of Naira?"

"He said that although her legs continue to give her trouble all else is fine with thy beloved Naira."

"I'm so worried about my mammy. She just can't walk very well, but I must take her with me," said Esther with emotion.

"Do not worry," said Mark, "thee will find a way. Tomorrow we will work out the final details of our plan."

Esther stretched her weary body out on the boards of the wagon. She rested her head against her canvas bag and closed her eyes. In the background, Mark and Claudia were happily exchanging news about their children. Suddenly, it occurred to

Esther that she had come home to the land of her childhood. As the wagon creaked slowly down the road in the balmy night air, the particular sounds and smells of the Tidewater country filled her senses with a heightened intensity. And Esther gathered it all inside. The woods, the fields, and the marshes yielded a hundred familiar memories of a time when a young slave girl was learning to find her way in the world.

"Good morning, Esther," greeted Mark. "I hope that thee slept comfortably in thy bed."

Mark, his wife Rebecca, and their two sons sat at the breakfast table with Claudia. "I had a restful night's sleep," answered Esther, a bit embarrassed that she had slept in later than her hosts. "Thank you."

"Please come and join us at the table," requested Rebecca warmly. "These are our two boys, Elijah and Benjamin."

Esther sat at the table and kindly shook hands with the boys. "It's so nice to finally meet you. How old are you?"

"I am fourteen," offered Elijah, who looked very much like his father.

"I will be twelve in November," added Benjamin. The fair-haired Benjamin had blue eyes and favored his mother.

"Boys," said Mark, "Please see to the cows. I will join thee in a while. I need to visit with thy Aunt Claudia and friend Esther for a few minutes."

"Sure, Pa," said Elijah, "take thy time. Ben and I will get started with the day's chores."

"They're wonderful boys," praised Esther as she watched the boys leave.

"Thank thee," answered Rebecca. "They are a big help to Mark and me. I do not think we could run this dairy farm without them."

Large loaves of bread and several varieties of cheese rested in the center of the table. A plain white china bowl held plump apples. Rebecca filled Esther's glass with fresh milk and loaded her plate with food. Esther was hungry. The aroma and crusty texture of the warm bread complimented the nutty flavors of the savory cheeses. "I don't think I've ever tasted cheese like this in the North. Are these your own special recipes?"

"They are," beamed Mark. We enjoy making our cheese and have several varieties. "I will set aside a supply for thy journey north."

When Esther had satisfied her hunger, Mark asked her to join him in the sitting room while Claudia and Rebecca cleared away the leftovers from the breakfast table. Mark invited Esther to sit on a small couch. The simple furniture was comfortably arranged around a large brick fireplace with large gray slate stones covering the floor near the hearth. "Esther, it is vital to our cause that thee are not traced back to this farm. If I could, I would lend thee my wagon to bring thy mammy, but that is just too risky. Thee will have to think of a way to get Naira and the children safely away from the plantation on your own."

"I have given this much thought over the past weeks, and I'm still not set on a plan," Esther groaned. "I'm certain that something will show itself to me. I've come too far to fail."

"We will be able to hide thee until it is safe to go to the next station, once thy family is here." Mark rose from his seat and walked over to the fireplace. He beckoned Esther to join him as he pointed to a large flat gray stone that lay among other similar stones in front of the large fireplace. Esther saw nothing unusual about the stone other than it had a small chip at one edge. Nothing however seemed out of order.

"What do thee see?" asked Mark.

"A flat gray stone with a small chip."

."Esther, if thou might be so kind to help me move this stone," Mark requested. Esther looked on as Mark lifted an iron poker from a large canister that also held a broom and small shovel. He carefully wedged the sharp end of the rod into the chip, which enabled him to pry the stone from its spot. Using one hand as a lever, Mark steadied the stone as Esther bent over and helped him lift the large slab of slate from the hearth. Esther was astonished. The stone fit so well into the hearth that it was impossible to see that it was not permanently mortared into place like the rest of the stones. After setting the stone to the side, Mark opened a wooden door-hatch that rested underneath the stone, and Esther found herself staring down into a dark hole.

"What is this secret place?" asked Esther.

Mark lit a small lantern with a bit of flint. "Please come and see for thyself," he invited. Mark led Esther down a ladder to a small earthen cave supported by wooden beams and held the lantern away from his chest. A five-gallon wooden keg of water with a metal cup lashed to its lid was located on a small wooden stool. A metal chest labeled RATIONS rested on a shelf cleverly built into the wall of the cave. Two rag dolls and a carved wooden horse lay on top of the chest. Esther noticed a small lantern holding a single candle securely nailed into one of the beams. A small metal chamber pot lay in the corner near a stack of woolen blankets. To Esther, the cave appeared to be about sixteen by sixteen feet wide and perhaps five feet high. Although Esther could stand up straight, she noticed that the taller Mark Singer had to stoop over a bit as to not bang his head against the sturdy beams that had been constructed to keep the cave from collapsing.

"This hideout is astonishing, but how can a person breathe down here?"

Mark smiled. "That is what I am most proud of, Esther." Mark walked to the far end of the cave and pointed to a large pipe extending out from a hole in the wall. "A small breathing passageway extends from this cave all the way to an outdoor pipe underneath the kitchen window. It is hidden from sight by a hedge, but if someone were to look closely, the pipe merely looks like one of the drainpipes from the kitchen sink. This arrangement provides ample air for our passengers to breathe. We have concealed a dozen people safely in this cave at one time," Mark offered proudly.

"Has your home ever been searched?"

"Many times. The homes of all Quaker families are searched, but so far no one has ever discovered our secret cave."

"Can you burn wood in the fireplace?" asked Esther.

"Absolutely. That is what is so unique about our design. No slave catchers have ever suspected that we would hide someone under a live fire. I must add though, it can get a little warm for our passengers in the cave, so we try and keep the fire small. No one seems to mind the inconvenience though," he laughed.

"What about the children? Can you hear the sound of crying?"

"The cave absorbs much of the sound, but it is important for all our passengers to be as quiet as possible."

Esther nodded. "This cave represents a lot of work." Esther looked at Mark and added sincerely, "It touches my heart to know that there are good people like your family who would go to such lengths that others might be free."

Mark shrugged. "It is the way of the Society of Friends. We do not believe that any man, woman, or child should be the property of another. I am only one of many who have done the same. It is what we regard as God's commandment."

"But to risk your own safety for people you don't even know is beyond kindness. Your spiritual reward will surely be great." Esther shook her head in admiration as she climbed the wooden ladder that led to the sitting room.

Chapter 18 ~ September 1853 – Big Buckwater

Esther crept through the woods with a strangely familiar ease. It was hard for her to imagine that three years had passed since she had escaped from the King Plantation with Bucky. Coming back to her childhood home filled Esther with both happy and unsettling memories. Esther fondly summoned to mind the summers of enlightenment and discovering the gifts of the forest from her teacher, Old Jed. She recalled the warm summer nights in the cabin, whispering the gossip of the day as she cuddled with her mammy on their pallets. But she shuddered with fear when she recalled the sting of the whip at the hands of Shelby Moss, and the hurtful taunts of Mandy and her friends. Esther patted the leather case and felt the outline of the Bronze Bottle at her side. She forced the disturbing images from her mind and concentrated on the mission before her. The predictable smells and sounds of the forest calmed Esther's misgivings and helped to quiet her heart, which she felt was beating as fast as the wings of a hummingbird.

The former slave girl wore coarse black cotton pants tied at the waist with a rope, a dark blue shirt and soft leather ankle boots. She had secured her hair inside a floppy black felt hat, which was pulled low over her forehead. Moving silently through the underbrush, she came to the precise spot for which she had been told to search for Old Jed. Esther crouched low in the bushes and carefully spread the branches. From her vantage point in the shadows, Esther could see a large granite rock and the bowed trunk of an ancient oak tree that swayed like the curved back of an old horse. The old tree protruded from the bank and stretched over the glistening black waters of the Big

Buckwater as if drawn by its mighty flow. A waxing full moon cast a soft glow on the bank of the river and caused shadows from the leaves of the oak branches to dance in the night breeze on the sandy bank. Esther looked around for her old friend and teacher.

Earlier in the day, Mark had described the spot where Old Jed would be waiting for Esther. Claudia and Mark knew that it would be foolish for them to go to the King Plantation. If Quakers were caught anywhere near the quarters, there would be trouble with the law, so they nervously waited for the fugitives back at the Singer farm. The first part of the escape would be entrusted to Esther's able hands.

Esther put her hands to her mouth and made the hooting call of an owl. She sat back on her haunches to wait. She listened to the rippling sound of water as it flowed down river. The young woman knew well that this might be her last moment of peaceful solitude for many days to come.

In the distance, Esther heard the soft hoot of an owl. She answered its call. In another moment, the hooting sound cut into the soft hum of the night. Esther stared from her place in the shadows but could see no movement along the path by the bank. She crouched in her hiding place in the bushes for several minutes in nervous anticipation of the task that lay before her. The jumpy girl startled when a soft nudge brushed against the top of her hat. Esther snapped her head and turned around in one swift movement to twist her body into a crouching position like a frog. Blood coursed through her veins, and the hairs on her arms stood on end as she tensed her body. Slowly, she lifted her head to confront the unknown challenge. Esther saw Old Jed smiling down at her.

The young girl let out a relieved sigh and whispered, "Bucky and I never could track through the underbrush like you, Old Jed. You still tread through the forest with the silence of fog."

"I guess I've had a lot more practice over the years," Old Jed offered with a wink. His lips parted in a smile to show the straight white teeth and knowing smile that Esther had grown to love and respect from her youth.

Esther crawled out of the underbrush and threw herself into the arms of the old trapper. "It's been too long since I've seen your enduring smile my old friend. I've dreamed of this moment for three years." Esther pulled away from Jed and looked into his eyes. His face looked exactly the same as the last time Esther had seen him on the night she and Bucky had fled the plantation when she was a girl of fourteen. To Esther, it seemed fitting that they should reunite for the first time alone in the woods where she had spent so many happy hours learning from her mentor.

"Why, look at you, Esther." Old Jed gently removed Esther's hat, stepped back and folded his arms over his chest. "You've grown into a beautiful young lady. You may be dressed like a boy, but these clothes barely hide the striking young woman I see before me." Jed smiled again and shook his head. "All of a sudden, I'm feelin' like the old man that I am."

"That's not true. You look exactly the same to me, my friend," said Esther with honesty.

"How's Bucky? I was hoping he might make this journey with you."

"Oh, he wanted to, Old Jed, but he was needed up north." Esther smiled and added, "I've so much to tell you about Bucky, and the wonderful work he's doing with the orphanage. He's been studying these past three years with a group of other men. He knows about so many things, Jed. The children at the orphanage just love him," said Esther with liveliness in her voice.

Old Jed looked at Esther. As a slow grin spread across his face, he nodded his head. "Bucky was always a quick learner," he said, "but so were you, Esther. I'm happy that you two are using your gifts to help others."

Esther was quiet for a moment. She caught her breath and asked. "How's my Mammy Naira, Jed?"

"I'm not going to lie to you, Esther. Naira has dropped a lot of weight since she lost her job in the kitchen, and that may be a bit of a shock to you. Her bones ache a might more than she'd like. But Mammy Naira's been getting 'round the quarters with a little more bounce in her step these past weeks knowing that she'd be looking at the face of her sweet daughter. It's been a bit of a trial to go about our business pretending that nothing out of the ordinary is about to change our lives."

"What about the children? Do they know that we are leaving the plantation tonight?"

"No, we thought it best to not say anything to the smaller children. Everyone in the quarters has been under suspicion for many weeks now, and Shelby Moss has made it his particular pleasure to terrorize all the slave children on the plantation. Fortunately, he has not been able to get the information he so desperately wants. In the beginning, many extra privileges were taken from the slaves, but in the last few days, things have gradually returned to normal. Rumor has it that Shelby may be questioning whether or not Mandy might have made this whole situation up to gain extra favors from the tedious Mrs. King."

"The names of Shelby Moss and Mandy conjure up memories that I'd like to leave buried along with my life as a slave," said Esther with a shudder. "How will Mammy and the others get away from the quarters?"

"Well, last night I had the chance to get young Sampson alone and ask for his help. He's a good boy, Esther, and reminds me a lot of Bucky as a youngster. I knew that we'd not be able to get the little ones away without his aid. He invited the boys to go bullfrog hunting with him after supper tonight. Saturday nights are always a happy time in the quarters. With luck, the boys will not be missed when they don't come back."

"What about Mammy and the twins?" asked Esther.

"Naira has plans to get Franny aside just before they go to sleep to tell her that they are going to play a joke on Flossy. Mammy will tap Franny on the shoulder and wake her from sleeping. Franny is to pretend that she has a stomach ache, and Mammy Naira will take her to the outhouse."

"Why did Mammy not tell, Flossy?"

"Well, our little Flossy is a bit of a magpie and does most of the talking for Franny. Always has. That child could talk the ears off a rabbit." Old Jed chuckled. "Our Flossy also happens to be very protective of Franny. Flossy would be hard-pressed to keep a secret from her sister. Now Franny, on the other hand, hardly opens her mouth and seems to be happy to let Flossy do most of the talking for them both. Mammy Naira figured that if she only let Franny in on the game, she could keep silent. Flossy is so protective of Franny, Mammy felt certain that she would follow her sick sister to the outhouse. The plan is for everyone to meet here by the swayback oak at around midnight."

"How are Mammy's legs, Jed? It's about five miles to the Singer farm. Will she be able to walk there?"

"No, but I think I have a plan. What we need, Esther, is a horse."

"What's the biggest bullfrog you ever caught, Sampson?" asked Noah.

Sampson, Moses, and Noah were seated around a small fire roasting frog legs on sticks. "Well, Noah, that's a mighty interesting question. When I was a little older than you, I worked for a miserable little Frenchman named Charles Dupree in a large city to the south of here called New Orleans. Summers were hot and sticky in the French Quarter where Master Dupree kept a home. Many people died from strange diseases that mysteriously appeared with the heat of the summer, so the Frenchman always sent his family out to his plantation home in the country, where the cool breezes from a big river called the Mississippi made life a bit more tolerable for his family. At that time, I was alone in the world and just learning to speak a new language. The Frenchman had no wish to call me by my African name, Osombo, so he gave me the name of Sampson. Although he spoke French to his family, he taught me to speak the English language.

"You see, Master Dupree had a love of gambling, and he tried to keep this little secret hidden from his nosey wife. So, it was my job to run around the city and place bets for him with the group of English gentlemen he gambled with in the English Quarter. Those men would bet among themselves on almost anything – cock fights, horse races, boxing matches, and even gentlemen's dueling fights with pistols or swords. He was pleasant to me when he won, but if he lost a bet, he tended to drink a bit too much. He liked to take his aggravation out on me with a switch. I grew to live in fear of his mean-tempered ways."

"But what about the bullfrog?" asked Moses impatiently. "Everyone knows dat cock fights and bullfrogs ain't got nothin' to do with each other."

Sampson laughed. "It takes *time* to spin a good yarn, Moses, but I guess you're too young to appreciate the art of good storytelling, so I'll get to the point of my story. At the height of the summer, I got mighty sick with the fever. Now, the Frenchman knew that he could trust me to run around the city and make bets for him and keep my mouth shut around his family. He didn't want me to die because then he would have to train a new slave. So, he sent me out to his summer plantation to get nursed back to health from one of his slaves. An old medicine woman from Jamaica was well known for her healing powers and Master Dupree entrusted me to her care. My progress was uncertain for a while. But, when I felt better, the slave woman told me to leave my pallet in the quarters and go for walks to build up the strength in my legs.

"One day, I was walking along the shores of that forceful river, the Mississippi, late in the afternoon. Suddenly, I spied an enormous bullfrog warming himself on a flat boulder near the bank of the river. When I reached out to grab him, why that wily ol' frog just leapt off the rock and jumped into the shallow shores of the river. Then a funny thing happened. I swear that brash amphibian poked his head out of the waters of the Mississippi and smiled at me!"

"Come on, Sampson," said Moses, "everyone knows dat frogs can't smile."

"Áll I know, boys, is that I reckoned I just *had* to catch that fat ol' frog."

"How'd ya do it Sampson? What'd ya use to trap that ol' boy?" asked Noah with excitement.

"Now you boys know as well as I do that there are many ways to catch a frog," declared Sampson. "Some folks use their hands…like we did tonight, while others like to clobber 'em with a large rock, but my favorite method for frog-catchin' is using the element of surprise. And it was during this period of my confinement that I discovered the butter-frog method of ambush," said Sampson with a wink. He could see that the boys were really enjoying the story, and that was exactly the distraction that he was hoping for.

"What in blazes is *dat*?" asked Noah as he scratched his head.

Sampson looked at the boys and spoke dramatically. "Well, when I was gettin' nursed back to health, I noticed that the Frenchman's daughters liked to run in the flower garden and catch butterflies with a net attached to a wire hoop and a handle. I observed that it was a skilled way to trap the little winged creatures as they fluttered from flower to flower. Havin' more than a little time on my hands, I came to wonder if the same idea would work with frogs."

"How's *dat* goin' to work, Sampson?" asked Noah. "Everybody knows full well that frogs can't fly!"

"That's all well and true, my young friend," agreed Sampson.

"But frogs can jump, Noah!" interjected Moses turning to his best friend.

"That's mighty observant of you, Moses," praised Sampson, "and entirely correct. So when I was feeling stronger, I set about to weed the old woman's vegetable garden behind her cabin to win her favor and formulate my plan to outwit that ol' frog. And sure enough, to show her thanks, the woman gave me the worn burlap sack I had my eye on. I set about to findin' a flexible branch from a pine tree and bent it in the shape of a hoop. I attached a wooden branch to the hoop with a small length of rusty wire I found near the barn to form a handle. Finally, I attached the opened end of the burlap bag to the hoop with river grasses that I weaved into holes I cut.

"It was a mighty fine day as I took off toward the river with my...er...butter-frog sack. You can see, in your mind's eye, my extreme joy when I saw that fat ol' frog sunning itself on that same ol' rock."

"What happened then?" asked Noah with fervor.

"Well, Noah, I snuck up behind that old frog and wham! My, ahem, butter-frog sack trapped that frog afore he even had time to wake up and hop away."

"What happened then?" questioned Moses impatiently.

"Well naturally, I wanted to look at my prisoner, so I reached inside and slowly pulled him from the sack and held him up to my face until we were staring at each other eye-to-eye," Sampson continued.

"How big was he?" inquired Moses.

"You know Master King's fat calico cat that catches mice in the stable?" offered Sampson.

"Yeah," said the boys in awe.

"Well that bullfrog was just about the size of the master's calico cat."

The boys' eyes had grown as big and round as flapjacks. "What'd you do with it?" asked Noah in wonder.

Sampson smiled, "Well, boys, I'm thinkin'…I'll be eatin' some plump frog legs for my supper. It was then, that big ol' frog made me jump outta my skin, because in a croaking voice he bellowed, 'You must not eat me, young man!'"

The boys let out a gasp and opened their eyes even wider. Sampson drew closer to the boys. "I, naturally, was very surprised and somewhat unnerved to discover that the fat ol' frog could speak, so I thought I best listen to what the clever bullfrog had to say."

"What'd he say?" inquired Moses suspiciously.

"That bullfrog told me that he was really a handsome young prince who'd been turned into a frog by an old crone who was in actual fact a witch. He said he had been waitin' for a young lady to come by and kiss him, for that was the only way he might be released from the evil spell of the old crone. The frog also promised me that if I let him go, so he could meet a beautiful young woman, good fortune would come to me."

"What'd you do?" asked Moses.

Sampson smiled at the two little boys and said with a wink, "I let him go, of course."

"You let him go? Did good fortune come to you?" asked Noah.

"Well, I guess I can never be absolutely sure," offered Sampson, "but a few weeks later I was back in the city and witnessed first hand the fury from my master losing in a game of cards. Dupree, who had been drinking whiskey all afternoon, threw his cards on the table and recklessly accused a river boat captain of cheating during their last hand of poker. The enraged man jumped from his chair and challenged the Frenchman to a duel. The captain presented the challenge in the form of pistols or swords. I watched from a corner as a bead of sweat dripped from the side of Master Dupree's face. Even though my master was not a very good shot, he was useless at fencing, so the uneasy Frenchman chose pistols. Dupree was bound by gentlemen's agreement to face the captain the next morning at dawn."

"What happened?" asked Moses in an anxious voice.

"Word quickly spread through the city. Everyone felt certain that the Frenchman had signed his own death warrant. I later found out that even Dupree's English gambling friends had wagered gambling bets against the Frenchman, they felt so certain that he would lose. At dawn, Charles Dupree faced the captain with a look of sheer terror at a place called Jackson Square."

"Tell us what happened," commanded Noah.

"Well, the loose-lipped Frenchman was killed when a single bullet from the captain's gun entered his heart. Dupree hit the ground without firing a shot from his dueling pistol." Sampson sat back and let out a long sigh.

"What's so lucky 'bout dat?" asked Moses.

Sampson let out a short laugh. "Well, with the death of Master Dupree, his wife decided she had no use for me. So, a few weeks later I was sold and came to live at the King Plantation. Before coming here, I never remembered what it felt like to be loved the way my young mammy had once loved me. Then I met Old Jed, Mammy Naira, Flossy and Franny, and the two of you rascals, and we became kinda like a family." Sampson paused and sighed, "So letting that ol' frog go was indeed good fortune for me." Sampson looked over at the two young boys and noticed that they were grinning from ear to ear.

"Sampson," questioned Noah through squinting eyes, "is dat frog story true?"

"That, my young friends, you will have to decide for yourselves. Now help me put out this fire. I want y'all to take a little walk with me yonder."

Moses and Noah cheerfully began to spread dirt over the fire pit. They were happy to be able to stay out longer with their adopted older brother.

A frail Mammy Naira took Franny and Flossy to the outhouse when, on cue, Franny had sat up on her pallet and complained of pains in her stomach. She spoke softly to the girls once they were inside the small wooden shack. "Y'all listen to your mammy. We be goin' to take a little walk down to de river, and y'all must be very quiet. Lots of folks be sleepin' in d'quarters, and we don't want to wake dem up. Y'all be good girls and help Mammy Naira make her way to de path dat will lead us to the Big Buckwater." The girls knew that something out of the ordinary was about to happen because they had never been further from the cabin than the outhouse at night.

It was dark inside the outhouse, but the light of the full moon fell through a small hole near the roof, and cast a soft light so that the three could see each other. Flossy, who wore the same tow-linen dress she had worn during the day, noticed that Mammy Naira wore her day dress under her big old nightdress. Confused, Flossy opened her mouth to say something, but Mammy put her fingers to Flossy's lips and added, "It be mighty important for my little Flossy to stay quiet. Mammy Naira wants ya to put dis stick in yo' mouth. Put it straight across yo' mouth like y'all sees de Master's dog when he carries a bone." Naira placed the wood in Flossy's mouth. "Good! Dis stick will remind you dat it be most important for Flossy not to talk."

Flossy looked at Mammy and opened her mouth to speak. The twig would have fallen in the dirt of the outhouse, but Mammy Naira cupped her hands under Flossy's chin, and the stick fell into her hands. The action so shocked Flossy that she instinctively shoved her hands to her mouth as if to remind herself that she must not speak.

"Dat's right Flossy. Mammy Naira is going to put d'stick back in yo' mouth. I want to see if you can keep it dere 'til we all get to de river." This time Flossy nodded her head, but her teeth remained tightly clamped over the small branch in her mouth.

Esther and Old Jed squatted in the shadows watching the old plow horse standing on some grass near the edge of the meadow. "Is that Sally?" asked Esther with amazement. "Why, that mare was older than dirt when I lived on the plantation. It looks as though Sally's been put out to pasture," remarked Esther while looking at the condition of the old mare. Esther noticed that Sally's back was even more bowed than she remembered as she stood sleeping under a big oak tree.

"Sally may be old, but she still can move about, and that's good enough for me. What we need to do, Esther, is convince her to come with us." Old Jed smiled and pulled a length of rope and a carrot from his pocket.

"You've clearly given some thought to this plan," said Esther with respect in her voice. "Are we going to steal Sally?"

"Nah, we're merely going to borrow her. When we get to the Singer farm, we'll just pat her on the rump, and she will most likely find her way back here to her meadow."

It took Esther and Old Jed just under five minutes to entice the even-tempered Sally across the meadow to eat the carrot. While Esther slowly fed the crunchy bait to the mare, Old Jed deftly tied a slipknot with the rope and slid the noose over the horse's neck and wrapped it around the old mare's nose to fashion a halter. Then Esther and Old Jed gently led Sally in the direction of the Big Buckwater River.

Chapter 19 ~ September 1853 – Big Buckwater

Mammy Naira was worn out when she reached the granite rock and the swaybacked oak tree hanging over the bank of the Big Buckwater. It took over an hour to walk nearly a mile from the quarters to the place where it had been decided that the family would meet. The old mammy had to stop and rest about every ten minutes. She wearily sat on a fallen log and motioned for the girls to come and sit with her. Naira smiled kindly as she removed the small wooden branch from Flossy's mouth. Two neat rows of small teeth marks were etched into the sides of the twig. Mammy Naira looked at Flossy with affection and said, "I know dat must have been hard for you, Flossy. But ya did just fine, child."

A stunned Flossy looked at Mammy Naira but did not speak. It was as though the stick had caused her jaw to freeze up like the icy water in the hogs' trough in winter. Franny stared at her sister with a concerned look on her face. "It's okay, Flossy, you can talk now," she whispered.

The sound of Franny's voice abruptly freed Flossy's jaw from its frozen position. She looked at her mammy and released a flood of words that poured from her mouth like bees from a hive. "Why'd you make me promise to chomp down on dat stick Mammy Naira? That was really hard. I thought dat my jaw would lock up forever. What're we doin' here so far from the quarters? We should be sleepin' in the cabin. Y'all know dat I ain't never been out of the cabin at night. 'Cept of course to go to the outhouse. I heard strange and scary noises on dat dark ol' path out dere. I'll be mighty cranky tomorrow if'n I don't get my rest…"

Flossy might have gone on talking for some time, but at that moment Sampson, Noah and Moses stepped into view. Sampson looked at Flossy and said, "Y'all will hafta try and be more quiet, Flossy. Me and the boys could hear you jabberin' clear up the path."

"You know dat our Flossy can't never stay quiet," said Moses to Sampson.

Seeing the three boys, Flossy's voice clogged as though another stick had been placed in her mouth. The talkative young girl was too stunned to speak, so she turned to her mammy looking for help. The mammy motioned all the children to her side. She told them to sit in the sandy soil so she could talk to them.

"Y'all know dat Miz King and Shelby Moss have most recently made life miserable for de children on dis here plantation." The children stared up at their mammy and nodded.

Flossy dropped her head on her chest and spoke to her mammy. "Does dis have something to do 'bout dat time I was talking to Franny near the outhouse 'bout learnin' the letters?" asked Flossy.

Mammy Naira nodded her head. "Y'all have done powerful good to keep quiet 'bout de secrets of Night School, but Old Jed and I have known for some time dat it was no longer safe for our children to stay in dis place. Old Jed and Mammy Naira did not be wantin' to scare y'all, so we felt it best to keep our plan a secret 'til dis night. We're not yet out of danger, and we'll not be fully safe for many days to come. Dis journey is mighty risky. You must listen to what we all ask you to do, even if you don't understand it."

At that moment, a crazed sound terrified the group. It cut through the night air and made them jump with fear. "I *always* knew dat I heard what I heard dat time when I was in de outhouse," yelled Mandy as she crashed through the bushes.

She faced the small group of children who had moved closer to Mammy Naira. Her voice and body shook, and the group could see that she was very agitated. "I been watchin' from de shadows every night in d'quarters, and tonight I saw y'all go into dat outhouse. When y'all didn't go back to de cabin, I knew dat somethin' was muddled, so I followed Mammy Naira to dis place and hid in de bushes. Is dis where y'all be learnin' de readin'? What's all dis talk 'bout leavin'? Why, with yo' crippled ol' legs, y'all could hardly git to dis place. I ain't never seen anyone walk so dern slow."

Mandy glared at the scared band of children huddling around their mammy. "Now y'all are goin' to come back to d'quarters with me," yelled Mandy with bravado. She knew that the children and the old mammy were no match for her strength. Even twelve-year-old Sampson seemed unnerved that she had threatened the little group of runaways with her intimidating words.

Naira knew that she needed to stall for time to delay making the dreaded trip back to the cabins. She prayed that Old Jed and Esther were on their way. She looked at Mandy and spoke in earnest. "Mandy, y'all don't want to be doin' dis. Why don't ya just go back to yo' cabin and forget 'bout what y'all have seen here tonight."

"Whatcha talkin' 'bout, ya crazy ol' mammy? Now, you know dat Mandy ain't goin' to do nothin' of de sort. Miz Wendy done promised me a reward, and a *reward* I aim to git! You and dese young'ns pick yo'selves up dis instant! Y'all will be comin' back to d'quarters now, and dat's all dere is to it. It be clear dat y'all ain't goin' to be travelin' nowhere fast, so if'n ya don't come now, I'll go git Boss Shelby and he'll bring de hounds, and dey'll rip y'all to shreds."

"Don't you talk to our mammy that way," bellowed Sampson through clenched teeth. He stood up and stepped in front of Naira and the four smaller children.

Mandy eyed the twelve-year old boy who was clearly on the verge of manhood, and decided that Sampson was still no match for a bully so unmistakably experienced at tormenting the young and the defenseless. She spat in the dirt and took two steps toward the boy, "Sampson, it would take a lot more dan d'likes of y'all to…"

"What about me, Mandy? Why not pick on someone more acquainted with your torments," declared Esther as she stepped into view from behind a large granite boulder. Old Jed hung back out of sight to tether Sally to a tree. Mammy gasped and motioned with her arms for the five children to stay in place. Everyone waited to see what Mandy would do.

Mandy stared with a confused look on her face at the unfamiliar young boy wearing a floppy felt hat and carrying a small leather pouch strapped to his side.

With a confident stride, Esther walked over to Mandy and took off her hat. Soft wispy brown curls streaked with strands of gold escaped from the pile of hair that had been pinned up to fit under the hat. "Remember me?" Esther asked Mandy.

It took Mandy a few moments to connect a link to the green-eyed girl, dressed in boy's clothing, standing before her. Mandy sucked her breath in sharply. Then, the sudden recollection of the girl she had tormented, as a child, caused Mandy's dark eyes to glaze over. "It's…it's *you!*" Mandy spit out.

"Yes, Mandy, it's me."

Mandy quickly studied her challenger to size up the situation. The young woman standing before her was clearly not the vulnerable child she had so cruelly taunted with her friends. As with most bullies, who are really cowards, Mandy wished she had thought to rouse Bertha or some of the other girls from their pallets to lend support. Still, it seemed clear to Mandy that the petite young woman would be no physical match for her. After all, she was a head taller than Esther and outweighed her by a hefty fifty pounds. Mandy boldly resolved to employ a technique that had served her well throughout her life. She decided to, once again, play the role of the bully.

"Well, look at what d'cat dragged in. If it ain't old *alligator* eyes come back to de plantation to rescue her crippled ol' mammy. Problem is, gal, y'all didn't reckon dat Mandy would be clever enough to spoil yo' plan." Mandy sneered as she circled Esther like a vulture waiting for the opportunity to pounce on its prey. "Ya thinkin' dat you might be strong enough to take on big Mandy, gator eyes. Why, I think dat Mandy needs to throw gator eyes in de river so she can go for a swim."

The tendons in Esther's neck tightened, and the hairs on her arms stood up with fear. She knew that she was no physical match for Mandy. Esther frantically searched her brain for a way that she might gain the upper hand over her oppressor. *It's doubtful that I am as strong as Mandy, but I am probably quicker and have more physical stamina. Perhaps, I can wear her down,* thought Esther as she moved a few paces away from Mandy. Suddenly, Esther thought that she detected a slight vibration from the bottle resting inside the leather pouch. The movement disturbed her thought, and Mandy was able to move close in and smack Esther on the side of her head with her hand. The stinging crack of the slap stunned Esther and she staggered sideways.

"Ya best give up gator eyes, 'cause ya ain't no match for Mandy!"

Esther jumped out of harm's reach just before Mandy was about to grab her arm. She instinctively moved away from where Mammy and the children were seated.

Is it my imagination? I seem to gather strength from the throb of this bottle that beats like the pulse of a heart at my side. Encouraged with the notion that she might possibly be growing physically stronger, Esther decided to test her intuition and face the assaults of her old bully. Stepping next to the swayback oak tree near the river, Esther bent into a crouching position and waited. She did not have to wait long.

Mandy let out a grunt and lunged like a bull with its head bent low, but this time Esther stood her ground. Mandy tried to seize Esther's waist, but Esther was able to twist sideways and wrap her right arm around Mandy's neck. Using the crook of her elbow and her opposite hand to apply pressure, Esther squeezed with all her strength. Mandy winced aloud in pain as she lifted Esther off the ground and carried her a few steps closer to the river. All Esther could do was increase the squeezing pressure to Mandy's neck.

Just as Old Jed stepped out from behind the rock into view, Mandy let out a horrific scream. The pain inflicted by the smaller girl surprised her. Desperate to escape the throbbing grip and gain the upper hand, Mandy let out an angry roar and twirled her body in a circle to throw Esther to the ground. The twirling motion caused Mandy to lose sight of her position near the river. As Mandy gave one last burst of energy to free herself from Esther, her head smashed into a low branch from the oak tree that hung over the river, and Mandy was knocked unconscious. Her legs crumpled as she crashed down the steep bank and into the rushing river. The thrust carried Esther into the dark waters with her.

Esther sank to the bottom of the river. She came sputtering to the surface of the chest-high water, and quickly gained her footing on the sandy bottom. The waters of the Big Buckwater ran swiftly in many places, but a bend in the river had carved out a small cove under the overhang of the swayback oak tree.

Over time, the natural erosion caused a pool of calmer water to form in that area. It took Esther a few minutes to gather her wits about her and realize that Mandy was still somewhere at the bottom of the inlet.

Esther looked up the steep bank of the river and saw Old Jed frantically searching the surface of the water. Esther looked toward her old friend for an instant, and then dove to the bottom of the cove. The water was so black and murky that Esther might as well have been blind. All she could do was reach-out to feel for Mandy's body. On her third try, Esther found Mandy's motionless body resting on the sandy bottom of the river. With strength she did not understand, Esther grabbed Mandy's limp arm and pulled the unconscious slave to the surface of the water. Esther positioned herself at Mandy's back and hoisted her slack body partially out of the water so that she could place her arms under the girl's ample armpits. Mandy's head slumped to the right and came to rest over Esther's forearm.

"Esther," directed Old Jed, "try and drag Mandy upstream if you can. There's a place up yonder where the bank's not so steep. I think we can pull the gal to safety. Sampson'll help you get her on shore."

With a mysterious intensity of purpose, Esther carefully backed up while lugging Mandy's lifeless form against the current of the river. Gradually, the water receded to Esther's knees. The muscles in her legs trembled with the efforts of her labor, and her arms burned with an aching throb. It was a relief to look over her shoulder and see Sampson wade toward her.

"Esther," called Sampson, "the slope's not so steep here. I think we can haul her safely to shore."

Esther was too exhausted to speak. She nodded her head and allowed Sampson to help her drag Mandy out of the river and roll her onto the sandy bank of the Big Buckwater. Old Jed joined them and the three crouched over Mandy's still body. With Sampson and Jed helping her, Esther turned Mandy onto her back. She put her face to Mandy's mouth, as Old Jed felt her wrist for a pulse.

"She's not breathing!" Esther shouted frantically. Esther impulsively grabbed for the bottle and pulled it from the wet leather case. "We must do something to save her, Old Jed. We can't let her die."

"Sampson, help me turn Mandy onto her side," instructed Old Jed. Sampson nodded and positioned the unconscious woman as directed. Old Jed turned to Esther and spoke. "I think she may have water inside her lungs and can't breathe. We must help her get the water out, or she'll have no chance."

Without thinking it through, Esther grabbed the Bronze Bottle at its neck and thumped it in the center of Mandy's back just below her shoulder blades. After each thump, Esther prayed for the lifeless form in front of her to breathe. She was on the brink of despair when, on the fifth blow, Mandy coughed twice and spit river water onto the sand. When it was clear that Mandy was finally breathing normally, they gently laid the revived slave on her back.

Mammy Naira and the other four children had come over and stood quietly off to the side. Despite being nervous about what Mandy might do next, the small group breathed a sigh of relief to see her coughing and spitting up water.

"Is Mandy gonna live, Old Jed?" asked Flossy.

"I think she's going to be just fine, Flossy," Old Jed said in a reassuring voice.

"I thought for sure dat big ol' gal was dead," Flossy rattled on. "She looked dead when Esther dragged her out of the Big Buckwater. I just don't know how Esther did dat...ya know, pullin' her like she weighed nothin' more dan a sack of potatoes. She be mighty darn little compared to dat big Mandy gal. Why, she looks to outweigh her double. And whatcha y'all doin' thumpin' her on the back with dat pretty bottle. I ain't never seen anything like it in my life...."

"Hush now, Flossy. It's all over now," murmured Naira as she placed her arm around the shoulder of the clearly distraught child.

For the first time in three years, Esther looked at her mammy. She was startled to note how much weight Naira had lost in the years since she had been away. The woman who had loved and cared for her in childhood looked so very frail, and Esther instinctively wanted to guard and protect her. She walked over to her with measured strides. "Mammy," said Esther in a voice that shook with emotion, "it makes me mighty happy to see your loving face after all this time." Esther wept as she cradled her mammy into her wet arms and body, just like she had been cradled by Naira in the days of her youth.

The groaning voice of Mandy caused everyone to look over in her direction. She sat up and looked around at the small group. "What happened? Did y'all try and drown me in the Big Buckwater?"

"Don't be thickheaded, Mandy. You were fightin' and got knocked out and fell in the river. Esther pulled you up from the bottom and carried your lifeless body to shore," said Sampson with fervor.

"You carried me out of d'river?" croaked Mandy in a raspy voice.

Esther nodded and water dripped from her hair.

"You hit your head against the limb of the tree, Mandy," continued Sampson. "You fell in the Big Buckwater and took Esther with you. I think you would've died if Esther hadn't dove to the bottom of the river to fetch you out of that murky black water. She carried you out of the river and thumped on your back 'til you started breathing again."

"Why'd ya do dat, gal?" asked the bewildered Mandy, looking into the green eyes of the girl she had tormented throughout most of her childhood. You could've let me drown, and no one would ever knowd that I caught ya tryin' to run away." Mandy continued to look at Esther, who was still cradling Mammy Naira with wet and muddy arms, and coughed. It took a few moments for Mandy to compose her thoughts. "Why'd ya save me after de way I tortured ya all dem years?" Mandy coughed again before shamefully looking up at Esther.

"I didn't even consider what you did to me while I was growing up, Mandy." Esther glanced at Old Jed before turning back to Mandy. "I forgave the way you treated me a long time ago. Tonight, you were just a girl in grave trouble."

Mandy shook her head and said, "I still can't believe y'all would risk yo' life to save me after de way I tortured ya as a child."

Esther looked at Mandy and implored, "That doesn't matter any more. Mandy, you've a chance here to make things right. Let us go. You know what Shelby Moss will do if he catches us. You've seen your own people suffer at the hand of his whip. Give these young children a chance to grow up free and be something other than slaves."

Mandy sat up and looked at the circle of people around her. The five young children, two old folks and an escaped slave seemed an unlikely group to try and escape from the King Plantation. She shook her head and laughed. "Y'all have 'bout as much chance of escaping Shelby Moss and his hound-dogs as a mule escaping d'bite of mosquitoes at sundown!"

Esther's body shook with despair. Then suddenly, Esther looked on in wonder as large tears welled up in Mandy's eyes. Great sobs issued from her chest, and it took Mandy a few moments to speak. "Y'all saved my life," Mandy choked out, "and I be knowin' for a fact dat I wouldn't have done de same for y'all. I don't understand none of it," murmured the bully, "but as the Lord be my witness, y'all will have no further trouble from me."

Slowly Mandy wrestled to her knees and sat back on her haunches. She looked around at the small rag-tag group – two old slaves, a young girl dressed in boy's clothes and five children. "I believe I'll be makin' tracks back to the quarters, and I'll go to sleep, and when mornin' comes, Mandy will go 'bout her business like nothin' happened last night other than a trip to de outhouse.

"You've done the right thing tonight, Mandy," said Old Jed with praise in his voice. He felt almost certain that she would not give them away.

"Come along with us, Mandy," implored Esther. "There's a better life for you out there."

Mandy wrinkled her brow in thought for a few seconds. With tears still in her eyes, she slowly shook her head. "Naw. I just don't think I have de courage to do what y'all be doin'. I think I only feel brave when I have Bertha and de other girls to back me up." She lowered her head in shame and added, "In fact, Esther, part of d'reason I think I always was so mean to ya…was…'cause I was jealous of de silent courage ya always showed in dem green eyes of yours when we said and did mean things to ya. I thank ya for askin', but dis be de only life I've ever known. Truth is, I'd be plum scared to try another."

"Are you certain, Mandy?" asked Esther.

"Yeah, now y'all best git goin'. With so many of ya gone, y'all will be bound to come up missed in de mornin'. Miz Wendy and Shelby Moss will be powerful mad. They'll have de dogs after ya for sure." Mandy shuddered when she thought of the hounds. "Every moment be mighty important."

Assisted by Sampson, Mandy stood up and brushed the wet sand off her dress. "I'm goin' now. Y'all best git as far a way from dis plantation as ya can." Mandy looked squarely at Esther. "Esther, I been mostly a fool and a bully all my life. Sorry fer what I done to ya. I promise dat your secret'll be safe with me."

As Mandy slowly walked up the trail that led back to the quarters, Esther asked Jed, "Do you think we can trust her?"

"I like to believe that there's goodness in all people. She seemed sincere, and I hope so," answered the old trapper shaking his head. "We've no choice but to go forward, and we best get movin'. Sampson, help me get Sally. Esther and I borrowed the master's old mare." Old Jed turned to Naira and smiled. "Mammy, tonight you're going to be escaping from the King Plantation in style!"

Chapter 20 ~ September 1853 – Singer Farm

Mammy rode on Sally while the others walked. The group stayed off the main roads, and it took most of the night to walk to the Singer farm. Old Jed guided the horse and little party of fugitives using all the safest trails that he had become so familiar with over the past years. Sampson carried Moses on his back, while Noah rode on Esther's back. No one spoke. Even Flossy seemed to understand the gravity of the situation. The twins held each other's hands and stumbled beside Old Jed, who led their mammy on the old mare. At times it seemed as though the travelers would not be able to go on, but then Esther would allow each a sip from the waters of the Big Buckwater that been thoughtfully placed in her Bronze Bottle. The liquid spilled life into their weary bodies and seemed to fortify the travelers with a mysterious energy that allowed them to continue under the friendly blanket of night. When they finally reached the edge of the cleared forest, the group sighed with joy upon seeing the Singer farm in the distance. As the dawn of dreaded daylight seemed in a hurry to wake in the east, the little group stared at the neat white house, which would hide them from their tormentors. The strain of mental and physical exhaustion began to slowly subside.

Esther faced the weary band and whispered, "We're not out of danger yet. Wait for my signal. If it's safe, I'll hold my right arm straight over my head. Don't hesitate. Walk quietly, but without panic, to the back door." Everyone nodded anxiously, but no one spoke. "Can you get Sally pointed in the direction of the King Plantation, Old Jed?"

"The horse is plum done in, Esther, but I'll slap her backside and hope she'll have the strength to make tracks home."

Esther tapped on the kitchen door. A voice asked, "Who are thee?"

"A friend with friends," said Esther, using the familiar password spoken up and down the line of the Underground Railroad.

Mark Singer opened the door six inches and whispered, "All is quiet. Signal thy friends to come forth." Esther raised her right hand over her head. The tired little band of fugitives helped Mammy Naira stumble the last few steps to their shelter.

It may have been from exhaustion or relief, but Mammy Naira nearly collapsed on the floor when she crossed the threshold to safety.

Claudia and Rebecca guided the weary mammy to the couch. The rest of the worn-out group tumbled to the floor in relief. A large platter of bread and cheese had been laid out on a small table with a huge pitcher of milk. "Please," beseeched Claudia, "thee must be famished. This food will nourish thy body and help thee sleep."

"A secure hideout has been prepared for thee," added Mark. "Fear not. During this day, thee will be able to sleep and regain thy strength over the next twelve hours. Tonight, we will see thee safely to the next station."

Chapter 21 ~ September 1853 – Singer Farm

Claudia Grigg nervously dropped a fork onto her plate when a loud banging at the door interrupted the Sunday meal she was sharing with her brother Mark and his family.

Mark looked at his sister and gently smiled. The gesture calmed her a little. "Continue with thy meal, family. Everything must appear as normal. I will see who is at the door."

Mark opened the door and caught sight of Shelby Moss and a group of four men holding two dogs and a tired old mare behind him.

"I think y'all remember who I am. But I'll introduce myself just in case. My name's Shelby Moss, and I be the overseer at the King Plantation." Shelby looked closely into the steady eyes of the tall man in plain clothes that stood holding the door of the farmhouse and watched for signs of tension.

Mark Singer met the overseer's gaze with calm eyes before he spoke. "I remember thee, Mr. Moss. What brings thee and thy men to my home on this Sabbath day as I share a midday meal with my family?"

"This morning two adult slaves, a young buck, and a litter of four young black tar-babies showed up missin' in the quarters." Shelby hooked his thumb over his shoulder in the direction of the King Plantation but never took his eyes off of the Quaker farmer who stood before him. "Me and my men found this mare eatin' grass near the river about a mile from your farm. We think the horse may have been stolen and used in the escape. My hounds seemed clearly agitated by the scent that led us to the nag. And it were evident when we found her that she had been rode sometime in the night."

Mark opened the door to his farmhouse further. He hoped the gesture would demonstrate that he had nothing to hide. He tried not to show his nervousness as he eyed the fangs of two dogs itching to be released from their tethers. Mark was thankful that Claudia and his family worked late into the previous night cleaning the entire house with a vinegar and water solution. He knew that the mixture could confuse a pack of dogs hot on the scent of escaped slaves. "I have been to Sunday Meeting with my family this morning and upon our return we noticed nothing out of the ordinary. I am sorry that I might not be better assistance to thee."

Shelby Moss spat on the rush doormat and spoke. "I doubt you or any Quaker would tell me if you had seen anything, anyway. If you have nothing to hide, then I s'pose you'd be agreeable to me and the boys searching yer farm."

"Thee have trampled over my property many times before, so it would be pointless for me to refuse," said Mark with a steady voice.

"You boys scatter over the farm. Search the barn and other possible hideouts." Shelby pointed to three men. "We'll have a look-see through the house." Shelby Moss and a hired hand named Jasper entered the parlor leaving small clumps of dried mud from their boots on the spotlessly clean pine floorboards of the parlor. A small fire burned in the large fireplace that stood against the interior wall of the room. If Shelby Moss had been a more astute man, he may have wondered why a fire was needed on such a gentle autumn day. Instead, he instructed Jasper to search every corner of the parlor as he headed into the dining room.

At the dining room table, he recognized the farmer's wife and his two boys. His eyes scanned to another pretty woman whom he did not recognize. She had delicate features and shiny brown hair that poked out from a white cap. Her eyes were cast down to the food she was not eating. Shelby decided to focus his attention on the stranger. "What be your name, little lady? I don't think we've had the pleasure of meetin'." A syrupy smile spread across Moss's face to reveal yellow-stained teeth and a moist wad of brown tobacco protruding from his lower lip. He eyed the gentle features of the woman with a leering stare.

Claudia called on all her inner strength to compose herself so that she did not look as nervous as she felt. She slowly looked up at the man, she secretly loathed, for the pain he had inflicted on Esther when she was a young defenseless girl. "My name is Mrs. Grigg, and I am paying my brother and his family a visit."

"Really," said Shelby, "and where might you be callin' home?"

"I live on a small farm just outside Philadelphia with my husband Donald and our two children."

"What made you travel to Maryland alone, without yer husband?"

"I appreciate thy interest in my family," said Claudia looking straight into the eyes of the man that has caused Esther so much grief, "but I wished to visit my brother and his family. My husband and our children are busy harvesting the last of the summer crops and could not leave the farm."

"And when might you be plannin' to make the trip home, Mrs. Grigg?"

"Oh, I have no definite plans. I guess I will take the train home when I get homesick for Donald and the twins."

Shelby studied the houseguest for a few moments. He sensed that something was not quite as it seemed, but he could not quite piece the puzzle together to make a clear picture of what his instinct was telling him. Shelby Moss sucked some saliva though his teeth and wished that he could spit the juice from the wad of tobacco resting in his cheek onto the floor. He called to Jasper, "Spread out and together we'll search every square inch of this house." Shelby turned on his heel and stomped up the narrow stairs that led to the upper rooms in the farmhouse.

Hidden below in the secret cave, Sampson held Moses and Noah tightly in his arms. He could feel the pounding of their small hearts as the fearful boys buried their faces into his neck. One small candle illuminated the underground cavern. Sampson looked across the small cave to see Naira whispering soothing words to Franny and Flossy. Old Jed sat crouched near the ladder that led up into the false floor of the parlor. He held his walking stick with a grip that made the sinews in his wiry arms bulge. A kneeling Esther crouched at Old Jed's side. She held both hands to her lips as a sign to the children that they must remain silent. Her eyes were closed and Sampson thought the gesture made her look more like an angel communicating some unspoken prayer to the heavens. The fugitives could hear the crashing of boots and the scraping of furniture against wooden floors as the rooms were thoroughly searched. Esther thought Shelby Moss and his men would surely tear up the floorboards, one by one until they found what they were hunting for.

Flossy tried to be brave, but her silent sobbing caused her to get an attack of the loudest hiccups Esther had ever heard. Flossy looked around the cave with wide eyes frozen in fear. She smothered her mouth with both of her hands, but as hard as she tried, she could not make the hiccups stop. Esther frantically wracked her brain for help. She looked at the Bronze Bottle resting in its case and scrambled across the earthen floor. She was at Flossy's side in an instant.

Taking the bottle from its leather pouch at her side, she whispered, "The water inside this bottle is mixed with enchanted minerals, Flossy. Place it against your lips and drink from it slowly. The special water will make your hiccups go away."

Flossy bobbed her head up and down as she desperately took the Bronze Bottle into her grasp. None in the cave could take their eyes off the trusting child as she tilted her head and placed the bottle to her lips. Flossy drank slowly, and the gesture caused her to breathe a little slower. She steadily took in the water from the bottle until it was empty. When Flossy drew her mouth away from the lip of the bottle, she waited. Everyone waited. Esther pushed a stream of air from her lungs when it became clear that the attack had mercifully subsided.

At length, the fugitives heard the muffled sound of boots beating a path to the door that led outside. Esther motioned for her family to stay calm and to try and get some rest. She knew it was going to be a long day and an even longer trip north. Esther looked around the room and saw five terrified children, an old man, and her crippled mammy. She whispered a silent prayer. *Help me Lord. Help me find a way to outwit Shelby Moss and lead my family away from his tyranny and north to freedom.*

The entire group, half hysterical from fear of being captured, tried to stifle their laughter when Flossy whispered, "Esther, I gotta go pee."

"I tell you, the Quaker be not as innocent as he claims," growled Boss Shelby to his men as they rode away from the Singer farm. "Too many clues lead the slaves to this farm. Yet again, they may have already moved them on to some other abolitionist sympathizer. Let's search the other farms in the area. If we can't find the runaways, we'll double back and search this area again. One old trapper, a crippled old mammy and five children just couldn't vanish into thin air."

The same scrawny field foreman, named Jasper, who had caught Esther drawing with a shard of charcoal so long ago, spoke up. "Boss Shelby, I've got an idea."

Shelby snarled at his hired hand, "What idea could you possibly have in your pea brain, Jasper, to make me want to listen to you?"

"Well, we all could ride up the road a bit, Boss Shelby, like we was goin' searchin' in a different direction. 'Cept I'll sneak back and stake out the Quaker's farm. If anythin' suspicious crops up, I'll be here to root it out. You and the boys can swing back this way if you run into a dead end." In truth, Jasper was a little tired of running after fugitive slaves and thought it would take a lot less effort to stake out the Singer farm than ride all over Dorchester County. He was surprised when his overseer agreed to his suggested plan.

"Jasper, if I come back here to find that you have been napping under some tree all day, I'll stake you to a tree and tan your hide with my whip."

"No need to worry 'bout me, boss. I'll be as alert as a fox guardin' a chicken coop," Jasper joked to hide the nervous feeling he felt in his stomach. He knew that Shelby Moss meant every word of his threat. He hoped that he could keep his promise. Jasper had been up late the night before playing checkers with another worker and was dog-tired.

"Pa, Benjamin and I spotted one of Boss Shelby's men resting against a tree at the edge of the forest as we were bringing some of the cows back from grazing near the river. We just tipped our hats to him and continued on our way," said Elijah. "We saw no other men spying on the property. Ben was thorough in his search."

"Thee did well, boys." Mark turned to Rebecca and Claudia and spoke. "We need to move our friends to the next station tonight, but that man could be a problem in achieving our goal."

Everyone was silent for a few moments, when at length Claudia spoke. "I have a plan." All eyes turned to Mark's sister. Claudia cleared her throat and said, "After...well, after little Emma passed away, the doctor gave Donald some medicine to calm my nerves and make me sleep. I don't know why, but I saw the bottle of Laudanum in a cupboard and something possessed me to put it in my luggage the day before we left Philadelphia. I think it could be of help to us now. Perhaps our Mr. Jasper is hungry and in need of some food and coffee to warm his insides. Coffee...that is...laced with a little sleeping potion," offered Claudia with a twinkle in her eyes.

It took Claudia the better part of an hour to convince Mark and his family that she should be the *Good Samaritan* and bring food and coffee to the man guarding their property. "If I am going to be of any help to Esther and her family, this is a perfect test to see if I am up to the task."

Rebecca brewed a fresh pot of coffee in the kitchen, while Claudia sliced up a portion of bread to place beside the large chunk of cheese she had put in a basket. "What if he can taste the Laudanum and won't drink the coffee?" asked Claudia nervously.

"Do not worry, Claudia. I shall add a fair quantity of sugar to the coffee and that should disguise any taste of the medicine. The question is, how much of the tonic shall we add to send the man to his slumber without killing him?" inquired Rebecca nervously.

Claudia read the printed instructions on the bottle. Take two spoonfuls every four hours to calm the nerves. She looked at Rebecca and shrugged, "Thy guess is as good as mine. Let us triple the dosage and pray to the Lord that it will only send him into a deep slumber and not to his eternal reward."

"Agreed," uttered Rebecca.

Sitting with his back resting against a small pine tree, the late afternoon sun made Jasper drowsy. His eyes drooped much like the weeds he sat staring at, as the heat scorched his body and wilted the bent stems of meadow-grass. His head bobbed forward as he struggled to stay awake. The sun had shifted direction again and its rays felt hot against his dirty woolen pants down to his sweaty old boots. The bored man struggled stiffly to his feet to move to a shadier spot, so he wouldn't be tempted to drift off to sleep. The threat of Boss Shelby's whip caused him to tremble. He cast his eyes in search of a more agreeable vantage point and noticed a slim attractive woman carrying a basket across the field walking in his direction. She wore a slate gray dress with a crisp white apron and matching white bonnet on her head. It was clear that she had also seen him, so he stretched to ease the soreness in his back and brushed the dust off his backside with his hands.

"Good afternoon," Claudia managed with a smile.

"Good afternoon to ya," the startled Jasper mumbled. He looked into the lady's face and thought she was very pretty despite the plainness of her dress. Encouraged by her smile, he stood and added, "My name's Jasper, Ma'am." Jasper tipped his dusty hat respectfully.

"Greetings, Mr. Jasper. My brother's sons said there was a man resting near the farm, so I thought I would bring thee something to eat and drink. I recognize thee from earlier today. Thee must be hungry having been here for such a quantity of time."

"Why'd ya want to do a thing like that for me?" said Jasper as he removed his felt hat and wiped a bead of sweat from his brow.

"We Friends believe that we should open our home and our hearts to those who are in need."

"Friends?"

"Why yes, that is what we call ourselves, The Society of Friends. Some people call us Quakers."

"I know y'all by that name. That's an odd name fer a religious group. Quakers. How'd y'all come by it?"

Claudia looked at Jasper and started to speak. She decided to practice speaking in the manner of her non-Quaker friends She hoped to put the man at ease with her words.

"Our founder was an Englishman named George Fox. He believed that all mankind should live in love and harmony with one another and not engage in inhumane wars. Mr. Fox began his mission of peace in 1647, and he walked the countryside with nothing but a suit he had stitched for himself from leather and a broad-brimmed hat to protect him from the elements of nature. Thus he began a lifelong pilgrimage to preach his philosophy of peace to any man, woman or child who might listen. Oddly enough, the words of this peaceful prophet, who slept in haystacks and in dampened grassy ditches made some men, rich with wealth and power, nervous and uneasy. Over time, our founder was arrested often and spent countless days inside damp prison walls. The religious leaders and nobles felt threatened because of his beliefs about men and war."

Jasper stared entranced at Claudia's lovely face. He felt he could listen to her talk forever. A more astute man might have noticed the change in her manner of speaking.

"In the year 1650, while appearing in court, George Fox told the judge to *quake* at the name of the Lord. It has been said that the action of his words caused the name Quaker to be associated with our people.

Jasper coughed and scratched his scalp to break the charming spell he was under. "Well, my boss thinks that you Quakers be a right pain in the backside. Pardon my bluntness, Ma'am."

Claudia Grigg cleared her throat to mask the giggle that was rising in her throat. She shifted her manner of speaking once more. *If thee only knew what was in store for thee, I am certain that thee would agree with thy boss.* "Sir, thee must be famished and thirsty from thy long day in wait. Please partake of this food and coffee to refresh thy spirit." Claudia held out the basket and prayed that Jasper would quickly accept it from her hands, which were beginning to shake from nervousness.

Jasper knew that Boss Shelby would not want him to take anything from the home of the Quaker family he was supposed to be guarding, but as he looked into the sweet face of the woman who looked more like an angel than the enemy, Jasper felt a growling in his stomach. He reached over and accepted her offerings. "Why thank ya kindly, Ma'am. I guess I do feel a bit rumbly in the stomach, and this here coffee will help me stay awake," added Jasper as he caught a whiff of the nutty cheese and hot coffee. "Might ya stay and break bread with me whilst I eat?" added Jasper hopefully.

"Thank thee kindly, Mr. Jasper, but there are some evening prayers I must attend to with the family. I will return in an hour to retrieve thy basket," declared Claudia as she backed away to leave. Claudia knew it would be impossible for her to stay and watch the man drink from the potion-laced pot of coffee.

"My name's just Jasper, Ma'am. No mister before it, and you'll find me under that tree yonder, waitin' for ya in one hour's time," Jasper said earnestly, pointing to the shady pine tree.

Claudia could tell by the tone of Jasper's voice that he was clearly smitten with her, and she prayed that when she returned in an hour's time he would be snoring under the appointed tree.

Mark Singer sighed with relief to see his sister approach the house from the parlor window. As she moved closer to the front door, he could see that she was flushed with color. Claudia entered the house and said to the family, seated anxiously in the parlor. "Well, I pray that went well, but I am glad that it is behind me." She walked over to a chair and collapsed into its seat, relieved that her mission was accomplished.

"Tell us what happened, sister. What did he say?" asked Rebecca

"He told me his name was Jasper, and thankfully he did not ask my name, for I would not have wanted to tell a lie. He asked me why I would do a kind deed for him, and I told him it was the way of us Friends." Claudia bit her lower lip.

"Do not berate thyself, Claudia," urged Mark. "Thee hast done nothing wrong. What else did he say?"

"He wanted me to stay with him whilst he ate, but I could not bear to watch him drink the coffee. So, I told him I would return in an hour to retrieve our basket."

"Thee will not have to face our watchdog alone. I will go with thee, sister. Thee have done well."

Claudia looked at Mark and breathed a long sigh. "Thank thee, Mark. I did not care for the way this man stared at me. It is a relief that I will not have to face him alone. Mark?"

"What, sister?"

"Can you share thy plans to get our passengers to the next station?"

Mark's eyes moved to the hearth, and he instinctively lowered his voice. "When we have checked on our friend, Jasper, and it is determined that we are safe to proceed, Elijah and Benjamin will be moving two wagons full of manure to Ted Lloyd's farm to fertilize his crops. Ted lives about five miles north of here."

Claudia's eyes opened wide with shock. "Surely, thee cannot ask our passengers to allow themselves to be buried under something as toxic as cow manure. How will they breathe?"

"We have moved many passengers to Ted's station using this method of transport. We have never failed to achieve our objective, and thy nephews are well seasoned in handling any slave catchers who might stop them on their journey."

"But, how can they breathe?"

"That is the miracle of our plan. The wagons are fitted with false bottoms. We have our passengers lie on their stomachs and breathe through small holes that have been drilled into the underbelly of the wagon. It is not the most comfortable method of transport, but we have never failed to pass an inspection. Most slave catchers are put off by the foul smell of the dung, but those who have poked through the fertilizer with sticks hit nothing but the false wooden bottom. There is one problem, however."

"What is that?"

"Old Jed and the small boys will be transported in one wagon and Mammy Naira and the twin girls will be driven in the second wagon early in the morning. The boys will leave around three o'clock."

"Does that not arouse suspicion?"

"No, the boys always relay the same story. They say that they must make the journey early so that they might return to help their father with the running of the farm. Most slave catchers think that we are an industrious group anyway, so no suspicions are aroused."

"What of Esther and Sampson. How will they reach Quaker Lloyd's farm?"

"Well, that is a problem, sister. There is not enough room for them in the wagons. Esther and young Sampson will have to make their way on foot to Ted Lloyd's farm. I have communicated this to Esther. She feels confident that she will be able to safely lead young Sampson to the farm. After all, she has done this work before."

"And what of me, Mark? How will I arrive at the next station?"

"It would not be safe for thee to leave just now, sister. It would arouse too much suspicion." Mark noticed that his sister looked disappointed. "In two day's time, Rebecca and I will drive thee over to visit Rebecca's cousin, Ethan Barkett. Thee will be staying with him before returning to Philadelphia."

Claudia wrinkled her brow and Mark knew she was puzzled. "Do not fret, sister. Rebecca's Cousin Ethan will be the third stationmaster along the Underground Railroad. Thee will meet up with thy friends soon enough. Now let's go check on thy new friend, Jasper."

An hour later, as Claudia and Mark neared the spot where Claudia had last seen Jasper, they knew that all was well. Before they even laid eyes on him, they could hear the sound of snoring so loud that it was all they could do to choke back their laughter. They tiptoed to where he lay sleeping and removed all traces of the contents of the basket. Wiping away their footprints with leafy branches, they took one last look at the peacefully sleeping Jasper and made their way back to the farmhouse. Claudia hoped that when the snoozing man finally woke up, he would wonder if their meeting had all been nothing more than a pleasant dream.

Chapter 22 ~ September 1853 – Steidley King

"Are thee certain, Ben?"

"Yes, father. Elijah and I scoured the property and the surrounding wooded area. We are certain that we are not being watched."

"What about our friend, Jasper?"

"He's still sleeping like a baby where thee said he would be."

"Let's move our passengers to the barn then."

The boys and Mark removed the false stone and beckoned their passengers to climb the steps to the parlor. With only the dim light of a single candle illuminating the roomful of young and old eyes, the passengers stared transfixed at Mark patiently waiting for guidance. Mark faced the scared group and explained how they would be transported to the next station. "In a few minutes thee will be moved to the barn where we will hide thee in the bottoms of two wagons positioned with false compartments. The wagons have already been filled on the top with cow manure. Jed, Moses, and Noah will ride in one and Mammy Naira, Flossy and Franny will ride in the other. It will be a bit uncomfortable, but the journey to thy next station is only an hour and a half away. Thee must be certain to stay absolutely quiet. Elijah and Benjamin may be stopped at some point, but the boys make this trip often and they should not arouse suspicion. We supply cow manure to several of the farms in the area for their farm crops."

"Pardon me for askin', Master Singer, but how'll my daughter Esther and young Sampson be getting' to the next station?"

"Please, Mammy Naira, you have no need to call me master. We Quakers firmly believe that no man has the right to be master over another. It goes against all laws of God and nature, and soon thy family will be free of this former life of tyranny and oppression. But to answer thy question, unfortunately, there is not enough room for all of thee to ride in the wagons, so Esther will use her skills as a conductor to guide Sampson to the next station using the woods and the veil of this night as assistance. Thou must not worry. They will see thee soon."

"Don't worry, Mammy. I'll be mighty careful." Esther smiled at Mammy Naira and patted her on the shoulder. Esther's smile masked the nervous feeling lodged in the pit of her stomach. She always felt the same emotions before leading a group of slaves to freedom, but this time it was worse. This time she held the future of her own family in her ability to keep a level head and guide them north to safety.

Esther and Sampson hid in a clump of bushes as the sound of a lone horse slowly made its way along a nearby path. They had been walking for twenty minutes when a series of ill-fated encounters were about to occur. From Esther's crouched position, she could make out the outline of a well-dressed gentleman in a wide brimmed hat and long gray cloak. The rider appeared to be in no hurry to reach his destination, and Esther wished that he would urge his horse forward at a faster pace. What happened next was clearly unfortunate. A large rat scurried across Sampson's back legs, as he lay shivering with fear on his stomach. The movement caused him to let out a frightened yelp before he could cover his mouth with both hands.

The rider pulled on the reins of his horse, drew his pistol and pointed it in the direction of the bushes. He then demanded in a stern voice. "Show yourselves or you will die in the dirt where you lay."

"I'm sorry, Esther," Sampson uttered fearfully. "I've ruined everything."

Esther's heart was racing. She scanned the woods looking for a way out of their situation, but knew it would be futile to try and outrun a man on a horse carrying a gun. She decided to meet the obstacle head on and hope for a lucky break. "Come on Sampson. Take my lead. It'll be all right."

Slowly, the pair stood up. Huddling shoulder to shoulder, they stepped into plain view. The rider trotted over to where they stood by the side of the road. He dismounted from his horse with his pistol still leveled at the pair. Esther gasped, realizing that she had stumbled straight into the path of her father, Steidley King.

"What are you two boys up to? Have you got passing documents? No? I thought not. What plantation have you escaped from? What is that bag around your shoulder, boy? Something you've stolen? Give it to me, now!" Esther remembered that she was wearing the same hat, pants and shirt from the previous night, and that the rider naturally thought she was a boy. With an inward groan, Esther carefully removed the leather case from around her shoulder. Casting her eyes downward so the rider could not see her face, she handed the beloved Bronze Bottle over to their tormentor. "Listen to me. I'm going to ask you some questions. You had better not lie to me, or things will go worse for you than they already are."

With a steely calm that surprised her, Esther lifted her head slightly and peeked from beneath the brim of her hat to get a better look at her father and hopefully devise a plan as to how she might outwit him. Instead, the calm evaporated with the shock of facing the man who had tossed her aside like garbage. She caught her breath as her knees buckled under her.

Sampson, who was clearly in a state of panic, quickly noticed Esther's distress. Without thinking, he caught her around the waist so she wouldn't fall. As Esther struggled to compose her thoughts, Sampson blurted out, "Don't worry none, Esther. It'll be all right." Esther shot Sampson a warning look, but it was too late.

For in that short moment, Steidley King had briefly glimpsed the face of his daughter who stood before him as he was returning home after his weekly poker game with Mason Waverly and other wealthy men in the area. Esther prayed that her father hadn't grasped the meaning of Sampson's words

With the gun in one hand, Steidley King slowly reached up and removed the floppy felt hat from Esther's head and let out a gasp as a stream of hair spilled onto the fugitive's shoulders. Hidden under the disguise of pants and shirt stood his daughter. He studied the features of the girl before him. The rich golden color of her skin set off curly light brown hair and unusually bright eyes. The shadowy memory of a shy slave-girl stealing furtive glances at him so many years ago caused King to catch his breath. Over the course of time, she had grown into a beautiful young woman, but there was no denying that she was his daughter. Esther's resemblance to her mother, Janet, and an uncanny likeness to many of his own features, stunned Steidley. All the blood seemed to drain from his face. For the first time in his life, Steidley King collided head-on with the uncomfortable truth of his past. "My God, Esther, what are you doing here? I thought I'd never see you again. I thought I'd lost you...just like I lost your mother."

Esther looked at her father for several seconds until, at last, the stinging bite of his words penetrated her brain and she found her voice. "Lost me forever? What words are these? You never once acknowledged that I *was* your daughter! How can you lose what you never claimed in the first place?"

Sampson stood with his arm still supporting Esther's waist. His heart raced with shock upon hearing the discovery that Esther stood confronting, not only the master of the King Plantation, but a man she was claiming to be her father. All Sampson could do was to listen and stay close to Esther to lend physical support.

Steidley King stared momentarily at his daughter then lowered his eyes in shame. "I...I wanted to...."

Esther's heart beat faster. "If only you might have smiled at me, just once, or met my glances with understanding or compassion, I'd have lived a happier childhood cherishing the thought that you at least cared. Instead, you sold my mother south and cast me aside like useless garbage."

"I didn't know Wendalyn was planning to do that to your mother until it was too late. In truth, I missed your mother terribly after she was gone."

"I was there! You made me feel...unwanted...no worse. I felt discarded. And because of the way I looked and the color of my eyes, I *never* fit in...not with the other slaves in the quarters and certainly not with any white folks, or even my half brothers and sisters. If it hadn't been for Mammy Naira, I think I would've...."

"My children do not know that you are their sister, Esther." Steidley King's shoulders slumped forward. "Wendalyn made it very clear to me that she would sell you south too, if I ever spoke to you or tried to help you in any way. And, in truth, you reminded me so much of your mother, it hurt me to see her lovely face living within you. But worse than that, the truth is…I am a coward."

Esther felt little pity for this man who had rejected her so coldheartedly. "I never expected that you might want to help me, but I *never* thought you would allow *them* to hurt me."

Steidley King lowered his gun and asked, "Who hurt you, Esther? I swear to you on my parents' grave, I never knew that anyone hurt you. I'll admit that I've been a coward, but I never would have allowed anyone to harm you. Please, tell me who hurt you!"

Esther gazed at the painful expression locked in the eyes of her father and knew that he was telling the truth. She wanted to scream out Shelby Moss's name and expose the truth about how much the whipping bruised her both inside and out. Instead she surprised herself by saying, "It doesn't matter now. It happened a long time ago. I've moved past all that. It's over. But please, just let us go!"

"But where will you go? What have you been doing all these years and why have you come back home now?"

"Home? This is not my home. This was never my home! This was my prison!"

Steidley King bent his head in shame. "I'm sorry, Esther. I treated you horribly, and I'm ashamed that I didn't have the courage to accept you as my daughter. For what little it's worth, I want you to know that I cared for your mother, but I was worried about my position in society and what others might think of me. It was wrong. Oh, how you must hate me."

Esther thought of Old Jed and the night around the campfire when he showed her his scars. She unexpectedly found herself looking at the face of her father with pity. "For many years, I carried a seed of hatred for you and your family in my heart, like a tumor that grows with deadly silence inside the body. But a man, who was kinder to me than any I have ever known, taught me that to hate is an abomination. He told me that I should forgive you and any others who hurt me. It has taken me a long time, but finally I understand his words." Esther looked at the sad face of her father with compassion. "I forgive you for the hurt and pain you inflicted upon me as a child."

Steidley King stared into the face of his daughter and wondered where her strength of character came. *Surely not from me*, he thought. He couldn't quite come to grips with the emotion that he was feeling. *All these wasted years, I have selfishly played the tragic Shakespearean figure, like Hamlet. My entire life has been woven around a loveless marriage and the raising of children whom I have selfishly spoiled just enough to make them boring and socially unattractive. Yet, look at the obstacles my daughter has scaled with so few advantages.* King unconsciously fidgeted with the leather pouch Esther had placed in his hand and asked quietly, "What will you do?"

"I'm a teacher now up north. There are children waiting for me to teach them to read and write, and that's just what I'm going to do." It suddenly occurred to Esther that this man, her father, had no hold on her because she had come too far. Her freedom and the life she knew with Bucky, Joanne Cody, and the orphans meant too much to her. She could never return to slavery. She had to bring Mammy Naira and her new family north so they might also taste the joy of freedom. Esther straightened her shoulders and spoke in a level voice. "I'm leaving now. The only way you can stop me will be to shoot me." Esther wrapped her arm around Sampson's waist and walking away from her father, she guided the boy down the dirt road.

"Esther!"

Sampson and Esther stopped in their tracks, but neither of them looked around.

"You forgot your leather pouch. Please, take it with you. For some reason, it feels unnatural in my hands. Meet me half way, and I will give it to you…daughter."

Daughter. The word danced in the air like a firefly. Slowly, Esther turned and walked back to unite with her father in the road. With the bottle in its pouch clutched in his outstretched hand, Steidley King offered Esther her beloved treasure. To Esther, the full moonlight seemed to reflect its glory. The object dangled between them, until at length, she gathered the leather pouch lovingly into her hands. Esther held the face of her father with her eyes. Neither spoke. It was he who was first to walk away. Slowly, Esther turned and moved with unsure steps toward Sampson. At that moment, her heart was aching from years of pent-up emotions. In their brief exchange, Esther King felt certain she had seen the glistening of a tear in the corner of her father's eye.

Chapter 23 ~ September 1853 – The Swamps

Shelby Moss was annoyed. After hours of fruitless searching for the runaways, he pulled on the reins of his horse and scratched an ample belly that had been steadily growling with hunger. A long slow swig on his canteen of water did nothing to abate his appetite. The irritated overseer pulled a wad of tobacco from his leather case and pushed the brown strands into his mouth. He and his band of slave-catchers had searched a wide expanse of the area all day and well into the night. Now it was after midnight, and Shelby knew that there would be hell to pay if another batch of Wendalyn King's slaves escaped to freedom. Both he and his men were tired and jumpy from lack of rest and food. Moss tied his canteen to his saddle and was just about ready to double back and check to see if Jasper had seen anything suspicious when one of the hounds became agitated with the scent of human flesh. The excitement of the dogs was contagious, and the slave-catchers' spirits perked up with renewed enthusiasm. "Let's ride boys," Moss ordered. "My mood be so sorely agitated that I think I could whip the hide off an alligator tonight!"

"We're almost there, Sampson," panted Esther in a winded voice. It was evident from the vicious yelps that a pack of hounds had picked up their trail. "When we get to the swamps we'll try and lose the dogs' scent." Esther and Sampson had been running from the sound of barking dogs for ten minutes. At first, the yapping noise was faint, though alarmingly frightening. But now, the howls of the baying pack reverberated with a frenzy that sent panic into the hearts of Esther and Sampson. The fleeing pair grew terrified as the thud of horses' hooves and the sounds of men's voices grew louder with each passing minute.

Esther searched desperately ahead as the narrow twisting trail plunged them into a darkness created by misshapen trees and hanging moss. She felt certain that this was the way to the swamp. The air had grown thick with the decaying earthy smell of plants and trees so familiar to her. Over time, she and many of her passengers had hidden in the safety of the marshes to escape the terror of a pack of dogs and the slave catchers who encouraged them. Guided by her instinct, Esther said, "Come this way, Sampson. Follow me!"

Sampson pounded barefoot along the unfamiliar path. His lungs throbbed in rhythm with the silent plea beating in his brain. It was a prayer to reach the elusive water that would break the scent of their trail. Something wrapped around his ankle and he pitched forward onto the muddy path and screamed, "A snake on my right ankle!"

Esther was at his side in an instant. Anticipating the worst, she sucked in a sharp breath of air and reached for Sampson's ankles. Slowly, she let out her breath and declared, "It's only a vine trailing across the path." Quickly, she untangled the pesky impediment. "Hurry, we must go. We're nearly there. I can feel it!"

The untimely incident had allowed the hunters to close the gap. Somewhere hidden in the expanse of night a sound made Sampson and Esther shudder with fear. Shelby Moss's familiar drawl cut through the trees as he instructed his men to abandon their horses and continue the chase on foot. "Unleash them hounds boys, and let's hope they don't have the vermin in shreds before we can have a little fun."

The familiar sound of the voice that had haunted Esther's dreams for years sent a cold chill down her spine. For an instant, she thought she might scream out in terror. Esther bit her lip so hard she could taste the saltiness of her own blood. The pain that followed helped ease the panic that gripped her brain. *I must keep my wits about me! I mustn't give in to this madness. THINK!*

Her heart continued to race as Esther abandoned the trail. She deftly guided Sampson forward into a veil of thick twisting branches and tall clumps of fern and grasses. The limbs that formed the treacherous barrier ahead slapped cruelly against her body, reminding her of the sting of Shelby Moss's whip. The pain reinforced the notion that there could be no turning back. Esther knew that their only chance was to continue forward and find the waters of the swamp.

At length, Esther pushed aside several tangled branches and vines, and despite the eminent closeness of her pursuers, she wisely slowed her pace a bit. The ground had suddenly become very moist. Esther quickly reached for Sampson's hand. She knew from experience that an area like this might be filled with quicksand. Although it had never happened to her, Esther had heard stories of others who had witnessed those unlucky souls who became stuck in the wet sands and swallowed alive. She motioned for Sampson to follow her closely. The stench of decaying vegetation penetrated her every breath and caused her eyes to sting. Then without warning, the low thick twisting branches suddenly gave way to a clearing. The full moon cast its glow over a large swamp filled with patchy reeds and the rotting branches of dead trees. Esther quickly pulled Sampson into the treacherous bog and began plodding across the marsh. The waters quickly reached waist-high. The Bronze Bottle at

Esther's side, harbored safely in its case, bounced playfully along its slippery surface.

Esther and Sampson could hear the splashes of men and dogs as they penetrated the edge of the swampy water. The marshy lake was about fifty yards wide, and Esther could see trees and ferns in the distance. Esther prayed that the lake was not too deep, but she determined that it would be better to drown in the rotting waters than face the wrath of Shelby Moss. Once again, the terrifying voice echoed over the water. "Stop, you filthy wads of slime, and I might go easy on you," Shelby Moss lied.

"Keep wading, Sampson," Esther whispered. "It's our only hope."

"I caution y'all to think 'bout yer actions." Shelby Moss drew out his gun and fired a warning shot into the air. He smiled inwardly savoring the taste of victory over the hunt. He knew that the frightened slaves would soon be in his grasp, and he licked his lips at the thought of the punishment he would inflict on the pair to extract the necessary information to find out where the others had fled. "Let's finish it, boys. I'm hungry." The angry mob ventured into the waters of the marsh then suddenly stopped.

"Swamp ghosts!" shouted several of the men.

"Don't be ridiculous!" yelled the overseer over the sudden mournful howling of the hounds. The spooked dogs had suddenly turned back with fear and began paddling their way to the edge of the marsh. The frightened dogs emerged from the swampy water and crouched behind their masters whimpering softly.

"There be no such thing...." Suddenly at a loss for words, Shelby Moss stared at the amazing sight before him. Trailing behind the fugitives was a series of flickering balls of fire. He had heard stories from the slaves in the fields about the *swamp ghosts*. The slaves often talked about the eerie balls of light that danced mysteriously across the waters in the swamp. In fact, he encouraged the tales because he thought the superstitions would keep the slaves from escaping through the marshes. He knew that the balls of fire were really rotting masses of reeds and other decaying plants. The fermenting vegetation sometimes released methane and other gasses that could spontaneously burst into flames. He had seen it happen once when a gas ball ignited into fire during a lightning storm. But he had never seen a display like the one unfolding before him and his men. Dozens of the glowing ghostlike orbs popped up on the surface of the lake like giant fireflies, leaving a wake of fire behind the two fugitives.

The intensity of light was so astounding that Esther and Sampson glanced briefly over their shoulders. To Esther, it seemed as though a wall of fire had positioned itself between her and the pack of men and the dogs at their heels. Like Shelby Moss, Esther knew the scientific explanation for the phenomenon. She and Bucky had discussed the possibility of it happening to them on one of their missions. Esther quickly turned ahead and decided to use the camouflage of fire as a tool in finding a method of escape.

Meanwhile, the exasperated Moss tried to calm the outrageous gibbering of his men. Finally, the furious overseer cracked his whip into the air, and a deathly silence fell over the swamp. Then, with angry threats of punishments, Shelby Moss urged his men onward across the swamp to finish what they had started. But try as he might, the overseer could persuade neither man nor dog to follow him into the inferno of light that blanketed the swamp. In a rage of impatience and spewing angry swear words, Shelby spit out his wad of tobacco, fired his pistol across the balls of fire, and plunged forth into the swampy water alone.

"I think we may have lost them, Sampson, but let's keep moving. I see a clearing up ahead. We'll take a short rest and I'll try and get my bearings." A weary Sampson nodded his head and plodded after Esther.

Esther tried to look calm, but in truth she was extremely nervous. The two had been walking for over an hour moving ever deeper into the interior of the swamp, and Esther had no idea where they were or in what direction they were heading. Patchy clouds spread across the sky. There was no time to stop and search for the North Star. Esther shuddered inwardly reflecting on the sight she and Sampson had earlier witnessed in a dense wooded section of the swamp.

Hanging from a sturdy branch of a sassafras tree dangled the lifeless body of a man. An iron collar attached to a long sturdy chain cruelly adorned the slave's neck. Esther knew from experience that the man must have fled to the swamp as a runaway. Esther wondered if the forlorn fugitive might have given up all hope of escaping from the swamp, or if angry slave-catchers had cornered him. Whatever the reason, the result was that his iron collar and chain had been callously fashioned into a noose. It now cruelly tethered his corpse to the limb of the tree. Buzzards and other birds of prey encircled the slave from the nearby branches of his tree. To Esther, it almost looked as though the squawking animals had come to pay homage to a king, but the conductor knew otherwise. Esther quickly ordered Sampson to look away, but she knew the haunting vision would be impossible to forget.

Esther motioned to Sampson and the tired pair dropped onto ferns to rest in the shadowy recesses of some trees. The spot gave them a good vantage point to look across the marshy clearing to see if they were being followed. Sampson took a short swig from a water vessel made from an animal bladder and attached to a strap. Mark Singer had entrusted Sampson with the water and a small supply of cheese and biscuits, which he had lost sometime during the night. He handed the water over to Esther as she scanned the sky looking for the North Star through the clouds.

"Thanks, Sampson. It's best that we drink as little water as we can. The waters in the swamps are impure. We must ration what little we have." Esther sipped a small amount of the liquid and swished it around her swollen tongue before swallowing it.

"This place is spooky, Esther, and I can't get the vision of that poor man out of my head. What happened to him?"

"I can't be sure, Sampson, but it looks as though he probably ran away from his owner. He may have been murdered, or he may have decided that ending his life was better than going back to his life as a slave. I've seen it happen many times. The sadness is always unbearable."

"He musta been mighty low to…."

"Hush Sampson, I think I hear something."

Shelby Moss fantasized about what he was going to do to the runaways when he caught up with them. He had been following them for over an hour, and he knew they must be tired and thirsty. Moss licked his swollen lips with his tongue. He cursed himself for leaving his canteen of water on the saddle of his horse. The scene with the gas balls of fire and the desertion of his men and dogs had thrown him off balance. He had already decided that the fugitives would pay dearly for the pain and aggravation they had caused him. He wouldn't even bother to haul them back to the plantation, but deliver his punishment in a more permanent fashion.

Esther and Sampson watched from the shadows of the trees. Esther shuddered as she saw the agitated Shelby Moss enter the marshy meadow alone carrying a rifle in his hand, a gun holstered to his side, and his whip strung over his shoulder. She quickly scanned the area looking for an advantage. She was just about to motion for Sampson to follow her deeper into the tangled area of vines when she heard the overseer curse out loud.

"Blessed nightmare! Well, ain't this be just 'bout my luck tonight." The overseer tried to step out of the slippery mud, but the effort only sucked him further into the pit of wet sand. He scanned the area and in panic yelled, "Help! I need help." Common sense told Shelby Moss that his frantic cries were fruitless, but as he stood knee deep in the quicksand the terror inside him came out through his mouth. Each time the overseer tried to lift a leg up and out of the muck, it caused him to sink further into the quagmire.

Esther wondered if her old overseer was setting a trap, but as she slowly rose up and looked over in his direction, it appeared that he was indeed sinking into the muddy ground. Then Shelby Moss screamed out in horror. To Esther, the sound reminded her of a bear she had once come across in the forest that had been trapped in irons.

"What'll we do, Esther?"

Esther shook her head. She stood motionless staring at the man who had beaten her with a whip for drawing a spider in its trap. The irony of Shelby Moss's situation was not lost on her. And at that moment, her first instinct was to turn and run for freedom. Sampson must have had the same thought because she felt him tugging on her sleeve.

"Let's go, Esther."

Esther nodded and together they stepped into the clearing and began moving away from the marsh and Shelby Moss. The overseer saw his only chance walking away.

"Hey! You can't leave me to die like this. Come back here and help me. I got money in my pocket. Get me outta here and I'll give it to ya. Then y'all can be on yer way. I promise."

"What are ya stoppin' for, Esther."

"I don't know, Sampson, but something's telling me that if I don't help, I'll always feel I was no better than him. Esther turned toward Shelby Moss and shouted a warning. "Throw your rifle and your gun out of reach, and we'll come help you. And we don't want your money!" Reluctantly, the overseer tossed the firearms as directed. The action caused him to sink further into the quicksand and he screamed again.

From the time it took Esther and Sampson to carefully thread their way over to Shelby Moss, he had sunk into the quicksand up to his waist. Beads of sweat trickled down his face and his eyes held a blank terror as he looked up into the faces of the slaves he had so callously hunted.

"We need something to help pull you out," declared Esther. Throw us your whip."

Shelby Moss looked suspiciously at the light-skinned young man in a floppy hat and inwardly shuddered in disgust. *A filthy half-breed,* he reflected. Although there was something familiar about him, he couldn't place the half-caste boy as one of Wendalyn King's slaves. *Must be a conductor,* he thought.

The overseer's natural distrust of people slowed his thoughts about handing over the whip until Esther shouted, "You're wasting valuable time. Throw me the whip!"

With resignation, Moss nodded and removed the coil of rawhide from his shoulder and tossed it to Esther. The action caused him to fall further into the sinking sand until it was above his waist. He screamed out, "Hurry you stupid baboons. Can't you see I'm sinking?"

Esther winced, and the tone of Moss's voice caused Sampson to jump. "Come on, Esther. Let's go. Just leave him and walk away."

Esther looked down at the man who had caused her so much suffering. "No, Sampson. That'd make us no better than him. I know he's not worth it, but we have to try."

Esther tied a loop around the tip of the rawhide whip and tossed it back to Moss. "Put your hands through the circle, and we'll try and pull you out," Esther instructed.

"Grab the handle, Sampson. We'll pull together on the count of three." Veins popped out on their arms as the tired pair pulled on the implement of torture that had given Esther nightmares. In direct hindrance to their labors, Shelby Moss thrashed his legs, and the action only caused him to sink further into the mush.

"You must lie still," shouted Esther. "Your panic defeats our efforts."

"Help me!" screamed the overseer as the quicksand sucked his chest further into the muddy grave.

Esther and Sampson gave one last mighty tug on the whip. Shelby Moss screeched out in terror as his muddy hands slipped from the noose Esther had so cleverly fashioned. With the whip still in their hands, the pair fell backwards onto their bottoms. In stunned silence, they watched as the horrified slave hunter flailed his hands to the heavens in panic. The screaming face of Shelby Moss disappeared as it was gulped into the depths of the mud. Esther and Sampson looked on in horror as the overseers hands flailed above the mud like two puppets performing a dance. Then, it was over.

A chilly silence embraced the swamp. Panting from the effort of their labors, Esther and Sampson sat helplessly looking at the tranquil mud. Neither spoke for a few minutes. Esther suddenly felt the presence of the bottle strapped to her side. She briefly wondered why she had not felt the same surge of strength from it as she had during her encounter with Mandy. *I wonder if he would have kept his promise and let us go?*

"I wanna get outta here Esther," Sampson cried.

"I know, Sampson, so do I. There's nothing we can do for him now." Esther stood up and gathered up the pistol, rifle and whip. One by one, she threw them into the quicksand. "Once they sink, there'll be no trace of Shelby Moss. I wonder if his men will miss him and come looking for him." Esther doubted that the slaves would shed a tear for the loss. She knew that Shelby Moss had not recognized her as the young girl that he had so cruelly whipped when she was only a child. But why would he? She was but one of many he had tortured with the instrument she buried with him now.

Esther and Sampson walked away from the marsh and in time found a footpath. They plodded on for most of the night. Daylight broke in the east blocking any chance of finding the North Star. The rising eastern sun announced the way north, but Esther and Bucky were still hopelessly lost. At length they came to a fork in the path.

"What'll we do, Esther? Which way should we go?"

"I'm not sure." Esther took the Bronze Bottle out of its case and looked into its depths for an answer. Then, without questioning the reasoning behind her thoughts, Esther placed the bottle sideways on the path between the middle of the fork and twisted the bottle into a spin. The Bronze Bottle came to rest with its top pointing toward the center of the trail on Esther's right. Esther looked up into the quizzical stare on Sampson's face. "Let's try this again." She spun the bottle once more and again the bottle pointed to the path on the right. A third spin convinced Esther that the way out of the swamp was taking the path to the right. She gathered the bottle to her chest and laughed. "Let's go find our family, Sampson!"

Chapter 24 ~ September 1853 – Ted Lloyd's Farm

Esther and Sampson walked for another ninety minutes before they made their way out of the swamp. Each time they came to a fork on the trail Esther would place the bottle on the path and the two would follow the direction of its spin. From there it was easy to stay off the main road and follow the landmarks that Mark Singer had given them to find Ted Lloyd's farm. The pair watched a lone farmer tending his fields in the midmorning sun from the shelter of the woods. The wooded area rested adjacent to a large expanse of farmland, and a charming wooden-framed white house and barn.

"Look, Sampson," Esther whispered. Watch that farmer hoeing his fields. Look at the way he stops to wipe his brow with his bandana. He scans the area like he's admiring his land, but I think he's looking for something." Esther smiled into the haggard eyes of the young boy crouching next to her in the dirt. "I think he's looking for us."

Esther cupped her hands together and made the hooting sound of an owl with her mouth. The farmer casually placed his hoe in his wheelbarrow and removed a jug from its interior. As he slowly drank from its contents, he turned and looked in the direction of the sound. Esther repeated the hooting twice more. The farmer picked up an axe from the wheelbarrow and rearranged it to make room for his water-jug. Placing the axe on the top of his gear, he then pushed the wheelbarrow toward the wooded area. To the casual observer, it might have appeared that he was going into the woods to chop some wood for his fireplace. At length, the man entered the cool interior of the woods. Once inside, he asked in a soft voice. "Who goes there?"

Esther answered, "A friend with friends." She knew that this password, used up and down the Underground Railroad, would let the farmer know who they were, and that they had recognized that he was a friend who would help.

Esther and Sampson stood up and stepped into view. The farmer was tall and muscular with light brown hair and blue eyes. Esther observed that the man's blue eyes looked as though they were smiling from the white creases near the corners of his eyes, which stood out against his tan skin. He looked exactly like Mark Singer had described him. "You must be Ted Lloyd. My name is Esther and this is Sampson. We've been traveling all night to find you.

"Esther, Sampson, it is so nice to finally meet thee. We have been extremely concerned about thee, as we expected thee to arrive late last night."

"We ran into a bit of trouble with some slave-catchers, but we were able to lose them in the swamps. But please sir, give me the news of my family. Are they safely with you?"

"Yes, Old Jed, Naira, and the four children all arrived safely before dawn. Ben and Elijah hid them in the barn then unloaded the manure to an area outside the barn. The ride was a bit jarring for thy mother, but she seems quite well now. They all have been worried about thee. I can see that thee look very tired, and I imagine that thee are hungry and thirsty." Ted Lloyd looked around him to make sure no one was lurking in the shadows of the trees. When he felt all was as it should be, he pulled a gunnysack from his wheelbarrow and handed it to Esther. "There is food and water in here. Nourish thyselves and keep out of sight until dark. At sundown, carefully make thy way to my barn door and knock three times, then twice more and I will know it is thee. All has been quiet in this area. I think the search for the missing slaves from the King Plantation may have been called off.

Esther and Sampson glanced into each other's eyes for a moment before Esther said, "I think you might be right."

Esther and Sampson crept quietly to the barn door under the mantle of night. They had slept most of the day in the shelter of the underbrush. The food and water revived their bodies and spirits. At length, they safely reached the barn door and Esther knocked softly – three times, pausing, and then twice more. In an instant the barn door was heaved open, and Farmer Lloyd pulled the pair inside and closed the door.

"Follow me, please."

The inside of the barn was dark, but Farmer Lloyd had a small lantern, which illuminated their way. Esther and Sampson followed the farmer up a ladder and onto a hayloft. The smell of the hay reminded Esther of Bucky when they, as runaways, had spent a day nested inside the top of a haystack and were nearly discovered by Shelby Moss and his men. The memory reminded Esther how much she missed her old friend.

A large mound of hay was stacked in a corner of the barn. Ted Lloyd used a pitchfork to pull back some of the hay near the sidewall of the barn. After a time, he pulled open a small door and pointed inside to a small shed hidden under the mound of hay. The room appeared small, cramped, and dark.

"I have brought thee the remainder of thy family, Naira," whispered Ted into the darkness. Farmer Lloyd turned to Esther and Sampson. "I must return to my house. Rest here this night and thee will be moved to the next station in the morning." As

Esther and Sampson edged their way into the interior of the dim room, the farmer quickly closed the door. Esther could hear hay being replaced over the area that had been disturbed only moments before.

"Esther, Sampson, I be mighty happy dat you have finally found your way to dis station. We been prayin' for y'all." The moon had not come up yet, and there was barely any light in the cramped room, but Esther followed the sound of Naira's voice and crossed the few steps from the door to the shadowy form of her mammy who rested on a blanket in the corner.

"We're so happy to have caught up with you, Mammy," said Esther as she dropped to the floor to hug her mother. Esther and Sampson took turns telling the group the events that led to their reunion in the barn. Even Flossy was unusually quiet as the story unfolded with the rising of the waning full moon in the sky. The moonlight, casting its gentle glow through the cracks of the barn, not only illuminated the space, but the spirits of the little group.

"Y'all have been through a lot," murmured Old Jed. "I'm glad Master King did the right thing and let you go. It'll take some time to put things in order with your heart, but I expect you'll have lots of time to sort that out when you get home."

Esther nodded.

"I never want to see the inside of a swamp again," added Sampson. "It's gonna take me a mighty long time to get the sight of that poor man hanging from his own iron collar and chain in a tree. Or the sound of Boss Shelby screamin' as he was sucked into the quicksand after losin' grip of his own whip."

"I know that, Sampson," declared Old Jed. "Seems fittin' though, that the weapon that he held most dear, failed him when he needed it most."

"It's strange," mused Esther, "that I didn't feel the same surge of strength from the bottle as I did when helping Mandy." Esther removed the case from around her shoulder and opened the top. She pulled the bottle from its resting place and placed it in the middle of the room for all to admire. The light from the moon glistened upon its surface, and the tiny gold and silver specks sparkled just like stars. As Esther admired the bottle, she felt something hard resting in the bottom of the leather case.

"That's odd. A rock must've gotten trapped inside the bottle's case as we were escaping from the swamp." Slowly, Esther reached to the bottom of the pouch to remove the impediment. When she opened her hand, a large gold ring with the initials S.K. embedded with small diamonds on black onyx sat exposed in her palm for all to see. Everyone in the room stared at the object in front of them in silence. "That's *his* ring," whispered Esther.

"I don't understand," commented Sampson.

Esther let out a sigh to release the emotion of what the ring represented. "My father must have taken it off his finger, Sampson, and placed it in the case before giving the bottle back to me."

"What are you gonna to do with it, Esther?" asked Old Jed.

"I'm not sure, but for some reason, I'm happy to have it."

Mammy Naira said, "Ya know, 'bout a year ago, Master King came over to me one day as I be watchin' de babies in the quarters. He asked me if I ever heard from you. I was scared and shook my head. At de time, I worried that he might be thinkin' of doin' ya harm, but maybe he just wanted to know dat you was okay."

Large tears formed in the corners of Esther's green eyes. "I guess he must have cared at least a little about me after all."

Esther awoke early the next morning with a new sense of purpose. The early light of the dawn did little to brighten the hidden room, but she could see the faint outline of her family asleep on beds of hay. She was determined, more than ever, to guide her family safely north to the new school in St. Catharines. For the first time in her life, Esther felt as though she knew where she fit in, and how her life was finally full and complete. She reached into the leather case and found her father's ring and placed it in the palm of her hand. *I think I might wear this around my neck with a cord. It'll remind me of our last time together. I know that I'll never see you again. Yet, I feel that in giving me this ring, you showed me that you cared a little about the daughter you never knew.* Esther sighed and put the ring in the leather case.

Esther had learned from the group that the entire family would be traveling to the next station as part of a funeral procession, and that Mammy Naira would be riding in style in a casket, as the *dearly-departed,* pulled along in a horse-drawn wagon. The rest of the group would walk along behind as part of the funeral procession. Clean clothes had already been given to the family so that they would look like they had worn their Sunday best to pay their last respects to the deceased. Ted Lloyd cleverly dressed all the children in girls' clothing with large bonnets that covered their hair and faces. He reasoned that slave-catchers would be looking for three young boys and two young girls. A procession with five girls might throw them off-guard. Esther smiled thinking what a nice change it would be to pass through a series of towns in broad daylight to get to their intended safe house. She hoped Claudia Grigg would be waiting for her. It seemed a lifetime since she had seen her friend.

A knock at the door signaled the family that it was time to get ready to leave.

The small group of mourners gathered in the lower section of the barn. They surrounded a buckboard with a simple wooden casket tied onto the back. Naira sat up in the coffin waiting to close the lid and begin the procession.

"Are you sure you want to do this, Mammy?" asked Esther. "Even though the casket had holes drilled into the bottom for air, it could be a might confining."

Naira looked at her daughter and chuckled. "Dis mammy be goin' north to the Promised Land in style, child, and dat be the Lord's truth. Y'all don't be worryin' none 'bout me." Naira looked into Esther's eyes with determination. "I be tastin' freedom."

Esther suddenly remembered a story Tara Maguire had shared with her when her dog Bailey had been hidden inside an enclosed box. On impulse, she removed the leather case from her shoulder and placed it into Naira's hands. "Mammy, I'd like you to hang on to this for me until we get to our next station. I think it will be safer riding with you."

Naira looked at the bottle in its case and then at Esther. "It gives me a sense of calm to have it with me." The mammy yawned and laid her head back on the canvas pillow.

"I think she's ready, Mr. Lloyd."

"Do not worry, Naira. The day is overcast with a chill of autumn in the air. I think that thee will be quite comfortable in thy place of rest." The farmer nodded at Naira's smiling face and closed the lid of the casket.

"Here is thy written pass, Jed. This note gives thee and thy family the right to transport the deceased slave, known as Ina, to her final resting place in Ingleside to be buried alongside her husband at his plantation, and thy safe passage back to your plantation in Hillsboro. The truth is, the owner of the Henson Plantation over in Hillsboro signed this document for a family of his slaves last year. It came into our hands a while back and we have been using it from time to time to move some of our passengers north. Thy next contact is Rebecca Singer's cousin and his wife who have a farm near Ingleside. His name is Ethan Barkett, and he is expecting thee. Ethan will return the note and the wagon to me in a few days. Thee best be getting on the road before the sun comes up. Thee have a long journey ahead."

Esther and Old Jed bid a final farewell to Ted Lloyd. The younger children would take turns sitting up on the front seat of the wagon with Old Jed as he urged the sturdy brown mare forward. Esther and Sampson would walk next to the casket near the back. Ted Lloyd gave one last wave as the little procession turned onto the road that led away from Quaker Lloyd's farm. Esther looked to the sky in the east and could see that the sun was just about to open its sleepy eyes to the dawn of a new day.

The day progressed smoothly. The sky was mostly cloudy with light rain showers, which they could see coming in the distance. Esther made up a game for the children to pass the time away. "Estimate how long it will take for the rain from that cloud to get to us before passing overhead and moving off to the east by counting. Every ten steps will represent one number."

When the children tired of that, Old Jed explained that most storms come from the west and move toward the east. "It's when a storm comes up from the south that can cause all sorts of commotion, 'cause the clouds and wind can be unstable. Sometimes they might be bringin' hurricane winds with them," said Old Jed.

Esther smiled to hear the old trapper talk about the weather. She realized how comforting it was to hear him teaching again, just like he did when she was a young girl. The mood of the little group was happy, but they made an effort to look somber just in case they were being watched.

"How much longer to go, Esther?" asked Flossy who was taking her turn riding next to Jed on the wagon.

"The signs to Ingleside say five miles, so we should arrive before long."

Esther looked up ahead and spied four men sitting astride their horses blocking the road. Inwardly, she groaned. Under her breath she whispered the word *paddyrollers* to Old Jed. He nodded his head. It was not uncommon to see groups of slave-catchers, not attached to any particular plantation roam the countryside looking to catch runaway slaves and sell them back to their masters for profit. They were known to terrorize slaves throughout the south.

Esther slowly turned around to make eye contact with the five children. "Y'all stay quiet, alright. Let Old Jed and me do the talking." The children looked at Esther through wide eyes and slowly nodded their heads.

"Halt!" shouted a man sporting a scraggly black beard and mustache. Old Jed pulled on the reins of the horse and brought the little caravan to a stop. "Now, what've we got here? Looks

like y'all are up to no good to me. What d'you think boys?"
Laughter poured into the air.

"We got papers, Massa," said Old Jed in a submissive tone
of voice. Esther and Old Jed knew that most paddyrollers
expected black people to act and talk in a certain way, and they
were only too happy to oblige.

"Do you know what this paper says old man?"

"I been told what de paper say, sir, though I don't be
knowin' the words." Old Jed kept his eyes lowered toward the
ground.

"Well this paper says you be transporting a dead body to be
buried on a plantation up near Ingleside. And after the funeral,
you and the dead gal's kids will be headin' back to the Henson
Plantation near Hillsboro. Is that 'bout right?"

Old Jed nodded.

The one paddyroller, who had been doing all the talking,
dismounted his horse and climbed up onto the back of the
wagon. "Well, just in case y'all might be trying to pull
somethin' over on us, I'll be takin' a look at this here body."
Esther inwardly shuddered as she looked up to see the
paddyroller pry open the top of the wooden box with the muzzle
of his gun.

Flossy was about to say something to the man, when Esther
shot her a warning glance. From her vantage point on the seat of
the wagon, Flossy stared at the form of Mammy Naira who did
indeed look as peaceful as one who had recently passed over to
the other side. Mammy's face was motionless and calm with not
a breath seeming to pass from her mouth. The man stared at the
woman for a while. He started to replace the lid when he asked
suspiciously, "What's that old gal holdin' in her hands?"

Esther remembered the Bronze Bottle in its leather case that
she had placed in Naira's hands. Before Esther had time to think
of something clever, she heard Flossy's voice.

"Why that be my mammy's bottle o'molasses. Mammy always said that when she goes to heaven she want to take plenty o'molasses with her. That way, she can sit on a fluffy white cloud and eat cornbread n'molasses 'til her belly swells up like a melon. My mammy sure did like cornbread n'molasses." Then Flossy started to cry. She set out to bawling so loud that even the paddyroller was beginning to feel uncomfortable.

Esther looked over at Flossy and observed that she appeared to be very believable. She even thought she saw a tear well up in her eye. Esther decided that Flossy might make a good conductor someday.

The paddyroller looked at the outline of the bottle under its leather pouch, then over to Flossy. "You people have mighty peculiar notions. Do you really think…?" He looked into the cheerless face of the little girl and decided to let the dumb family believe what they might. Quickly, he replaced the lid, handed the pass back to Old Jed and said, "Let's go boys. There's nothin' out of the ordinary goin' on here."

"Look, Old Jed. I think that's the woods Ted Lloyd told us about. He said it was about fifty yards beyond the little stone bridge we just crossed."

The band of mourners pulled the wagon slowly up the road until they noticed a small sign with the name Barkett carved into the wood. The road narrowed to a smaller opening cutting a path through some trees. Esther and Old Jed looked up and down the main road. All seemed quiet. Esther spoke softly, "Looks clear. Pull the wagon off the road and we'll follow the wagon tracks that cut through the forest."

The soft shade from the trees blanketed the group and helped give them a sense of calm that the next stage of their journey would soon be over. Esther watched as the woods gave way to a large meadow that had been cleared for pastureland. The runaways had been told to leave the horse and wagon in the shelter of the woods. Esther would make her way to the house and if all went well, she would signal the others to join her. First, she decided to check on Naira. She hopped up on the wagon and anxiously watched Sampson and Old Jed loosened the lid of the wooden casket. Mammy Naira lay quiet and peaceful in the box, and for a moment Esther worried that her beloved mother may have indeed passed over on the long ride to their destination. But when she bent over and removed the bottle from her mammy's hands, Naira opened her eyes and smiled up into the faces of Jed, Esther, and Sampson.

"Lordy, I declare, dat was just 'bout d'best nap I've had in a long time. Seems like I just closed my eyes. Are we here already?"

Esther looked down into the face of her mother and smiled. "Yes, Mammy, we're almost here. Let Jed and Sampson help you up. I'll go check on things up at the house."

Esther was just about to knock on the back door of the farmhouse, when the door swung open. "Why, Esther, I'm so glad to see thee. I trust that all went well?" Claudia Grigg pulled her friend into the interior of the kitchen and gave her a tender hug. "I was hoping that thee might run into Rebecca and Mark on the road. They left early this morning."

"We didn't pass them, but we got off the road whenever we heard horses up ahead."

Claudia turned and introduced Esther to Ethan and Illean Barkett. The young good-looking couple had been married for just over three years. It had taken them a year to clear the land, and with the help of other Quaker families in the area, another to build the house and small barn. Although the farm was modest, Esther could see that it had great potential for growth.

"I'll bring the rest of the family up to the house," said Ethan. "A place has been prepared for thee in the attic."

"Esther, it is wonderful to look upon thy face," proclaimed Claudia.

"I'm happy to see you too. There's much to talk about, my friend."

Chapter 25 ~ September 1853 – The Road North

Esther and Claudia talked long into the night as the others slept on the floor of the attic. It was good that Esther could share with her friend all of the events that had happened since they had parted. It helped Esther sort things in her head. Claudia held the ring in her hands. She thought the beautiful initials embedded with diamonds were a bit too ornate for a Quaker's taste, but she was pleased that Steidley King had given a token of himself to his daughter. Then she promised to remember Shelby Moss in prayer the next time she went to meeting. Both women discussed why some people chose to be cruel in life while others went out of their way to end the misery of others. It had been decided that the group would rest at Ethan's and Illean's farm all day. The group had been pushing hard since Saturday and they needed the rest. Then under the veil of night, they would walk to the next station.

Claudia Grigg spoke softly as she handed the ring back to Esther. "A family of freeborn Negroes owns a farm on the outskirts of town just across the state line into Delaware. They go by the name of Jefferson because their ancestors used to work for Thomas Jefferson on his place at Monticello until Mr. Jefferson gave them their freedom, shortly before he died. Ethan told me that they are pretty much left alone because of their reputation of being connected to the third president of the United States."

"Can they take a group as large as us?"

"Yes. Ethan and Illean told me that they have helped folks out many times before. The family conceals runaways in a shed not far from their home. Word has been sent on ahead, and they will be expecting us, Esther. What about Mammy Naira? How is she fairing?"

"It's odd Claudia, but the restful sleep she had on the trip from Quaker Lloyd's farm seems to have done her a world of good. She walks with a new bounce in her step and says she feels years younger, but I don't think she can walk that far."

"Thy mammy will not have to. Ethan is loaning us one of his mules. Once we get to our destination, one of Jefferson's sons will bring it back in a few days. Just like Ethan will return the wagon to Ted Lloyd. People help each other on this railroad."

Esther shook her head. "Goodness never ceases to amaze me. I'm learning that there is a kind and trusting nature in most people. I just wish we all could get along."

"That has always been the hope of the *Friends*."

A three-quarter moon spilled light onto the floor of the woods as the group marched in silent procession behind Old Jed through the night. He seemed to have the uncanny knack of finding paths made by man or animal, which made the journey more bearable. Moses and Noah rode with Mammy on the large sturdy field mule known as Fulton. The mule was easy to handle and gently followed along as Sampson led it by its halter. Franny and Flossy held hands as they moved silently through the forest. Flossy had come to learn the importance of staying quiet. It seemed as though all the children had grown up a lot over the past few days. Esther and Claudia walked behind to make sure that all the children were within their eyesight.

Suddenly Old Jed stopped and held up an arm to signal the others to halt in their tracks. A low growling sound issued from somewhere ahead in the road. Esther slowly walked to stand next to the old trapper and whispered, "What do you think is out there?"

"Don't know for sure, Esther. It could be wolves or a pack of wild dogs. One thing's for certain. They've smelled us and know we're here."

Esther looked back. Sampson and Claudia were in the process of putting the girls up on the mule with Mammy Naira and the boys. Sampson held onto the reins of Fulton who was beginning to get jittery. He spoke to the mule in soothing tones.

"This isn't good, Jed." Esther murmured. The conductor knew that a pack of dogs could be a runaway slave's worst nightmare. Sometimes, these wild dogs had become separated from their owners – the very slave catchers who had trained them to attack humans at will. The fierce hunting dogs had been known to sometimes join with other feral dogs to run wild and kill whatever they might find to stave off hunger. She didn't blame the dogs. It was their nature to survive in any way possible. Esther secretly hoped the growls were from a pack of wolves. In her experience, wolves seemed less interested in people.

Esther's heart sank. Three large wild dogs stood together blocking the road ahead. As they growled, the light from the moon revealed large yellow teeth inside mouths dripping with saliva. The dogs looked half starved with ribs that poked through the sides of their scraggly torsos. The largest dog had yellow matted fir. Another was brown and black, and the third had white fur with patches of brown on its face and torso. The white-furred dog had dried blood matted to its coat from a large gash on its neck. Esther assumed it was the result of a fight with another animal. She knew that something must be done fast.

The children would be in serious danger if their mule, Fulton, decided to rear up and race away in panic.

Other than sticks, the group had nothing with which to fend off an attack from the hungry canines. As a last resort, Esther decided to use the Bronze Bottle, which had faithfully helped her out of so many situations already. Slowly, as to not startle the dogs, she loosened the top of the pouch and pulled the bottle from its case. She held the bottle at arms length in front of her and cautiously stepped forward and began to talk to the dogs in soothing tones. It occurred to Esther that if these dogs had in fact belonged to slave catchers, they might respond to commands. After all, they once were taught to obey the verbal authority of humans. Walking ahead slowly, Esther demanded, "Sit boys! Sit down! No one's gonna hurt you here. Be good dogs." At first, the three dogs persisted in issuing a low and steady growl, but as Esther continued to move forward and speak in a calm yet commanding voice, they gradually ceased to snarl. They perked their ears up and seemed to listen to her words.

Esther's heart raced so fast that she thought it might become impossible for her to use her voice. Yet she knew to gain the upper hand over the dogs, she must appear calm. "That's right. Easy boys. Down ya go. Sit down."

Then, to Esther's amazement, the three dogs lowered their haunches into the dirt and started whimpering like a litter of pups. Without turning around, Esther said, "Mammy, untie the gunny sack from Fulton and hand it to Jed." Naira obliged and Old Jed brought the bag to Esther as she turned her attention back to the dogs. "You're just hungry. That's why you're feelin' so grumpy."

"Think I know where this might be headin'," murmured Jed as he cautiously handed Esther the sack of food.

"While I distract them with the food, you and Sampson move the others up the trail out of harm's way." Jed nodded and relayed the plan to Sampson.

"I'll lead them through the woods and pick up the road down yonder. You be careful now, Esther," Jed whispered.

Esther nodded and let out a slow breath of air. She reached into the sack and got down on her knees. Sitting back on her heels, Esther murmured, "Steady pals. I know y'all are mighty hungry, so we're gonna share our dinner with ya." It saddened Esther that the children would not have as large a meal as Illean and Ethan had planned, but there was no other way of getting around their situation. Esther placed the Bronze Bottle near her knees on the dirt road. Curiously, the dogs began inching forward toward Esther and the bottle until they crawled within a few feet from where she sat. The nervous conductor, reached into the burlap sack and pulled out three pieces of fried chicken, and gently placed one piece of fried chicken in front of each anxious dog. The animals tore into the meat with a famished enthusiasm. Esther continued to talk to the pack in soft easy tones as Sampson and Jed quietly guided the mule off the road into the woods to lead Mammy and the children away from harm. The dogs ate hungrily. In seconds they had devoured the chicken. They sniffed the air and let out another low growl.

"Still hungry? Let's see what we can find for y'all." Esther started to reach for the burlap bag. To her surprise, the largest dog with yellow fur crept closer and began to sniff the Bronze Bottle positioned in the road. "Are you thirsty, fella?" Esther slowly picked the bottle up from the dirt and removed the stopper. She poured a small amount of water into the palm of her hand and held it out to see what the yellow dog would do. With a hand that Esther willed not to shake, she closed her eyes and waited to see if the dog would drink from her hand or bite it off. Esther felt a blast of hot breath and the brush of whiskers against her skin, as the beast sniffed the water. Then, the rough warm brush of a tongue washed over her palm as the canine lapped up the water in her hand. Esther continued the procedure twice more. The two other dogs had edged nearer to the yellow dog, and whined as though they too were thirsty. Slowly, Esther repeated the process until all the dogs had sampled the water from the bottle. Then, one by one, the dogs began to curl up together in a bunch. To Esther, they looked like a litter of pups in search of a good nap. Esther sat in the dirt petting the dogs' fur until they were snoring gently. "Well, I gotta go friends," whispered Esther. She reached into the gunnysack, unwrapped a bandana and removed three pieces of corn bread. Esther thoughtfully placed them near the sleeping dogs' muzzles. "Here's a little something to say thanks when y'all wake up."

Esther picked up the Bronze Bottle and looked at it with renewed respect. *Just want to say thanks to you as well.* Esther looked at the white dog with the large gash on its neck and shrugged. *Don't know if this'll do any good, but it couldn't hurt.* She poured the rest of the water over the wound. The dog stirred then settled back into its slumber. *I must remember to fill this again at the next stream.* Esther returned the bottle to its case and gathered the gunnysack of food over her shoulder. Slowly, she backed away from the bundle of sleeping dogs. Thinking of nothing more than finding her family, she stepped off to the side of the strays, and trotted down the road to face whatever lay up the road on her journey north.

Chapter 26 ~ September 1853 –
The Jefferson Farm

Albert and Suzie Jefferson ran a profitable little business making large oak barrels on their farm. The Jeffersons and their seven children were a family of free Negroes who lived in Hockessin, Delaware. President Thomas Jefferson freed Albert's grandparents, who had worked as slaves on his plantation called Monticello. Over time, the freed slaves were able to purchase twenty acres of prime land in a wooded area. The property had proudly been in the family for over thirty years. Forests of black and white oak trees provided the necessary hardwoods to craft the barrels. Albert Jefferson and his four boys: Casey, Gary, Ace, and Jared cut the oak trees in the warm summer months, while Suzie and the girls, Carrie Lynn, Barbara Anne, and Beverly Sue tended the large garden, which provided food for the family.

During the cold months of winter, the entire family cut, and shaped the oak into big barrels in a sizeable barn near their sturdy log cabin. Local farmers, with the need to ship agricultural goods, created a steady demand for their high-quality hand-crafted product. The Jeffersons also shipped a quantity of empty large oaken barrels to suppliers, by train and in cargo boats up and down the eastern seaboard of the United States. An especially good market for the barrels existed among the sugar planters of the West Indies. The hard-working family had long earned the respect of their neighbors. It would have come as a surprise to learn that they were active stationmasters for the Underground Railroad.

Esther had safely guided Claudia and the little band of fugitives to the Jefferson's barn. They currently rested in a large storage shed that was used to dry the oaken barrels until ready for shipping. A false room had been created behind the barrels, and the group rested comfortably on wooden stools and mounds of hay.

"Are ya certain dat it'll work?" asked Mammy Naira.

Albert Jefferson smiled at the concerned mammy and spoke, "I know it might seem extreme, but we have transported over fifty slaves using this method, and we've never failed to get our cargo to its destination."

"But to be shipped in barrels like we was nothin' more dan a tub of oats seems mighty uncomfortable, Mr. Jefferson," pronounced Mammy. "I'm troubled for d'little ones."

"I understand your concern," said Jefferson, but the bottoms and sides of the barrels are lined with cotton and small holes are drilled into the top for breathing. We've shipped children before. It's a might uncomfortable, but the trip to your next station in Philadelphia is only three hours by train. Our contacts, who work as shipping clerks, unload our cargo and take it to a nearby warehouse. Just think how great it'll be. You'll truly be in the North, Mammy. From there, y'all will be given a ticket and the proper papers, so that ya can travel as passengers on the train the rest of the way to St. Catharines. Once that train crosses into Canada, all your troubles will be over. Trust me when I say, the worst of your journey is behind you. In a few more days, y'all will be free."

Naira looked into the face of Albert Jefferson and sighed. She then turned to Esther. Large wet tears welled in the corners of the mammy's eyes. "I never thought dis ol' slave would ever be able to call herself free. I prayed dat it might happen to de children...but I never thought dat it would happen to me,"

Mammy sobbed. "*You* made dis happen Esther. You and Miz Grigg, and all de other fine folks dat helped us along d'way."

Esther got up from her stool and crossed over to where Mammy Naira sat. She knelt before her mother and said, "I never gave up hope of seeing you again, Mammy. In all the time that Bucky and I spent in New York, I prayed that we could be together again as a family. Then, almost like a miracle, the Griggs and Mark Singer's family helped make it happen."

Esther reached over to Old Jed, who sat on a stool next to Naira. She gathered his leathery hands into hers. Years of making and baiting traps had caused them to become coarse and calloused, but to Esther they represented experience and wisdom. "You know, old friend, none of this would have happened without your kindness to me. Remember that first day we met? You rescued me from Mandy and the other girls when they threw me in the muddy shores of the Big Buckwater. It was the first time in my life that anyone, other than Mammy, ever came to my defense. Then you taught Bucky and me to read at Night School all those summers chopping trees in the forest. You kept telling us to *read the signs of the forest and the signs of the road,* and your instruction convinced us that we could escape north. But mostly, you taught me how to forgive. From you, I learned to find the goodness in people, and not blame all for the wrong-doings of a few."

"I only planted a few ideas in your head, Esther. I knew that one day you would sort things out so they'd make sense to you. I must say, *pretty alligator eyes,* I'm very proud of the beautiful lady you've turned out to be both inside and out."

Esther smiled at her friend. "I hadn't thought of that name in years before making this trip to the King plantaion. Thanks to you and mammy...and...well...Bucky, I've grown to finally appreciate the different color of my eyes."

Nine large barrels marked **POTATOES** rested in neat rows on a large flatbed wagon. The four sturdy horses that had been hitched to the wagon seemed anxious to be called to duty to haul their goods to the train station. Their enthusiasm mirrored the mood of the little group who stood near the wagon.

Claudia Grigg could have easily made the trip in the comfort of the passenger car, but made the decision to be transported in the manner of her traveling companions. She told the little group that she wanted to be able to tell Donald and the twins what it truly was like to be a passenger on the Underground Railroad. She reasoned that it would be a great story to tell her grandchildren one day. She said she also hoped that she would be able to tell them that the Underground Railroad was a thing of the past, because the practice of slavery had been abolished.

When the little group arrived safely in Philadelphia, Claudia would part company with her companions and make her way home to Donald and the twins, Seth and Hannah. She privately promised herself that one of the first things she would do when she reached the farm, would be to walk up the little hill where baby Emma rested in her tiny coffin and recall to her daughter the incredible journey. Then she would say a prayer and bid her daughter well until they might see each other again in the future. Finally she promised herself that she would get on with the joy of living and watching her children grow up.

The Jefferson family had treated them with such kindness in the two days that they had rested at their farm, that it was hard to say goodbye. Each member of the fugitive group had been given an apple and some peanuts for the short train ride to Philadelphia.

"I guess y"all better climb on up into the barrels. The train to Philadelphia leaves in a few hours. Me and the boys will need the time to place the barrels on the cargo train. You remember what I told y'all last night?" Sampson and the four little ones nodded their heads.

"I remember, Mr. Jefferson! Let me tell it!"

"Okay, Flossy. Why don't you tell us what's gonna happen."

"We're gonna ride in the big barrels. Sometimes the barrels will get shaken about, and sometimes we might get rolled around like we was doin' summersaults, but we're not to get scared or cry out. The cotton paddin' inside the barrels will keep us safe so we should think of it as somethin' fun. We should rest easy and wait 'til the men at the train station pry the tops off of our barrels. When that happens, we will be in the North, and Boss Shelby will never again be able to git after us with the whip, and we won't have to spit tobacco on Miz King's roses." Flossy grinned at Albert Jefferson. "I added that last bit, myself. Cuz you don't know nothin' about Boss Shelby and Miz King...."

"That's just fine, Flossy," interrupted Old Jed warmly. "My, my, but you sure remembered well. You're gonna make a great student." He looked over at Sampson and Esther. "I guess none of us will hafta worry 'bout Shelby Moss when we get to the North." Esther nodded at her mentor and then shuddered remembering the last image of the overseer.

Esther shook away the thought and turned and faced her family. "Something happened back on the road with the wild dogs, and I've been thinking about it all morning. I want y'all to take a small sip of water from the Bronze Bottle. If things work out like I hope…well it just might make the trip north in the barrels a little more comfortable."

After a final goodbye to thank the Jeffersons for their kindness, Esther passed the bottle among the group and each took a swallow of the cool wet liquid, then one by one, they climbed onto the wagon and into the barrels. The Jeffersons' oldest boy, Casey, hammered the lids shut with nails.

Esther sat crouched against the padded cotton of her barrel. It suddenly occurred to her that she had not sipped water from the Bronze Bottle still clutched in her hands. She felt for the stopper and removed it from the bottle. Slowly she passed the refreshing water to her lips. As she did so she said a prayer. *Heavenly father, protect my family from all harm and guide them on this last part of our journey north to the Promised Land.* Esther replaced the lid and put the bottle back into its sturdy leather case. A powerful sense of calm washed over her like a cloak. Her last thought, before she drifted off to sleep, was of her long-time friend, Bucky. *I've missed you, my friend. But I'm almost home, and I'll be happy to see your face again.*

Epilogue ~ March 1854 – New York City

Esther and Bucky held hands as they walked down Pearl Street toward Doctor Simpson's office. "It'll be good to see Tommy again," said Bucky.

Esther looked over at her tall friend and nodded. "I love living with Mammy Naira and Old Jed in Canada, and the children are blossoming at the school, but New York is so alive with activity. It's great being here again."

It had been three months since the good doctor had asked them to make the train trip from St. Catharines to New York to rescue more abandoned children from the slums of an area known as Five Points.

Dr. Thomas Simpson lived with his mother, wife, and four children on the second and third floors of a comfortable townhouse on Pearl Street, near Broadway Avenue. The first floor was used as an office for his thriving medical practice. He was well thought of among his colleagues and patients. The doctor read all the latest medical journals from America and England. His office was clean and well lighted. He washed his hands with soap after treating each patient without fully understanding that what he did helped contain the spread of germs. Dr. Simpson charged ample sums to those of his clients who could afford his services, but he was also more than generous to his working-class cliental. And each Saturday, he set up his office as a free clinic to assist the sick and worn-down people of Five Points who could not pay. The doctor had a special love of children and felt it was his sacred calling to ease the misery of the many abandoned children who lived in the rat-infested area known as Five Points. He often made trips to the slum to hand out bread and fruit, to clean and mend wounds, or to encourage hollow-eyed mothers to bring their sickly children to the clinic. Suspicious at first, the miserable tide of humanity that dwelled in Five Points came to accept Doc Simpson as a man who was easy to talk to and someone they could trust.

It made Thomas angry when he overheard his colleagues proclaim that the Negroes and mostly Irish who lived in Five Points were lazy by nature. The doctor believed it made them feel better to make such statements. Then, they wouldn't have to help mend the atrocities that had been heaped upon the two races of people for years. He openly disagreed with his overfed associates. He campaigned tirelessly against slum landlords and the lack of sanitation and proper drinking water in the Lower East Side of Manhattan.

The doctor understood that the poor immigrants of Five Points accepted their appalling living conditions as a matter-of-course. Most of them had spent their entire lives scraping up from the bottom of the heap. He also knew that most of them wanted to work, but with signs stating, **No Negroes or Irish Need Apply**, made it almost impossible for them to climb out of their miserable existence.

The slim forty-year-old doctor, with kindly blue eyes and light brown hair, knew first hand of their troubles. His own dear Irish mother had worked long hours as a maid to a rich family in Dublin so that her bright young son could be sent to England to feed his hungry mind. In time, Thomas received a scholarship to Cambridge University to study medicine. It was there that the brilliant young scholar lost his Irish accent, but he never lost his love for his country, and the many underprivileged immigrants who came to America to find a better life.

Esther and Bucky sat in Dr. Simpson's consulting room having a cup of tea with the doctor. Esther asked, "Why can't we get the people out of that horrible place and into decent houses?"

The doctor smiled. "Esther, your outrage reflects my original feelings about their situation, but I soon learned that to help the immigrants, we must think with our heads and not our hearts. America has an open-door policy to anyone who wants to come here. Millions come each year, yet there are no agencies to make sure there is work and proper housing for them. The run-down houses in Five Points were once nice homes. As the homeowners moved out of the area, they rented out their old houses to the newly arrived immigrants. When the poor couldn't afford to pay rent for the whole house, rooms were leased to families – sometimes forty or fifty people living in a house intended for one family. With no agencies to monitor living conditions, the houses quickly became rat-infested ramshackle dwellings." Dr. Simpson sighed. "In time, we may find a solution to the problem, but my concern at the moment is with the children."

Bucky looked across the room at Esther with admiration and thought, *She's so pretty, and she cares so much for the downtrodden. I love her courage and determination.* Bucky coughed to help focus his attention back to the people of Five Points and inquired, "What have you uncovered this time, Tommy?"

Dr. Simpson explained the situation with the latest batch of homeless orphans he had seen in Five Points. "I've made contact with a recent immigrant from Russia named Otto. It has taken time, but I think he finally trusts me. The boy is only twelve, but from what he's told me, he's seen more in his short life than he should have. Under the decree of Czar Nicholas, Otto was taken from his village and was scripted to work at sea as a cabin boy. A year ago, he escaped from the cargo ship as it lay in harbor here in Manhattan. I'm amazed at how well he speaks English. I guess being forced to survive in a new country made him quickly find a way to communicate. I think he's very smart. He acts tough, but underneath there's compassion. Otto has become a parent-figure to some of the smaller children. You won't believe where they live. It's known as Rats Hallow. I'll take you to meet them when we finish our tea."

Otto Stanoff hated drizzle. *Why the devil won't it just rain and then be done with it,* he silently cursed. The light rain had been coming down as a misty sprinkle for over a week. The precipitation drenched his clothes and matted his dirty brown hair. The moisture had made the dirty streets turn to mud and it coated his pant-legs and bare feet. Otto's face was covered in grime from a day of rag-picking. It hid a handsome face with a strong jawbone and rich brown eyes – the color of mahogany wood. Because he could not get his thin clothes to stay dry, he was chilled to the bone. The cold made his lean body shiver and his empty stomach rumble. *Borshch. What I wouldn't give for a hot steamy bowl of beet soup, just like Mama's.*

Otto stepped off the wooden sidewalk and slogged across the muddy street to the grog shop. The boy smirked as he looked at the faded lettering on the glass. Although Otto could not read English, he had been told what the word meant. *It might **say** "Groceries" on the window, but everyone knows the smell of cheap liquor and cigars gives away what type of trade really goes on in here.* A man Otto knew only as *Irish* stepped out the door and onto the street with a bottle wrapped in old newspaper. Otto smelled urine on the man as he passed him going into the shop.

"What've you got for me today, Otto?"

Otto emptied the contents of his muddy cloth sack onto the counter. "I done real good today, Tabby."

"I'll be the judge of that," Tabby said brusquely. The greedy little shop owner pulled at the scraggly gray whiskers on his chin and stared at the booty through narrow dark brown eyes. Tabby sorted though the rags, corks and bottle tops placing the loot in neat piles as he went. He stopped when he saw the copper pipe, then, trying not to look too enthusiastic, said. "I'll give you three cents for the lot.

"Come on, Tabby. The copper alone is worth a nickel. Deal me a fair hand. I've been picking all day, and I'm hungry."

Tabby looked sharply at the skinny boy and briefly thought about throwing him out of his shop. But, he knew he could get a dime for the pipe and wanted to make the trade. "I'll tell you what. I got a hunk of cheese and a loaf of bread in the back. I'll trade ya straight up."

Otto knew he was getting the worst end of the deal, but there was little he could do. The children would be hungry, and he couldn't come back empty handed. Otto looked around the shop weighing his options. "Throw in that withered cabbage sitting in the window and you've got a deal." The boy sighed. *Shchi. Yes, a hearty cabbage soup would taste almost as good as Borshch.*

Tabby wiped his hands on his dirty apron. "You deal a hard bargain, Otto. Is that 'cause you're a Jew?"

Otto wearily looked up at Tabby and remarked with a scowl. "Maybe…but it's more likely because I'm hungry!"

Dr. Simpson led Bucky and Esther down Pearl Street past colorful shop windows decorated with hats and fancy cakes. A series of left and right turns brought the three to a shabby area with narrow unpaved streets. Esther gasped at the sudden decline in the area. *Five minutes ago I saw fancy carriages and beautiful shops, and now this.* Huddled in doorways to escape the dampness, Esther met the faces of suspicious people staring at her through the rainwater dripping from the roofs. Suddenly, Esther stepped into a hole in the rotten wooden sidewalk and found herself ankle deep in mud mixed with filth. Bucky grabbed her waist thus avoiding a fall. Esther retrieved her balance and looked up to see ancient sagging houses leaning at crazy angles. Most of the windows were broken and parts of the roofs were missing. Ill-tempered dogs, so thin Esther could see every rib, snarled and snapped at each other. A pig rooted hungrily in the wet muck. This pig was not like the fat pink creatures on Claudia's farm. This swine was a skinny fearsome beast caked in filth. A pock-faced boy with bright red hair and oozing sores on his arms crossed to the other side of the street as if to avoid them. Esther heard the weak wailing of a newborn baby. She clutched the Bronze Bottle in its case at her side and said a quick prayer that the infant would survive the night.

"This is it," said Thomas Simpson as he wiped the rain off his oilskin cape. The three had dressed for the weather back at Simpson's office and looked alike in their rain gear. If all went as planned, they would bring the children back to the doctor's office to be washed and fed, to check for infections, and to perform any other medical procedures that might be needed. In time, a train would transport the orphans with Bucky and Esther back to St. Catharines.

The house known as Rats Hallow stood at the end of a narrow street off by itself. Two crumbling brick chimneys in elaborate twisting patterns told Esther that the house was probably a beautiful home at one time. Looking at it through the mist, gave her an eerie feeling. The boarded up windows and the misshapen branches of ivy vines that climbed across the slate roof made the place look haunted. The house had no front door. Through the gaping hole, Esther could see women with small children huddled on the stairs and against the walls on the floor staring blankly at the miserable weather outside.

Dr. Simpson quickly led Esther and Bucky around the side of the house. An area where weeds had been trodden down revealed a small opening at the base of the house that seemed to lead to a cellar. Thomas knelt down in the muddy weeds and lit the candle inside the lantern he had brought with him. "I'll poke my head into the hole and take a look to see if Otto's here."

The light from the lantern illuminated the interior of the cavern, and the sight made Thomas gasp. A half dozen pairs of eyes huddling around a small fire stared at him. One of the younger children started crying. "Don't be afraid. I'm looking for Otto."

"Is that you, Doc?" Otto Stanoff stepped out from behind a rotting timber with a sturdy stick clutched in his hand. "I thought you might be someone from another gang coming here to pinch our dinner."

"Tell the children not to be alarmed. I've brought my friends. You remember, the ones I told you about. They've come to help. Can we come down?'

Otto talked to the others in whispered tones and then said, "Bring 'em in."

First Bucky and then Esther followed Dr. Simpson through the hole. Esther established footing on a box crate set up under the hole, but when she stepped off the box she caught her breath. Icy cold water penetrated through the leather in her shoes and chilled her feet. The smell inside the cellar was appalling, but she willed herself to smile.

"Please don't be afraid. We're here to help," Esther pleaded. The waifs huddled together around a tiny fire built inside a rusty bucket. The makeshift stove had been cleverly propped up out of the slimy water with bricks. A dented pot sat directly on top of the coals brewing something over the small fire. Esther could not imagine what they might be cooking for supper, but it did not look hearty enough to feed one let alone seven. The six small children clung to each other in fear. The children were nearly naked and they looked half starved.Esther could see that the oldest was no more than seven. A sudden overwhelming desire to help the little urchins wiped away her disgust at the putrid smell.

Bucky looked at the thick branch in the hands of the boy the doctor had described as Otto and spoke. "Have you been robbed before?"

"Sometimes. We been at this place 'bout a month. Most older gangs leave us alone 'cause this place is foul. I thought maybe they smelled cabbage soup and wanted to eat our dinner."

Thomas introduced Bucky and Esther. "These are the friends I told you about, and they've come to help. Please Otto, won't you introduce us to the children?"

As he spoke, Otto pointed to the pitiful children dressed in rags. "This boy is called Blackie, two girls here be Meg and Star. Over here we got Rat, Crow, and Porky.

Esther's feet were beginning to get numb with the dirty water that saturated her shoes. "Do any of you have parents?" The children did not answer her. They only stared up with large sad eyes. Judging from the sounds of most of their names, Esther thought they must have been alone for some time.

"Have you talked to them, Otto?"

"I tried, Doc, but they just cry and say they don't want to leave me. Thing is, I can't find enough food for us to eat. I told 'em they'll be better off with your friends."

"Boys and girls, my name is Doc Simpson. My friends and I are here to help you. We want you to come with us now. We're going to take you to my house. Once there, you'll get a warm bath, a hot meal and new clothes. I promise, we won't hurt you."

Blackie spoke to the adults revealing two missing teeth, "Can Otto come with us too?"

"Of course he can," proclaimed Esther, "and Otto can stay with us for as long as he likes." At that moment she trembled. A vibration from the bottle sent a wave of heat down her legs all the way to her icy wet toes.

With the children washed, fed, and put to sleep for the night on cots set up at the back of the infirmary, Esther and Bucky got a chance to talk to Otto after Thomas left to join his family upstairs. Now that the grime had been removed from Otto's body and hair, Esther thought that he had a fine looking face.

"Where did you find them, Otto?" asked Bucky.

"Here and there…on streets, in alleyways…left out to rot like garbage. No one wanted 'em so I took to looking out for 'em. They been with me 'bout six months.

"But some of the babies are only two. How'd ya do it, and why?" Esther questioned.

"Mostly, cause I was lonely and they remind me of my own brothers and sisters. They were someone to talk to, and they teach me English so I can sell my junk to grog shop.

"Where are you from, Otto?" asked Bucky.

I been to many ports in Europe since leaving Russia and coming to New York. I was taken from my mama when I was ten. Back then, soldiers come to village and take all boys to work for Czar Nicholas. Mama knew what they were gonna do, 'cause they took my older brother, Ivan, two years before. He was fifteen at the time. Ivan was sent to work on the western border of Siberia, but he escaped to Europe through Poland. We know this, 'cause we get letter from him saying he is out west in America. When ship lay anchor in New York, I escape to go look for Ivan. I try to earn money, but money hard to get."

"America's a big place, Otto. Do you know where in America?" asked Bucky.

"Yes…place called…California. Ivan go there to search for gold. He wants to find much gold and then bring Mama and family to this place, but I have not heard from him since leaving home."

"Oh," said Bucky. "California is a large area of land that became the thirty-first state in the union just a few years ago. It's a long way from here, Otto."

"But people still go there. I ask where is gold? People say place near *Fransico*. They follow on a train filled with wagons."

Bucky tried not to laugh. He knew that this was serious to Otto, and he remembered what it felt like to ache with longing when he and Esther wanted to go north. "That's called a wagon train, Otto. It's a lot of people walking and riding in wagons together for thousands of miles through Indian Territory. The town you seek is called San Francisco. Lots of people have been going out west because of the gold that was discovered in California a few years ago. A friend of Doc Simpson and mine is a wagon master and he takes a group west each spring. I met him when I used to live in New York. His name is Cornelius P.

McCauliffe. If you really want to go west in search of your brother, I think we may be able to help. "

Esther became somewhat alarmed when another surge of warmth began to radiate from the Bronze Bottle resting at her side. She decided to take the bottle out of its case and examine it. She gently removed it and placed it on her lap. Bucky and Otto were in an animated discussion about cowboys and going west. They seemed to have forgotten about her for the moment.

Esther sighed with happiness. The bottle charmed her as much today as it had the first time she had seen it in Tara Maguire's china cabinet a little over six months ago. But now, she suddenly noticed that something was different. Cutting across the middle part of the bottle raced a streak of purple so vibrant it took Esther's breath away. The color split like a fork in a river and sent two lines of purple sprinting off in different directions.

Esther was so absorbed in what was taking place before her that she failed to notice that the room had grown quiet. Bucky and Otto had moved over closer to where she sat and were also looking at the event taking place. She almost jumped out of her chair when she heard Otto's voice.

"This bottle...I don't know why, but bottle remind me of Mama." Otto reached out and asked, "Could I hold...please?"

For an instant, Esther wanted to say no, but her generous nature took hold of her emotions and she answered, "Of course...Otto." Reverently, she placed the bottle in Otto's hands as he came to sit in the chair next to her.

Otto looked at the bottle with wonder. As soon as he had taken the bottle into his grasp, more streaks of purple and lavender began to cover over the existing bronze tones. "I don't understand, but color is so familiar to me." Otto placed the bottle in his lap and reached under his new woolen sweater and pulled out a small pendant in the shape of a crest attached to a rawhide strip of leather.

"That's a beautiful pendant, Otto. May I see it?" Esther asked.

Reluctantly, Otto removed the crest from his neck and handed it to Esther, who began studying it with an artist's eye. The Coat of Arms was slightly larger than the face of her father's ring, which she wore around her neck attached by a chain. Instinctively, she felt for the object hidden under her dress and sighed.

The shape of the shield was straight across the top, slightly rounded at its sides and narrowing into a point at the bottom. The bowed triangular shape reminded Esther of a miniature shield of armor that knights once wore in battle. The crest displayed a flat enamel background of purple. Attached to this was an embossed carving of a two-headed eagle with wings spread wide. An ornately carved gold crown lay suspended above the two heads of the eagle. Set in the middle of the gold crown was a beautiful purple gemstone, which Esther believed to be an amethyst. Esther gasped. The shade of the amethyst gem was exactly like the color now streaking across the Bronze Bottle. "This is lovely, Otto. Is it from your homeland?"

"Mama is second cousin to Czar Nikolas. As young girl, Mama spent every year at summer palace as a playmate for his children. That was until royal family send Mama away in disgrace because she fell in love with a gardener who worked at palace, He was my Papa. She asked the royal family if she could marry. But Papa was a Jew and a gardener. They tell her she will be banished from family if she tried to see him."

Otto sighed. "Their love was so great that Mama left her home to marry Papa anyway. She give away all life for him. Mama and Papa were very poor, but they were happy in our little village. Then four years ago, Papa died of fever. A year later the czar's soldiers take my brother Ivan. Mama write letter to her family. She beg them to ask that Czar Nicholas might not send Ivan away since her husband was dead, but she never heard back from them. When the czar's soldiers came to take me, Mama cried. She took me in the house and gave me crest from neck. Mama look into my sad eyes and said, 'Otto, wear this under shirt and never let anyone see it. Keep it safe and a part of me will be with you always.' It was a most precious thing from her former life. I have kept it hidden under shirt until tonight. It makes me feel so close to her."

Esther was sad that the bottle had been with her for such a short time. She locked eyes with Bucky for several seconds as some knowing words silently passed between them. Esther nodded and handed the pendant back to Otto. "I'm happy that you like my bottle, Otto, because it's yours."

Otto looked at Esther and Bucky with surprise. "I could not possibly take a gift as fine as this." Esther and Bucky only smiled back at him. After a moment, he looked down at the bottle in his lap and nearly woke the children with a loud yelp.

The beautiful Bronze Bottle resting in his lap was now nearly half covered in several stunning shades of violet. Tiny streaks of silver and gold were racing into the mix. Otto was somewhat surprised to see that he bottle perfectly matched the colors of his mother's pendant.

"But how…how can this be? asked Otto.

"Otto, it's a long story, but before we go home to St. Catharines, I promise I'll tell you everything I know about the bottle," murmured Esther. "But you must know, that this is not an ordinary bottle, and it will help you on your journey. With good fortune, the mysterious Amethyst Bottle may help you find your brother, Ivan. It may even reunite you with your family one day."

* * * * * *

Author's note: The practice of owning slaves in the United States officially stopped when the Civil War between the northern and southern states ended in 1865. Many people believe that slavery is a thing of the past. Unfortunately, it is estimated that more than 25 million people remain enslaved throughout the world today.

CPSIA information can be obtained
at www.ICGtesting.com
Printed in the USA
BVHW081928310720
585155BV00002B/137